Autumn in the Vineyard

A St. Helena Vineyard Novel

Also in Marina Adair's St. Helena Vineyard Series

Kissing Under the Mistletoe
Summer in Napa

Autumn in the Vineyard

A St. Helena Vineyard Novel

MARINA ADAIR

Printed in the United States of America.

Published by Montlake Romance, Seattle

www.apub.com

ISBN-13: 9781477848135
ISBN-10: 1477848134
Library of Congress Control Number: 2013909204

For Rocco, my own personal hero.

Thank you for loving me even when

I didn't know how to love myself.

CHAPTER 1

It had taken three years, some tricky negotiating, her entire life savings, and a lot of ball busting—but Francesca
Baudouin was finally a vineyard owner. Well, she was the owner
of ten acres of prime St. Helena appellation soil, which would
take another five years of sweat and, quite possibly, selling off a
few of her vital organs before it fully became a quality producing vineyard.

But Sorrento Ranch, the most sought after property in the
valley, and all of its belongings, was hers. She bought it right
out from under the DeLucas' noses. In part because the owner,
Mrs. Sorrento, had played darts with Frankie and Frankie's great
aunt every Friday night for the past fifteen years, so her loyalties
were clear, but mostly because Mrs. Sorrento knew that selling
the land to either family involved in the great DeLuca-Baudouin
feud would piss off her ex-husband.

"One more inch and I'll shoot," Frankie said to the alpaca in
front of her, a four-legged garbage disposal whose mouth was
currently wrapped around the plastic casing of the water tank.

She stomped her ball-busting, steeled-toed combat boot in his direction for added emphasis.

The alpaca's beady eyes narrowed and dropped to her feet. Extending its lips in her direction, it made a loud raspberry sound, stomped an aggressive hoof and then went back to nibbling. Yeah, ball-buster or not, hooves beat boots.

But Frankie wasn't about to let some hardheaded alpaca with shaggy hair and buck teeth stick it to her on her first week in business. As the youngest of four, and the only girl, Frankie was a pro at dealing with stubborn males who excelled at ignoring her completely, while messing with her life wholeheartedly.

She cocked her rifle.

"The only thing separating you from becoming a pair of next season's mittens is my trigger finger, Camel Boy." Because the only thing separating *them* from ten-thousand gallons of well water was the thin plastic seam-binding on the water tank, which "Mittens" had managed to chew loose. She didn't want to deal with the cleanup and couldn't afford a new irrigation tank. "I mean it, one more bite and the only identifying male trait you'll have left is stupidity."

That got his attention. In fact, the animal straightened and fluffed out the fur around his face, making him look like a cross between a camel, a koala, and Clifford the Big Red Dog. When he wasn't destroying her property, he was kind of cute. In a big, dumb, oafy kind of way.

Mittens was the sole remaining alpaca from Mrs. Sorrento's farm. The rest of his hooved brethren were living it up at Alberta's Paradise Alpaca Farm and Pet Sanctuary. Mittens hadn't even set one hoof in the back of the moving truck when the rest of the heard gathered their spit and took aim. Poor Mittens had been kicked out of his own family and before

Frankie or Alberta had been able to catch him, his fluffy butt disappeared, and Alberta had left instructions to call when Frankie secured the runaway. That had been four days, two patio chairs, and a motorcycle tire ago.

"See?" Frankie lowered her rifle to the ground, picking up the cushion from Mr. Sorrento's old recliner in one hand and a rope in the other. "That wasn't so bad. Now just come over here and I'll give you a treat."

Eyes glued to the nubby avocado-green cushion, the alpaca took a tentative step forward.

"Then you can go to your new house." Another step. "Where they feed you gourmet hay and mud tires, and there are kids around all the time to play with you." Step. "And you'll get to see your family."

The alpaca stopped, squared its body, and let out an ear-piercing bleat, which sounded like a cross between *wark* and Chewbacca screaming, right before he sank his teeth into the plastic casing and pulled. Hard.

"Mittens!"

"*Wark!*"

"No—"

The tank split at the seam and before either of them could move, a wall of water came crashing out with enough force to topple Mittens into Frankie and send the two of them skidding back several feet.

When Frankie stopped moving and the water had receded into a pool of mud, she shoved the hair out of her eyes and took stock. She was flat on her back, with a stick poking into her right butt cheek and a drenched Mittens sprawled out over the top of her.

"Move." She shoved at the animal.

"Wark-wark!"

"I warned you! But did you listen?"

Mittens let out an apologetic nicker and dropped his head to Frankie's chest, his big brown eyes looking up at her through long lashes.

"You could be halfway to Paradise right now," she said, giving him a little rub behind the ears. "Just think, in a few months it will be grooming season and all the ladies will be prancing around in nothing but sheared skin. Plus, you'll have your family."

This time the nicker was almost sad. Ignoring the alpaca's wet dog smell, Frankie called a temporary truce and dug both hands in his thick fur to scratch his cheeks. "Yeah, I get it. Family sucks, but I can't let you stay here. Come spring, I'll start planting my vines and you'd eat them."

Mittens huffed, a burst of hot air hitting Frankie in the face.

"Liar." She worked her fingers around his temples and behind his ears. The animal's eyes slid closed in ecstasy. "You already cost me a water tank, which I can't afford to replace by the way."

His only response was to nuzzle Frankie's chest and hum loudly.

"So, there is no way I have the budget to keep replacing everything you decide to sink your teeth into."

Hum. Hum. Hum.

"I hope he bought you dinner first," a voice said.

With a groan, Frankie turned her head and, wishing she were standing so she could glare at him without having to shield her eyes, swore. Upside down or not, there was no mistaking the man who was currently towering over her—or the way her stomach gave a lame little flutter when he lifted his mirrored glasses and delivered a heart-stopping wink.

"Afternoon, Francesca," he said with enough practiced swagger that it made not rolling her eyes impossible.

Nathaniel DeLuca was six-plus feet of solid muscle, smug-male yumminess, and he smelled like sex. He was also extremely Italian, annoying as hell, and, for whatever reason, every time he entered Frankie's space she felt all dainty and feminine. Which pissed her off even more because at one time she'd trusted Nate with her heart and a promise of keeping her deepest secret.

And he'd broken them both.

Thank God she had on her ball-buster boots today. Too bad they were currently covered in mud, alpaca fur, and pointing at the sky.

"Go away, *Nathaniel*," she said by way of greeting.

Mittens hummed louder, arching into her hand as Frankie scratched down his spine.

"And leave a lady in need?" Nate asked, coming forward and squatting down to pluck a maple leaf off of Frankie's forehead. "Nonna ChiChi would have my ass."

"I know you're used to your women poised and proper. But I've got this handled."

"I didn't know you paid that much attention to my women, but now that you mentioned the difference . . ." He plucked a branch from her hair and flashed his perfectly straight teeth in her face. His smile, like his personality, was lethal and his entitled attitude was one-hundred percent DeLuca. "That's great," he continued, "because I won't have to worry that you'll cry when I tell you to stop exciting my alpaca and get the hell off my property."

His property?

He plucked off another branch, this time from her shirt, his fingers leaving a heated trail and stirring up all kinds of fire— and not the good kind. The last time she remembered being this close to killing him had been at the Summer Wine Showdown three months ago. He'd hard-balled her into sitting on the Tasting Tribunal, they argued over the winner, then he'd kissed her—right as her grandpa, a tsunami of irate old man, showed up.

No one had forced her to sit on that tasting tribunal, or to run her hands up his hard chest and into his hair when she'd kissed him back, but she blamed Nate anyway.

Frankie looked up at Nate and pinned him with her best *bring-it* glare. This land was hers. Her dream. Her fresh start. Her everything. And no one, especially not a DeLuca, was going to mess with that.

$\sim$

"Last time you threatened me, I think I promised to rip your face off," Francesca said, her voice eerily calm.

The calm before the storm, Nate thought, standing up and taking a large step back.

"With. My. Teeth."

One minute she was on the ground under a pile of wet alpaca, the next she was standing with her torn hip-huggers and black tank top plastered to her body, leaves stuck to her shapely butt, and enough curves and pissed off female vibes to level a guy. She was also clutching a shotgun, making her armed, sexy, and untouchable as ever.

It was no secret that Frankie hated Nate. Or that they argued all the time. She tried to fight with him about winemaking—which only continued the stupid-ass feud that had divided their families for over six decades—while all he fought was the idiotic urge to kiss her until she shut up.

Not that he'd give into the urge again. Even if hot-headed ball-busters with something to prove were his type—which they definitely were not—Nate didn't fight with people. Ever. It was a gigantic, ineffective energy suck. He was more the mild-mannered arbitrator. Always had been. And he was damn easy to get along with, even-tempered too—until he was nose to nose with Frankie.

Her temper was one of the many reasons on his ever growing *Why to Avoid Francesca Baudouin* list. Although, as of—he looked at his watch and smiled—two minutes ago, irritating her had him reevaluating said list.

"Beautiful—" he said, smiling as his gaze went from the barrel of the gun to her tank top, which was drooping with water and giving him an inspiring view of her breasts—"day, don't you think, Francesca?"

Clearly seeing the direction of his gaze, she dropped her aim—dangerously low. "Since I've been waiting months for a good excuse to shoot you, I'd have to say my day's looking pretty damn good."

Not for long, Nate thought, waiting for the sweet zing of victory to kick in. When it didn't, he had to wonder why.

Frankie's family wanted this land as much as his did. It wasn't just about the prime twenty-acre parcel. It was about righting a sixty-year old wrong that waged a feud between the two founding families of St. Helena. Back then, Charles

Baudouin had won. Today, the DeLucas had. But when Nate imagined this moment, and he'd imagined it plenty over the years since his parents died, he hadn't expected victory to feel like shit.

"Look, Francesca," Nate sighed, taking a small step toward her. This was going to be hard on her, and that bothered him. "Why don't you drop the gun, and let's go inside where we can talk?"

"I'll drop the gun as soon as I see your starched ass disappear over that fence." She waved the double barrels at the white fence that separated his family's vineyard from Sorrento Ranch.

Nate looked up at the sky and took in a calming, mild-mannered breath. "Unless you want to end up in cuffs, I suggest you put it down. The sheriff might be able to ignore the trespassing charge. But threatening a man with a gun brings this to a level even your brother can't make disappear."

"Well, since Mrs. Sorrento moved out, handing me the keys to the place, that would mean that *you're* the trespasser, so I think it would play out more like me protecting what's mine. So for old time's sake, I'll give you and your—" her eyes dropped and she grimaced—"loafers a two minute head start before I start shooting."

"Your property?" he asked, wondering what was wrong with his loafers.

"As of Monday," she clarified, a smug smile tilting up those luscious lips.

There were only a few things that could have made Nate's day any shittier. And that was one of them. Proof that Saul had officially screwed them over.

A crisp autumn breeze kicked up, rustling a leaf loose from Frankie's hair, but doing nothing for the suffocating feeling

Nate had pressing at his chest. The only thing he had going in his favor was that they had started escrow last Thursday, giving him a two business-day lead on the Baudouins. A man couldn't sell the same property to two people, and since it seemed like Nate had purchased it first, Francesca was two days too late.

"Look," he tried again. "Why don't we go inside and talk?"

"Oh, I'm done talking. All I ever get from listening to your dribble is a headache and a world of trouble with my family."

"Yeah, about that—" Nate ran a hand down his face, not wanting to think about her family or how many times he'd made her standing with them even more difficult and complicated.

Three months ago, Charles had boycotted the Summer Wine Showdown with the sole purpose of canceling the hundred year old fundraiser. He would have succeeded too, if Frankie hadn't agreed to fill in as the official Baudouin judge.

Nate hadn't seen much of her since—avoidance being something they had both mastered living in the same small town—so he didn't know what went down afterward. But that look on Charles's face when he saw Frankie sitting on the Tasting Tribunal was enough for Nate to understand that Frankie had gone too far over that line.

Judging by the dark smudges under her eyes and her taut, pale skin, these past few months had been hard on her. Guilt, and something he didn't want to acknowledge, shifted from his gut up to his chest, forming an angry knot.

He studied her face. "Frankie, about the—"

"Don't worry, golden boy," she interrupted, racking the gun's slide and obviously misunderstanding his attempt at an apology. Not that he blamed her. Apology wasn't something they had much experience with. "I won't shoot. Yet."

Nate sighed. He needed Rambo over there to put the gun down and be reasonable, just for two days, two freaking days and then escrow would close and the land would be his. Maybe if he approached Frankie with a generous enough offer he could salvage this screwed-up situation. He knew that her grandpa was having cash flow problems. If he—

Shit!

A police car's red and blue flashing lights sped down the dirt road, kicking up gravel and dust as it skidded toward them. Frankie raised her hand and squinted into the sun.

"Really?" She spun around and hit him with a very hostile glare. "You called my brother?"

"No," he said, confused as to why that would be an issue. If anything, her brother would find a way to haul his ass in while Frankie got away scot-free and his deal fell apart. "I called the *sheriff.* Your brother just happens to be the responding officer."

"Why am I not surprised?" Frankie rolled her eyes, going for annoyed, but he saw the way her gaze kept darting back to the passenger in the cruiser as it pulled to a stop.

"Afternoon, Nate. Frankie," Sheriff Bryant said, maneuvering his belly around the steering column and stepping out of the cruiser. "Got a call about an armed intruder."

"Armed intruder?" Francesca laughed, sliding Nate an amused look before lowering the gun and smiling up at the sheriff—who smiled back. "I was just walking my property, Sheriff."

Frankie's grin faded as her mountain of a brother, Deputy Jonah Baudouin, slid out of the passenger side of the car. He was impressively dangerous looking and, Nate reminded himself, packing. On a normal day, when unarmed, Nate could hold his own against the deputy. But he knew that when it came to protecting baby sisters, men could be ruthless. Hell, he'd do just about anything to make sure his sister Abby was happy and safe.

So when Jonah stood there, silently watching Frankie with a total lack of emotion on his face, Nate found himself wondering just what their relationship was like.

"Frankie," Jonah said ripping his hat as though she wasn't his sister. Then he turned to Nate with the same expressionless look. "What's going on?"

That's exactly what Nate wanted to know. Why did Frankie look like she'd been busted? And why was Jonah asking Nate when Frankie was the one holding the gun?

"I'm sorry," Frankie began, her voice shaking with something that did stupid things to Nate's chest. "I was going to tell you about the property, but I wanted to make sure—"

Frankie trailed off because—*holy shit*—Miss Bad Ass looked close to tears and Jonah wasn't even reacting, just patiently waiting for her to continue.

"Actually, it's my property," Nate clarified, wanting to get that on the record, and get everyone's attention off Frankie. "So there's nothing to tell except that she had a gun and I didn't know it was her, so I called you guys just in case. I know armed robberies carry four times the fatality rate."

"Let me guess, you read that in one of your fancy magazines," Frankie said with a small smile and Nate didn't respond because she was right, he'd read it in the *Wall Street Journal*—and because she didn't look like she was about to cry anymore.

Then her smile faded and her eyes narrowed, and damn it if he hadn't imagined the whole vulnerable woman act. "Wait! Just what are you accusing me of robbing?"

"My alpacas," he finally said, ignoring the way the two men exchanged shit-eating grins, and felt even stupider. "Last week there was a herd of them and I noticed this morning that they were all gone. Well, except for her."

Nate jerked his chin toward the animal who immediately started stomping her hooves in typical female fashion. Then her lips started working overtime and Nate took a giant step back. "Is she going to spit? I read online that alpacas spit when they get mad."

"So then you called to file a stolen property report?" the sheriff asked, his bushy eyebrows furrowed, his mustache twitching.

"The *property*, being the house and the alpaca, is mine," Frankie said, stroking the fluffball's head.

"So, there's no report then?" the sheriff asked.

Frankie ignored the sheriff and glared at Nate. "And *she* is male, which explains the need to stomp his hooves and spit when he's mad."

With a loud exhale, the sheriff unclipped his walkie-talkie. "Dispatch, this is Sheriff Bryant. Tell all units responding to Sorrento Ranch that they can go available." There was some squawking back, and then, "Nah, it's just a domestic dispute, we can handle this call."

"Domestic?" Frankie spat. "There is nothing domestic about us. I don't even like him." She flapped a hand furiously back and forth.

Nate leaned in. "That's not what I remember you panting a few months ago."

Frankie leaned in too, her full mouth so close he could feel her breath tease him—from his lips all the way down to his dick. Damn, he usually had better control.

"I was drunk and bored. You misunderstood. Plus, I like my men to pack a bigger set than me." She glanced down and then back up through her water spiked lashes. "Never going to happen, DeLuca."

"Who owns the land?" the sheriff interrupted loudly, taking off his hat and rubbing at his forehead.

"I do," they both said in unison. And Nate meant it. He was tired of being fucked with.

"So let me get this straight. You are both claiming ownership of the house, guardianship of . . . that there," Sheriff Bryant nodded at the alpaca, who nuzzled Frankie's hair and started humming. "And there's arguing, threats, and loaded weapons on the premises?"

Frankie shrugged.

"Sounds like a domestic dispute to me." The sheriff looked at Jonah, who ran a hand down his face.

"God damn it, Frankie," Jonah said on a long exhale, his cool fading. Nate found himself relating to the guy. "I have to haul both of you in."

Hell, no. That was not going to happen. "How about I drop the charges? Francesca and I can settle this like rational adults."

"Rational?" The deputy pushed his sunglasses down to the end of his nose and looked at Nate over the rims. "We are talking about the same girl and the same piece of land, right? Because my sister knows how to use that thing and she will shoot you if you try to take this place."

"I wouldn't shoot him," Frankie said. Jonah spared her a disbelieving glance. "Fine, I might shoot *at* him, but I wouldn't *shoot* him."

Nate had to smile. Gun or not, it was hard to feel threatened by a woman who had once, long ago, cried herself hoarse in his arms.

"Either way, I'd be called back out and the town would think that I was somehow aiding in this stupid old feud." Jonah walked around the back of the cruiser and opened the back door. "Now you both going to go easy or do I need to get out the cuffs?"

CHAPTER 2

Investment-quality wine?" Jonah placed his hands, palms down, on the assessor's map and slid it across the table in the Sheriff's station break room, making sure to shove all of his big-brother disapproval in her face. "Please tell me this isn't why you cashed out your trust account?"

"Not that it's any of your business, but yes," Frankie said, shoving a little something of her own back.

"Christ, Frankie." Jonah unfolded himself from the too-small seat, rose to his full, six-foot-two height and started pacing. He did that a lot when dealing with her. "What were you thinking?"

"Gee, Jonah, I don't know." She leaned back in her metal chair and kicked her boots up on the table, going for unaffected. It was hard to pull off since Jonah never got agitated unless he was really pissed. Or worried. And Frankie hated worrying him. "That it couldn't be any more risky than Grandpa slapping one of the most respected names in wine on a bottle of supermarket Syrah? Or maybe, that one of the best plots in St. Helena Appalachian history went on the market and I actually had a shot at owning it." She paused. "Wait? How did you know?"

Jonah walked over to the coffee pot, but not before raising an eye at her feet, which she ceremoniously dropped to the floor. He filled two paper cups with coffee and went about doctoring them up. "Phoebe called. I guess she had to sign off on the transaction."

"What?" Oh my god, her mother knew. Frankie couldn't imagine a worse situation. Other than Nate owning that other parcel of land, which she was pretty sure he did. "She isn't coming here, is she?"

"No." Jonah rubbed the back of his neck. "Thankfully, she has an art show in Mendocino this weekend that she has to prepare for. Then she leaves Monday for a three week commune with her inner goddess."

"A commune with her inner what?"

"God, don't make me repeat it."

Frankie smiled and felt her shoulders relax. In the craziness of the morning, she'd forgotten about her mom's yearly trip to her favorite artists' commune in Arizona. A trip that couldn't have come at a better time. The last thing she needed right now was her mom to pay her a visit and discover that Frankie had been fired. Phoebe would go all mama bear on Charles, who'd say something hurtful in return, then her brothers would feel obligated to intervene—and once again her family would get caught up in some nasty fight with Frankie at the center.

She studied Jonah, who was adding copious amounts of sugar and cream to the cups. "Why'd she call you?"

Although Frankie and her brothers shared a dad, they had different moms. Phoebe was wife 2.0 and quickly learned that loving a man who was clearly in love with his first wife, dead or not, only led to resentment. Especially when that man admitted that marrying a replacement after you'd had the real thing never worked.

"She called me because you haven't bothered to return any of her messages and when the bank informed her about your latest purchase she got worried."

She was worried? Frankie knew that her brothers wouldn't understand why she had to do this, but she never imagined that her mother wouldn't believe in her. She hated that the only time she felt like a loser was when it came to her family.

"That doesn't make sense. She hasn't been on that account since I turned eighteen."

Jonah set the coffee on the table between them and then seated himself. Resting forward on his elbows, he leaned in, eyes serious and full of concern. Frankie shifted in her seat.

"Katie told her." Jonah lifted the cup closest to him and took a sip. "Claims that Mom's name is on the account and she was doing her due diligence by notifying the executor."

"Shady Katie" was married to Charles's other grandson, Kenneth, a man who was more interested in the value of the land than actually working it. Unfortunately for him, his dad lost his ass in a pet supply dot-com company and was forced to sell their portion of Baudouin Vineyards to Grandpa Charles and, as Katie so often claims, robbed her Kenneth of his rightful legacy.

"She's so full of it," Frankie said, picturing Katie brown-nosing the old man first chance she got. "She just wanted an excuse to rat me out to Grandpa. Show him he made a bad decision in choosing me over Kenneth as the enologist for the winery."

Not that Frankie was Baudouin Vineyard's head grape expert anymore. Actually, she wasn't even employed by her grandfather's company. Nope. Nate had ruined that too.

"Well, she'll be happy to know that Charles hasn't spoken to me since the Summer Wine Showdown, when *I* apparently disgraced the family."

Then, instead of apologizing, she explained why buying a four hundred acre vineyard when they were already having cash flow problems was a bad move. Especially when said vineyard specialized in bulk wine intended for wholesale warehouses across the country and Baudouin was known for their higher quality and higher price points. That was when Charles told her that her opinions, expertise, and services as head enologist for Baudouin Vineyards—the place she'd dedicated her entire career to—were no longer required.

"Aw, Frankie." Jonah rested his hand on hers and there it was. That familiar sucker punch to the stomach. The one that reminded her of the scared little girl who, once again, hoped that this was the moment when everything would go back to before the divorce, when everyone pretended that they were a happy family and that she belonged.

Uncomfortable, Frankie dragged her cup closer and studied it so she wouldn't have to maintain eye contact. It was more milk and sugar than coffee, and was enough to squash the urge to care.

"Is that why you're doing this? As some kind of screwed up apology?" Jonah asked, his voice steady. It was always steady, controlled. "Or is this your way of proving him wrong for not listening to you about going after the collectors' market?"

"Neither," Frankie said. This was about her dream. About making the kind of wine that only the top percent of enologists ever got the chance to make. She was good enough and wanted to compete with the best and this was her chance. "How do you know I'm not doing this for me?"

"Because if you were, you wouldn't have blown your entire savings on a piece of land that is too small to be anything other than boutique. I know the kind of vineyard you want to run. That land isn't it."

Which went to show how little her brother really knew her. She knew he cared, but had a hard time listening. A boutique winery was Frankie's dream. Had been for the past ten years.

"I didn't *blow* all my money." *Just most of it.*

She hated how his eyes probed her and how his department issued tactics made her feel like spilling her entire life story. Which would be stupid, because he'd been there for most of the gory parts.

"Good, because I'd hate to find out you were doing all this to prove to Gramps what we already know," Jonah said softly.

"This is a smart move. It might be a small parcel, but it's the best in the valley. Plus, Saul had vines. Nothing big, barely a gentleman's vineyard, but they're old and well taken care of and about ready to be harvested." She knew this to be a fact because she had been secretly buying Saul's grapes for the past three years.

"There is enough to make about four hundred cases and my saplings will be ready for planting this upcoming spring. Until then, Aunt Lucinda's letting me keep them in the greenhouse," she said, thinking of the nearly two thousand saplings she'd grown from collecting cuttings that came from her family's hundred year old vines.

"Those saplings will take at least three years to produce. Another two to age. Even longer if you're considering collectors and boutique wine shops as your target buyers."

Frankie stuffed the urge to roll her eyes. "I'm not stupid, Jonah. I've done my research and have a respected wine broker interested in buying my entire bottled inventory. As for my wine skills, I've been working Grandpa's vineyard since I could say 'merlot'."

"Yeah, well you should still be working it, especially with harvest coming up." Jonah shook his head. "I give it two weeks before Grandpa comes crawling back. He needs you, Frankie."

Which was what made this whole situation so screwed up. Charles needed an heir to take over the vineyard and the only one qualified or interested was Frankie. Too bad she wasn't "man" enough.

"Look, we've been talking," Jonah said. *We* meant everyone but Frankie had been a part of a discussion *about* her. "And we all agree that a united front is the best bet. So unless Grandpa apologizes, he's on his own for harvest. We all walked away from that bullshit once before and we'll do it again."

Something she'd do anything to avoid. After her dad passed, his assets were divided among his four kids—all of his assets except the shares in the family business. Those went to only his three sons as per her dad's wishes.

Frankie was crushed and in a moment of weakness, she did something she'd never done before: confided in someone—who went directly to her brothers. And everything went to hell.

"I never asked you to walk away," Frankie said.

"I never said you did." Jonah's face went from confused to soft understanding. Frankie would have preferred the first. "Is that what you thought?"

She shrugged. What else was she supposed to think? She blabbered to a nosy Italian and her family had imploded.

"Frankie, Dad cutting you out of your shares in the vine-yard and Grandpa refusing to equally redistribute them was part of it, a small part." Frankie straightened. She'd never heard this before. "You were too young to remember, but that vine-yard destroyed this family."

She may have been six, but she remembered. Remembered sitting in the courtroom while her parents argued, her mom demanding custody, her dad saying the boys would be raised with him on the family vineyard. Frankie was too young to de-termine what words like 'prenup' and 'divorce' meant, but old enough to understand that she was an object to argue over, just like her dad's motorcycle and the beach house in Pacific Grove. She remembered the day her parents divorced was also the day their dad had stopped loving her.

"It destroyed Dad and Grandpa's relationship, their mar-riages, their connection with their kids, and in the end they wound up alone. We didn't want that kind of life." Jonah reached across the table and gently nudged her hand with his. "And I sure as hell don't want that for you."

"And I don't want you guys to make this any harder on Grandpa. He's had a rough year and things are already strained enough between everyone. As for why I bought Sorrento Ranch, I've waited my whole life for this chance. It's what *I* want, for me."

"As long you aren't doing this to prove to Grandpa what we already know, you've got my support," Jonah said softly and something inside Frankie warmed.

And just when she almost leaned across the table to give the guy a hug, he added, "Because Adam, Dax, and I all agree that living outside the old man's world of grapes is nice and it's about time that you tried it."

That was easy for him to say. He had his brothers. Always had. Always would. Whereas Frankie was always too female, too young, and after the divorce, too limited to weekends and rotating holidays to be anything but peripheral in her half-brothers' lives.

She was pretty much on her own. And as long as she remembered that, she wouldn't be let down.

"Now that this *kum bay ya* moment is over, can I go?"

Jonah smiled. He actually smiled. "Not until you tell me what all that was about back at the ranch."

"All what?"

"The name calling, the pissy stares, shanking DeLuca with your elbow in the back of the cruiser."

"It's called irritation." That much was true. The man irritated her into warm fuzzies.

"Really? Because from where I stood, it looked a lot like foreplay. Especially since everyone is talking about how the two of you were sucking face at the Showdown."

"Who says 'sucking face'? What are we, twelve? And he kissed me!" Frankie snapped, her face going red.

Jonah just smiled bigger. "Have you seen the picture?"

Yes, she had. Everyone in town had after Nora Kinkaid insisted on including it in her Summer Wine Showdown Facebook Photo Album. "I am so not having this conversation with you."

Frankie stood, grabbing her plastic bag of personal items that Jonah had confiscated when taking his sweet time locking her in a cell. Unzipping the bag, she started angrily pulling items out and shoving them in her pockets.

"Hey, I didn't mean to upset you." Smile gone. "Sit down, finish your coffee, and tell me how you've been."

Without looking up, she smashed lip balm in her back pocket and jerked her chin toward the cup. "I assume that's not soy."

"No. And since when did you go all tree hugger?"

"Since I'm allergic to milk."

"When did that happen?"

She lifted her head and stared at him. For a long moment, she couldn't even speak. When she did, it came out harsher that she'd hoped. "At birth." He opened his mouth, most likely to apologize since that guilt was now piling high on his oh-so-capable shoulders, which were starting to sag. "If you're done with the touchy-feely shit, I have an alpaca to feed and property to defend."

Jonah looked at her for a long minute. His expression said *I'm worried about you.* Frankie knew that look. Knew it meant he was going to try to fix her life. Which meant he'd call in reinforcements.

"You aren't going to tell Mom and Grandpa about me going to court Friday over the land, are you?"

Jonah was quiet, considering his options. Suddenly, her stomach felt way too small for the three ham and double cheese croissants she'd had at the Sweet and Savory Bistro. Having to argue with Nate in an open court of law over a piece of land that was rightfully hers was bad enough. Having her mom and grandpa there to witness the moment would only make it worse.

"I should," he said. "Maybe she could talk some sense into you. But that would mean she'd be staying at my place and driving me insane. So you're safe. For now."

"Thanks," Frankie whispered.

"As long as you promise to come over for dinner soon. We only live five minutes from each other, Frankie, so you don't have to wait for Phoebe to visit to see me. You know how much I love these talks," he added, his chest extending with a laugh.

Heading toward the exit, Frankie did a little extending of her own, with the middle finger fully engaged. "Maybe next time I'll bring some wine coolers and we can get drunk and then take turns braiding each other's hair."

She was nearly out the door when Jonah said, "Hey, Frankie?"

Everything inside her stilled and her heart, which had been beating too fast all morning, stopped in her chest. Back to him, she closed her eyes and willed herself to breathe.

Frankie knew that after three tours in Iraq, their brother Dax was coming home for only four days. Just like she knew that Jonah and Adam were headed to San Francisco on Friday to pick him up and welcome him home. She also knew she would never insist on tagging along, but if they invited her, she would drop everything to be a part of that. Even if it meant begging Judge Pricket to change the court date.

"Did you know that Saul had split the land before you bought it?" he asked.

Frankie hated herself for being stupid enough to hope.

Ignoring the pain rippling through her chest, she turned to face her brother. When she did, the ripple became a full tsunami of hurt. One look at the deputy standing across from her was the reality check she needed.

Jonah was a mountain of a man, sharing the same deep blue eyes, dirty blond hair, and trademark Baudouin intensity as her two other brothers. Aside from her unnatural height and inability to connect to others, Frankie was nothing like them.

Something she'd spent her whole life trying to overcome, with no luck.

"Yup." She choked out a laugh, while forcing herself to suck it up before she did something totally undignified, like cry. "I did my homework before I signed anything. I didn't know it was DeLuca who'd bought the other parcel, though. Mrs. Sorrento told me Saul had sold it to a developer."

Jonah nodded, a flash of pride flickering in his eyes. "You think he knows?"

"Since when do you care what the DeLucas are doing?"

"I don't," he said. Frankie knew that admitting he cared meant admitting he was affected by losing Grandpa's good opinion. "I was just curious."

"By the look on Nate's face when he saw me on the property, I'm betting, no."

Working side by side with Nate wasn't ideal, but it wouldn't affect her end goal. She wouldn't let it. As for him, once he learned how the property was divided—Frankie smiled. "But I'd give anything to see the look on his face when he figures it all out."

~

After a morning spent at the sheriff's department, and an afternoon stranded in town without his car, Nate needed a cold drink and some time to come up with a plan. He was due in court Friday morning, and if he didn't figure out a solution, he might lose everything.

Nate opened the door to the Spigot, the only bar in town that served mostly locals instead of tourists and always straight-up. The chilly evening air was replaced with the smell of buffalo wings and greasy fries, reminding him that he hadn't eaten since breakfast. Football played on the old television perched above the bar and, despite the fact that the wine cave turned sports saloon was in desperate need of an overhaul, a decent happy hour crowd already filled the tables.

Nate started for the bar to grab an empty stool and—*son of a bitch.*

His two younger brothers sat at a booth in the back, huddled around a pitcher of beer, tossing back a few as though Nate hadn't spent the past four hours in the planning commission's basement alone. They hadn't bothered to answer a single one of his ten phone calls.

"Well, look who it is," Trey, the youngest, and at the moment the most annoying sibling, said, raising a frosty mug in greeting.

"About time," Marco, the next oldest said, staring at his phone, thumbs flying over the keys.

"You'd better be texting me that your phone was broken and that's why you didn't return any of my calls," Nate said, dropping down onto the chair across from Marc.

"Nope, telling Lexi that you made bail so she can stop trying to hide a fingernail file in one of her éclairs," Marco said, a goofy grin on his face. The same grin that had taken up permanent residence ever since his high school crush Lexi moved back to town—and into his bed. Now that Lexi was wearing his brother's ring, she was about to become family. And Nate couldn't be happier for them. Although right now, he had a hard time feeling happy about anything.

"He's been texting her all evening," Trey said, exasperated.

"Yeah, well what the hell have you been doing?" Nate challenged, stealing his beer and draining it in a swallow.

"Besides trying not to gag on the level of domestication sticking up the family?" Trey didn't even balk at the empty glass Nate set back down; he just flagged the waitress for an-other mug.

"What's that supposed to mean?" Marc shot back.

"I'm in town for two days," Trey pointed out. "Two days, Marc. I haven't seen Gabe since Sofia was born. Nate spent his day playing domestic dress-up with Frankie—"

"I was in jail."

"And I wasted most of today trying to convince you to meet me for a drink," Trey said to Marc.

"It took you all day to convince me because Lexi was cook-ing up something sweet in the kitchen." Not only was Lexi a great chef, she was great for Marc.

"I thought the bistro was closed on Wednesdays," Trey said.

"It is." Marc grinned, way too big. His phone pinged. There went the thumbs again.

Trey shook his head. "Come on, I leave tomorrow and you haven't stopped sexting since you got here."

"I'm not sexting," Marc said eyes glued to his screen. He smiled. The phone pinged. Fingers back to work. "I was just telling her that I miss her."

"Aw, man don't admit that," Trey groaned, shaking his head. "At least sexting sounds manly."

"Nope. Being a man is having the balls to admit that I'd rather spend the day with Lexi in the kitchen than drinking beer and watching ball."

Trey froze, his eyes wide and accusing. "You drank the Kool Aid didn't you? How many times have I told you sip, but never swallow?"

"If you two are done acting like a bunch of little girls, we have a problem," Nate snapped.

"Wow, man." Marc looked up from his phone for the first time since Nate sat down. "Jail made you hard."

"Yeah," Trey agreed. "You don't have to yell."

"I'm not yelling," Nate said, using every ounce of control he had not to do just that.

"Okay, so you're not yelling, but your eyes are all mean and there's a hard edge to your voice. It's hurtful." Trey shrugged and Nate wanted to punch him.

"Kind of like how he was acting after the showdown when he kissed Frankie and she rammed his left testicle into his throat."

Yeah, that had been a bad call. Not the kissing part, but the forgetting to protect his package part.

"This is serious. Can you focus for just one minute?" Nate ran a hand over his face and willed himself to focus. Problem was he'd been on edge since his encounter with Frankie. An afternoon arguing with the planning commissioner and an ill-equipped legal team hadn't helped.

"Right. Sorry." Trey elbowed Marc and they both bit back a smile. "What's on your mind?"

"While you were here ignoring my calls, Charles snatched the land right out from under us," Nate said, happy to see their stupid grins fade.

"What? But we close escrow Friday," Marc said. "Wait, start from the beginning."

Nate unrolled the assessor's map and spread it across the table. His brothers huddled around. "Tanner delivered this earlier this morning."

Jack Tanner, NFL legend and home-grown celebrity, was not just a booming land developer in the Napa Valley. He was also, luckily, *not* a DeLuca or a Baudouin, which was why after

Saul's wife filed for a divorce, Saul quietly approached Tanner and offered him Sorrento Ranch. Tanner had no interest in a twenty-acre vineyard. His interest lie in wine caves not vines, so he agreed to act as the front man with Saul, securing the land for Nate and his family, if Tanner Construction would be named the exclusive builder for all future DeLuca projects.

It was a win-win.

Except for the fact that Nate couldn't do his usual background check on the land prior to escrow closing without risking their anonymity. And if Saul Sorrento discovered he was really selling to a DeLuca, he would have pulled his offer indefinitely.

"What am I looking at?" Trey picked up the map.

"It's different from the one filed with the bank."

"Different, how?" Marc asked, leaning forward, phone forgotten, focused.

"Different as in we are screwed." Nate smoothed the assessor's map across the booth top and pointed to a strange line on the map that cut diagonally through the property. "This wasn't on the map Saul filed with the bank. That one didn't have this easement dividing the property."

"Dividing?" Trey said. "It hacks it in half. Are you telling me we paid seven and a half million dollars for twenty acres of cow pasture that the city is planning to cut a road down the middle of?"

If only they were so lucky. His brothers had been hesitant to pay Saul's insane asking price to begin with. Thinking he was selling to a developer, Saul jacked up the price. And it wasn't as though Nate could call the greedy twerp on it. This was the only chance Nate and his family would have to own this land and finish what Grandpa Geno had started. So he'd convinced his brothers of the long term potential and made the offer. Only he hadn't done his homework and now they were screwed.

"Actually, we paid seven point five million for ten acres," Nate said, sitting back in the chair. "That isn't a road, it's a property line. From what I can find out, about fifteen years ago Saul had the land split into two separate parcels. We bought the south parcel."

"Holy shit," Marc said, slumping back in his chair. Nate knew what he was seeing. Every plan they'd made was going up in a fucking cloud of smoke. "We need all twenty acres to make this work."

As though Nate didn't fully understand. This was the proposed site of their premiere winery, Opus. A vineyard that yielded small quantities of high-end wine.

Nate's dad had spent every spare moment crossbreeding vines and experimenting with what he'd called his grand opus. As a teen, Nate had been right there with him, tinkering, as his dad called it, trying to find the perfect blend for an extraordinary wine. Nate never forgot those times with his dad, or their dream.

"Ninety percent of the vines are on the north parcel," Marc continued. "Without those, we won't have producing vines for at least three or four years."

"I finalized those grapes yesterday," Trey added, his face a little pale. "Susan Jance was so impressed with your pitch that she is positive her client will want every barrel."

Marc whistled. "Every barrel? That's a lot of wine for one collector."

"Not when the collector is Pierce Remington," Trey said.

"Of Remington Hotels?"

"The very same," Trey said and everyone fell silent.

"Shit," Nate sighed. Today was just getting better and better.

Susan Jance was a wine broker to the rich and entitled. Her clientele included some of the wealthiest wine collectors in the world, with Remington being at the top of her list. He was the new face to an old money hotel empire and as such liked to scout out the up-and-comers before their wines went to auction.

"Remington isn't just looking to grow his own collection. Susan says he's looking for a wine that is fine enough to grace his personal cellar while also wooing his high rollers in his hotels. Kind of a 'sample my life by sampling my collection' kind of treatment for his VIPers. Ten acres won't cut it and we can't lose this deal."

"I know," Nate said, pulling out his *GAILS CLUSTERFUCK LIST* and adding *TAKE SUSAN JANCE TO DINNER* in slot number seven.

When life got crazy, Nate made lists. Had since his parents died. It was his way of finding logic in otherwise emotional situations. And right now, he was staring down a tornado of emotion.

"How much is Saul asking for the other half?" Marc asked, after the waitress delivered a full pitcher and disappeared.

"It's already sold," Nate admitted. How had this even happened?

"Sold? To who?" Trey asked then started shaking his head. "No way. I thought the Baudouins were having money problems."

"Yeah, well Charles must have found the money somewhere," Nate said, remembering how Frankie was all but preening this morning in her wet, translucent tank top. Okay, so the top had been black, but it was still wet and if he stared hard enough, he could see her chilled nipples poking through the fabric.

"Seven million?" Trey challenged, emptying the pitcher into his mug and signaling the waitress for a refill. "Where does a guy who was willing to screw over the entire town to save his winery suddenly find seven and a half million?"

That was what Nate was trying to figure out. Just a few months ago, Charles had tried to ruin the Summer Wine Showdown in hopes of discrediting the DeLucas. Fortunately for Nate, the only name discredited had been Baudouin. Unfortunately for Charles, he'd lost several local accounts because of it.

"Saul didn't sell it and Charles doesn't own it," Gabe, head of the DeLuca family, said from behind.

Nate turned around and saw his older brother, looking like the daddy he was now, dressed in jeans, a faded—and very wrinkled—college t-shirt, and stubble from three days ago. He dropped his body onto the seat next to Nate, picked up Trey's new beer and downed it in one long swallow.

"I thought you weren't allowed to drink," Trey said, reaching for the empty glass.

"I *chose* not to drink and that was when Regan was pregnant. In case you haven't noticed, she isn't any more," Gabe said, eying Marc's mug.

Regan was Gabe's wife and not only was she no longer pregnant, but the dark circles and bloodshot eyes said Gabe still wasn't sleeping. At all. Whereas Nate's oldest niece Holly was a talker, his new little niece Sofia, adorable as she was, was a screamer. Baby Sofie had come home from the hospital three weeks ago and Gabe hadn't slept a wink since.

"How is Regan?" Marc asked.

"Amazing." Gabe smiled. And man his brother looked happy. That was all it took, just the mention of his sweet wife and he perked right up. Marc was the same way lately. Nate was happy for them, he genuinely was.

In fact, he wouldn't mind having a woman in his life. A sweet woman with a bright smile and a big heart. A picture of Frankie popped into his head and he flinched. *Sweet.* He wanted sweet. And a home, not a rundown alpaca farm.

"How are you handling things?" Nate asked.

"How the hell do you think?" Gabe said, his smile fading, but there was no anger in his voice. He was too tired for anger. "I haven't slept in what feels like a year, my daughter cries every time I hold her, Holly is already asking for another sister—she wants to return her for one who doesn't cry all the time—and Regan's OBGYN told her that after the C-section she needs to take it easy for at least another few weeks. Somehow my wife took 'bed rest' to mean 'I'm throwing Sofie a one-month birthday party. By the way, you're all invited.'"

Gabe pulled three pink envelopes out of his pocket and slid them across the table. Inside was an even pinker card, shaped like two baby booties. But what had Nate smiling was the frilly embossed cursive, which looked more wedding invitation than baby's birthday and read: COME CELEBRATE ST. HELENA'S OFFICIAL HARVEST BABY'S FIRST MONTH-DAY.

"Official harvest baby?" Nate laughed.

"Wait, this is on the same day as the Cork Crawl," Trey pointed out and Gabe groaned. Apparently this had been a point of contention.

In wine country, the harvest season brought out hundreds of thousands of visitors and their spending bucks to the valley. In St. Helena, harvest season brought the annual Cork Crawl. It was the Oscars of wine, where the biggest names in the valley went head to head in a tasting that declared the king of wines for the following year. Nate's family had reigned supreme as the undefeated Cork King since 1982.

"The Crawl is always over by late afternoon and this starts at six. Sharp," Gabe said to the group but was staring at Trey. "You will all be there, and on time, and you will all smile the entire fucking night, got it?"

They all nodded. Well, except for Trey who glared out the window.

"Great, now since we have that settled, can someone pour me another beer because Regan told me that Glow sold the north parcel to Frankie for just under a mill," Gabe said, and Marc immediately flagged down the waitress for another mug.

"One million?" Nate choked. "That land was worth at least—"

"You'd better say ten million, since you convinced us that ours was worth seven and we don't even have enough grapes to make a jar of freaking jam," Trey said.

Until recently, the direction and decisions concerning the wineries had been made based on marketability and returns. Now, after closing the biggest distribution deal in their company's history, DeLuca Wines had the money to "tinker." But tinkering came at double the price for half the land.

The waitress delivered the mug and Nate waited for Gabe to take a drink before he spoke. "She must have bought it for her grandpa."

Because why would she buy it for herself? Frankie's life was her family's vineyard. It was one of the few things that, outside of getting on each other's nerves, they had in common.

"Frankie no longer works for Baudouin Vineyards," Gabe said, pinning Nate with a look that he couldn't decipher.

"What?" Nate felt everything slow to a nauseating stop. "There's no way she'd quit."

"She didn't quit. She was fired. I overheard Regan on the phone with Frankie earlier, which is why I came here," Gabe said. "I guess Charles was so mad about Frankie helping with the Showdown that he fired her and kicked her out of the family business. According to Regan, Frankie is really upset. The old goat refuses to see or even speak to her."

Nate felt sick. For a girl who'd spent her life on the edge of the family unit looking in, kicking her out of the family business would have felt more like being kicked out of the family entirely.

"How did we not know this?" Nate asked, then answered his own question. She didn't want anyone to know.

His stomach knotted at the memory of how she'd looked at him all big eyes and—Christ, now that he thought about it, she was begging him for an out. A way to salvage the relationship she'd worked so hard to create with her grandfather and still not let the town down.

Instead of helping her, he stuck her square in the middle of the fight, a place that her family had resigned her to years ago. She knew that to make it an official vote, there had to be a member from each of the town's founding families.

So Frankie did what Frankie always does; she bucked up and took the brunt of the blow. Walked into that party, tight red dress and enough sex appeal to bring a man to his knees, and took her rightful seat. She had to have been scared to death, knowing that at any moment Charles could walk right in and cut her out of the family business once and for all.

He could have ruined the entire fundraiser. Instead he ruined Frankie's life.

"What now?" Trey asked and all the guys looked to Nate.

"We've got a hearing on Friday with Judge Pricket," Nate said hating what he was about to say.

He didn't mind taking down Charles. But taking on Frankie, knowing what he did about her past and what this land must mean to her now, wasn't something he wanted to do. Ever. But he also didn't want to let his dad down. Or let his family down. They had a lot of money tied up in this deal, and Frankie would rally. She always did. Plus it was just a business deal, nothing personal, just business.

"Frankie's dad left her some money when he passed," he began, knowing exactly how much she had inherited. "If she spent a million on the land, my guess is she's close to broke."

"Which helps us how?" Trey asked. "She already owns the land."

"Yeah," Nate said. "But Frankie doesn't plan, she just jumps in. I am betting come Friday, when she realizes she only has half the land and adds up how much a new water tank and pump are going to cost, not to mention the irrigation the land needs, she'll be open to an offer."

"You think she'll sell?" Gabe asked.

"It will be a slam dunk," Nate said, feeling good about his plan. "What kind of logical person would turn down double profit in less than a week when their only option is to go broke?"

CHAPTER 3

Well, since it looks as though both parties are accounted for and those who aren't will no doubt be caught up by lunch," Judge Pricket said, peering over his glasses at the packed courthouse, "Let's get started."

"We can't start without Lucinda," Nate's nonna said, her shoes clapping against the marble floors as she waddled down the aisle, waving to just about everyone she passed.

Judge Pricket looked at his watch and scowled. "I've got an urgent appointment in thirty minutes."

Based on the crisp white slacks, matching white polo, and custom carved mallet leaning against the wall behind the judge's bench, Nate figured his "appointment" was at Meadowood, St. Helena's premiere members-only club, and that "urgent" appointment was his weekly game of croquet with the mayor. One that had been going on since the man took the bench back when Eisenhower was in office. The judge was in his eighties now.

"Well, you can't let that poor child sit up there all by herself. Plus, Lucinda is on her way. She didn't know about the hearing." ChiChi shot a chiding look at Frankie, who rolled her eyes. "Or she would have rescheduled her mammogram appointment. She should be here in about fifteen minutes."

Dressed in some fancy pants suit, enough gold to fund the entire city for a year, and sculpted silver hair, Nate's nonna slid behind the prosecution table, forcing him, all of his brothers, and his lawyer to scoot down to make room.

Frankie, on the other hand, sat in the middle of the defense table, empty chairs on either side, wearing her dark hair pulled up into a ponytail, a pretty blue top and dark jeans—no holes today. Besides the biker boots and motorcycle helmet resting in front of her, she looked more sweet co-ed than smart-ass and—since the table practically swallowed her whole—almost fragile.

Nate refused to acknowledge the small tug in his heart because he knew better. Knew that nothing about Frankie was fragile. She was tougher than most men and would probably skin his nuts for thinking any differently. But, goddamn, she looked so small behind that massive mahogany table. She didn't even have a lawyer.

She should have one. At least one. Nate had nine. Drew might be the only one present, but the other eight were diligently working on his family's behalf. Making sure they not only kept their half of the land, but looking for loopholes that would screw Frankie out of hers.

Nate watched her worry her lower lip and frowned. Where were her brothers?

"I'm sorry," Judge Pricket said to Frankie, not sorry at all. "But between talking to Patsy down at the planning department, Katie Baudouin at the bank, and both Saul and Glow Sorrento, I haven't had time to use the facilities today, let alone enjoy a meal. This is also the third time I have had this cockamamy claim in my courtroom, so you understand that I am anxious to hear the evidence, make a ruling, and stop wasting more taxpayer dollars on something that should have been taken care of decades ago."

"Amen," ChiChi chimed in, giving Nate a quick flick to the ear as though *he* were the reason that they were all here today, wasting taxpayer dollars.

"It's all right, your honor. I'm as frustrated as you are about coming here today," Frankie said. Without looking back to see who was there, Frankie shrugged nonchalantly and, although he couldn't for the life of him read the expression on her face, there was nothing nonchalant about how hard her throat was working. "Since this isn't a family situation and I knew what I was getting into when I bought the land, I think I can handle this on my own."

"I'm glad we are on the same page, Miss Baudouin." Judge Pricket lowered his glasses and studied her empty table. "I take it you are waiving your right to legal counsel?"

"Yes, your honor," Frankie said, standing. The judge let out a groan. "I figured this was a pretty straightforward case. I bought the land from Mrs. Sorrento, I talked to her last night and she has no intentions of reneging on the deal, and neither do I, so we are good."

"Well, since I'm the one who has reviewed all the material, who has been dealing with this land and your two families for over sixty years, and am appointed by the great state of California . . . " The judge picked up the case file in front of him, the one Gabe and his brothers had spent all night preparing with the help of their legal team, and tossed it aside. "Why don't you take your seat and let me decide just how *good* we all are?"

"Um, yes, your honor," Frankie said. She didn't look happy.

Welcome to my world, Nate thought.

"You purchased the northern part of Sorrento Ranch from Mrs. Sorrento on the fifth of September. Is this correct?"

"Yes, your honor."

"And Nathaniel, you and your brothers purchased the south part of the property on the second of September from Saul Sorrento?"

"Yes, sir. Although at the time we were under the impression we were acquiring the entire twenty acres," Nate said, hoping to get a little sympathy sent their way.

"Yes, and at the time Saul thought he was selling his half of the property to Jackson Tanner, not DeLuca Wines," Judge Pricket said, sounding like a disappointed principal more than a judge. "Maybe if you'd taken more time doing your homework instead of trying to buy the property under false pretenses, you would have noticed that the land had been split fifteen years ago."

"Yes, sir." Nate felt thoroughly scolded.

"You would have also noticed that instead of Saul's inflated price of seven and a half million"—the entire courtroom went silent and Nate felt as though every eye were on him—"the other property was being offered at—"

Pricket looked down at his notes and laughed. He freaking laughed and Nate sank even lower in his chair. "Frankie, did you really get that land for nine-hundred thousand dollars?"

Frankie looked over her shoulder at Nate and blew him a kiss. "I did, Ed." Since when were the judge and Frankie on a first name basis? "Well, nine-hundred thousand and my 1948 Indian Chief."

"It was in mint condition," the judge said, as though throwing in a motorcycle evened things out. "And did you know you were purchasing just the ten acres?"

"Yes," she said all smiles and sunshine, which was Frankie shooting Nate the figurative finger. "Glow and I were both upfront about the entire transaction. She explained that Saul had split the land back in the nineties for their kids, but neither of them wanted it. So each received half in the divorce. Glow was under the impression Saul sold his share to a developer, not a DeLuca."

"Weren't we all," Pricket mumbled, shooting the prosecution table a similar glare.

Gabe leaned in and whispered, "Can Pricket sink this deal?"

Nate sure as hell hoped not. He'd tried to find out their legal standing. The money had already been wired to an escrow account, but since escrow hadn't officially closed, his lawyers weren't sure.

"We're fine," he whispered back.

"Really?" Trey leaned in. "Because this slam dunk hearing doesn't seem so slam dunk anymore and that makes me nervous. You know what makes me even more nervous? That Frankie isn't even breaking a sweat. "

Nate looked over and Frankie was smiling up at the judge, not an ounce of worry on her pretty face.

"I'll fix this," Nate whispered, then stood. "Your honor, if I may?"

"No, son, you may not." Judge Pricket's bushy brows furrowed in annoyance. "I've been listening to your families gripe about this land my entire career."

"Yes, your honor," Nate cut in, not wanting him to get any further. "And I'm sorry. But I don't think the past has any relevance on today's hearing. This sale has nothing to do with our grandparents' feud. We are a new generation who would like the opportunity to make this right."

"I am glad to hear you say that, but it still doesn't answer the problem about what to do with the house. The way Saul had the property line drawn, it goes right down the middle of the house. So I have a single residence dwelling with two owners. Not to mention the south property has access to the road and driveway, and the north property houses the well."

Yeah, Nate had noticed that too.

Judge Pricket took off his glasses and rubbed at his eyes. After a long, tense moment, he looked out at the courtroom. "Legally I can and should take that sucker down, knock you both out of escrow and force the Sorrentos to put the land on the market with all parties aware of the facts."

"Wait." Frankie stood. "Mrs. Sorrento would never agree to that. She is happy with the sale and so am I."

"Which is my problem, Miss Baudouin." The judge's expression softened. "Since you did your due diligence and Glow is adamant that escrow closes in a timely fashion, I have my hands tied. However, the house, which I believe you are living in, is still under my discretion. As for the other half of the property, Saul is open to other ideas." His gaze narrowed on Nate's table.

"So I am giving you both thirty days to get in there and prove to me that you can make this work. Thirty days is plenty of time to come up with some unique ideas, and believe me, I've had sixty years to start my list." He sent them both a stern smile. "One complaint, one bullet fired, one call to the sheriff, and the bulldozers come in and I get to go have a beer. Because at the end of your month, one way or another, this feud will no longer be my problem. Understand?"

"Yes, sir," they both said in unison.

"Good." The judge stood and whacked his gavel. "Now get out of my courtroom so I can go play croquet."

"Can he do that?" Nate asked his lawyer when Pricket disappeared back into his chambers.

"Can and would," Drew said to the table. "My advice is to do whatever it takes to avoid Judge Pricket. Find a way to make it work with Miss Baudouin."

Nate looked over at *Miss Baudouin*, who oddly enough wasn't celebrating her victory. She was staring at him, a million death threats shooting out of her pretty eyes, sharpening what appeared to be a pocket knife on the metal cap on her left boot.

"Or make her an offer she can't refuse." Drew followed his gaze and laughed. "Just be sure she holsters the blade before you start negotiations."

"There is no way she'll sell," Nate said, eyes still on Frankie. "Not now. Not when she knows how much we spent on the land." *Not when she knows how much I want it.*

"You need the other ten acres to fulfill your contracts, right? And our research shows that she is desperately short of liquid assets. So stop thinking with this," Drew patted his chest, "and start thinking up here. I'm sure that some kind of partnership between the two properties can be reached."

Nate laughed. "You obviously have no idea how Frankie works. She would never get involved with a DeLuca."

Nate knew that firsthand.

As though sensing she was the topic of conversation, Frankie dropped her feet to the floor, and, after pocketing her knife, strode toward him with enough purpose and attitude to scare even the manliest of men.

Nate leaned against the table, crossing his ankles, and smiled. "Hey, Francesca."

She stopped when they were toe to toe, her eyes narrowed into two irritated slits as she gave him a long onceover. He gave her an equally long assessment, taking in the way she smelled—freaking incredible—and how her blouse hugged her breasts. Breasts he had spent the past two days convincing himself couldn't be as perfect as he'd imagined.

They weren't. They were even better. Almost as impressive as her backside, not that he could see it right now with her staring him down, but he remembered.

When the tapping of her combat boots didn't get her desired results, she cleared her throat, letting him know he was caught staring. He raised his eyes and—*oh yeah*—her baby blues lit up, her face softened and she smiled. And his brain glitched. Just like that. One smile and he was so gone.

"Seven and a half million," she said, still smiling, and he was smiling back. "What an idiot."

By the time her words set in, she was already shoving her way through the crowd, proving them both right: He *was* an idiot and her ass was as sweet as he remembered.

"Good to see you too, Frankie," Nate called out.

"Bite me," she said over her shoulder, flipping him the bird as she made her way toward the exit.

"You're right," Drew laughed, clapping Nate on the back. "I don't know how that woman works, but you obviously do. How long have you two been circling each other?"

"Since high school," Trey said, his eyes equally as glued to Frankie's retreating backside as she pushed through the massive double doors. Nate elbowed him.

"Maybe it's time you let yourself get caught," Drew suggested, packing up his briefcase.

"Get caught?" Nate asked, dismayed. Not at the idea of Frankie's more than capable hand on him because, sweet Jesus, tangling with Frankie would be like skydiving, alligator wrestling, and silky, sweet curves all rolled into one. But because spending time with Frankie and not getting involved would be impossible.

No, Nate and Frankie as anything more than bitter friends would be a mistake. And Nate didn't do mistakes. Not ones that had the potential to blow up into a disaster of epic proportions.

"All I am saying is that Pricket can be a hard ass and I don't think he was joking. If you two can't find a way to play nice then you *will* lose that property and I guarantee that Pricket will make it so no one in your family for the next hundred years will be able to get their hands on it." Drew gave Nate a serious look. "You want that land? Maybe it's time to change up the rules."

∼

Frankie passed between the marble columns and down the front steps of town hall, which spanned the entire length of the building, heading toward the parking lot. A warm breeze blew past and the thin layer of maple leaves, so yellow that the town seemed tinted with the season, floated down Main Street, past each brick-faced storefront decorated with pumpkins, and under the festive banner advertising the upcoming harvest and Cork Crawl.

Shifting her helmet, she stepped off the curb by her motorcycle and stopped, her stomach plummeting to her toes.

Further down the two-lane street, exiting The Barrel Buyer—a specialty wine shoppe and tasting room—was her grandfather, briefcase in hand, scowl in place. He headed toward his sedan and was about to open the door when he looked up and spotted her.

Frankie forced her lips into an unsure smile, one she'd given a thousand times as a kid, and waited for him to respond. She watched him take a breath, a small step off the curb, another tentative one closer, and everything inside of her stilled.

It was stupid to think that Charles might have come to support her. Even stupider to hope he would tell her how proud he was of her for Red Steel Cellars, the wine she was making to target the collector's market. Not after the way he'd reacted when he'd discovered Red Steel. But she had still hoped.

During the hearing, she'd even managed to convince herself that Charles had been at the back of the courthouse, hidden among the crush of people. But that silly, childish hope was extinguished now when she raised her hand and waved—and he took a huge step back, into his car and further out of her life. The disapproval rolling off of him as he drove away was like a physical blow.

"Good to see you too," Frankie called out and kicked at a pile of leaves in the gutter. This was why she'd bought Sorrento Ranch. Charles was so easy to disappoint and too stubborn to forgive. And she was tired of trying to live up to unattainable expectations.

"Frankie?" Nate asked quietly.

With shaky hands, she set her helmet on the seat of her bike and fished though her pocket, not wanting to turn around. She knew if she did, she'd see Nate standing behind her, wanting to make sure she was okay while his team of lawyers and supportive family waited for him inside. Nate with his Italian swagger and warm brown eyes that had a way of looking at her until she felt as though she weren't all alone.

He didn't say a word but she could feel his concern radiating off him, drawing her in and she turned. Big mistake, because Frankie had never been a hugger, but for some reason she got one look at those arms—arms that made a woman feel safe—and wanted to walk right in and make herself at home. But like she said, she wasn't a hugger.

"If you're here to make me an offer on the land, the answer is no."

His eyes went warmer, if that were even possible. "We're prepared to offer you double what you paid."

"Wow. Did you expect me to jump up and down and say yes, when the entire town just discovered that the land is worth seven times what I paid?"

He took a step forward. Toward her. "Look, I just want to help. You and I both know that Saul screwed us."

"*You*, golden boy. He screwed *you*," she laughed. "I was straight up with Glow, did my homework, knew exactly what I was buying. And you heard the judge, I'll be just fine."

"What if you lose the house?"

"Then I sleep in the shed. Thanks for your concern." *Not.*

Frankie fumbled with unlatching the chin strap of her helmet, but her damn hands weren't working. Okay, maybe she wasn't going to be fine. Her personal life was nonexistent, her family life was a train wreck, and she really didn't want to think about how alone she'd felt in that courthouse. Even though she knew her brothers were in San Francisco picking up Dax, that Charles was probably never going to talk to her again, and that Aunt Lucinda would have had her back if Frankie had told her, some stupid part of her heart had held out hope that her family would come rushing in to stand by her side. Like Nate's had.

But she had the land and a house—well, for at least the next thirty days. And she wasn't going to screw this up. Now if she could just get Nate to stop looking at her like she was about to burst into tears at any minute she'd be fine.

"Francesca," Nate said, stepping closer and making her wish she was the kind of girl who could cry. Because then he'd give her a hug, and she really needed one. "I know how much a new tank costs. I also know that Charles never paid you a cent of what you were worth, because he knew you were trying to prove yourself. After buying the land and losing the water tank, you have to be low on funds. Take my offer."

When she was silent, hating that he knew her so well and wondering if maybe taking the money and moving somewhere else to start over was the best thing for her, he added, "I'm willing to raise it to two-point-five and offer you a job."

Oh my god. He'd done it. He knew she was upset about nobody showing up and he'd managed to humiliate her even more. This was why he'd come out here. Not to check on her or apologize. She knew better. "You are the most arrogant, idiotic jerk I have ever met. You actually think I'd take a job making wine for you?"

"You're right." He flung his hands in the air and he started to pace. It was a pissed off pace reserved for Frankie alone. With everyone else he was calm, collected—nice. "*I'm* the jerk. I can see how you came to that accurate conclusion. I'm offering you more than double what you paid and a way to continue doing what you love without having to go groveling back to your asshole of a family."

"My family members aren't assholes," she defended.

"Really?" he yelled—*yelled*. "Then please define 'asshole' for me, because I'm pretty sure it accurately describes a person who fires his granddaughter when she was just doing what's right."

Frankie wasn't sure how to answer that. She also wasn't sure how much longer she could hold his gaze, so she looked down at her helmet and fiddled with the strap. She'd been so sure that her day couldn't get any worse. Man, had she been wrong. Here she was facing down the one person who could make her feel vulnerable and safe at the same time, and once again they were on opposite sides of the war.

Nate's hand rested on top of hers, stilling her fingers. He took the helmet and placed it on her motorcycle. "I'm sorry about Charles. I know how much the winery and his relationship meant to you. And I'm sorry that all of this happened because I bullied you into sitting on the tribunal. I knew he'd be pissed if you helped us, but I had no idea he would retaliate like he did." He stopped, his chocolate colored eyes melting with understanding—she studied her boots. "But you knew, didn't you?"

Yeah, she knew.

Nate curled a finger under her chin and tilted her head up to meet his gaze. So she closed her eyes. "Why didn't you tell me?"

When it became obvious he wasn't going to leave until she answered him, she opened her eyes and—*whoa, big mistake.*

Nate was looking down at her like he couldn't decide if he wanted to hug her or kiss her. And her heart was praying for the first and her lady parts were partying like it was the second.

She remembered what his lips felt like on hers, warm and strong and, in that moment, right. So incredibly and cosmically right. The man could kiss. But then her grandpa had gone ballistic and Nate blurted out his apology—for kissing her. Not for screwing up her life or being a permanent pain in her butt, but for the kiss. As though it would take him a lifetime to get over the hardship.

And he'd never even called. Not the next day or even the next week. A guy shouldn't kiss a girl like that and then never call.

Then again, what did she expect? Nate's disappearing act went all the way back to high school when he kissed her and then the next day asked Sasha "I'm perky and petite and everything you'll never be" Dupree to prom.

"First off, I didn't sit on the tribunal to help you. I did it for the town and because, whether my grandpa believes it or not, I earned my right to be there." Which was only partly true. The other part, the seventeen-year-old girl who still had a crush on Nate, did it for him and his family. "And secondly, trusting you hasn't worked out so well for me in the past."

The minute she said the words, she wanted to take them back. She didn't want to talk about the past. Dealing with the present was hard enough.

"Forget it." She turned to leave but Nate's strong hand caught her wrist.

"No, you're right. I should've listened to you about the land and the tribunal, and I should never have kissed you."

It was impossible to speak. It was as though he'd socked her in the gut.

"There," he added on a long exhale. "Shit, I am totally screwing this up again. What I meant to say was that I'm sorry that I kissed you *there* where anyone could have walked in."

She wanted to say that it didn't matter anymore, that she didn't care, but for some silly reason she did. "But you did. Why?"

Nate cleared his throat, but his voice came out ragged. "Hell, Frankie I don't know. You were all pissy about the winner who *everyone else* felt deserved to win. Then you started yelling that it was unimaginative and predictable, with the poor guy standing twenty feet away, so I took you aside and kissing seemed like the only way to calm you down."

"To calm me down?" she said, suddenly feeling anything but calm.

"Yeah," he laughed. "And, trust me, I had every noble intention of leaving it as just a kiss, then you stuck your hand down my pants and I was a goner."

Frankie felt her face flush with embarrassment. She remembered how something had just snapped. Maybe it was the stress of disobeying her grandpa, or the disappointment over knowing that if she hadn't sat on the tasting tribunal, she could have entered her wine and won, or maybe it was just that she'd had a dry spell that had spanned two harvests. Whatever the reason, one touch of his lips and she'd been so aggressive, she'd practically knocked him over.

"You could have at least told me that my grandpa was in the room."

"I didn't see him," Nate defended.

"He was looking right at you!"

"Again," Nate said, pointing to his southern region. "Hands down my pants. Any guy getting a hand job would have had a hard time focusing."

"Half a hand job," she smiled. "I never finished."

"Believe me, I remember." So did Frankie. She remembered vividly how good he smelled, tasted, felt pressed against her body. "Anyway, what I am trying to say is that I'm sorry you lost your job over it."

"Yeah, me too." She'd lost so much more than just a job that night. Her grandfather walking away like he had, even after she explained she was just trying to help the town, had reaffirmed her greatest fears: For whatever reason, Frankie wasn't the kind of person who inspired unconditional love. "Although I think the final straw was my lecturing him on buying that land in Santa Ynez Valley."

Nate ran a hand through his hair. "If I had been thinking straight yesterday, I would have told the sheriff it was a misunderstanding."

Frankie raised a brow, challenging.

"Okay, maybe not. I was pretty ticked when you said it was your land. But I'm sorry I didn't listen."

"Thanks," she said, shoving on her helmet and adjusting the strap. "For the apology and that touching walk down memory lane, but I'm still not selling."

"Yeah, didn't think you would," he shrugged. "Can't blame a guy for making an offer, though."

Frankie climbed on the bike. She felt him watching her.

"Did you ever explain things to Charles? How what you did saved the event?"

She almost missed the question over the rumbling of her engine as she started her bike.

"Yeah," Frankie said, staring at the road and making sure not to betray herself. "He wasn't interested." Frankie flipped down the visor of her helmet and took off.

CHAPTER 4

Mittens was driving her insane.

Okay, to be fair, it wasn't the alpaca's fault that he'd eaten the mesh on the screen door and the top two boards off the first step of the porch. Frankie should have come straight home after the hearing and fed him. Instead, fired up and frustrated by the day's events, she burned up the pavement until she burned out the need to scream—or cry. The result: She was exhausted, Mittens had a stomachache, and now, instead of checking her vines to make sure none of the heavier clusters had broken from their ties, she was cutting down the boards to size.

"*Wark.*"

"Is that all you have to say for yourself?" Frankie asked, firing up the skill saw and making the last cut.

"*Wark. Wark. Wark.*"

Mittens, cured from his bellyache after eating every last flower in the flowerbed, pranced around proudly.

"Let's see if you're still strutting when I have to sell your manly coat to make next year's sweater sets so I can afford to buy new plants," Frankie muttered, wiping the sweat off her brow and picking up her nail gun. "You do this to even one of my vines and I'll be eating alpaca jerky for the next year. Got it?"

Mittens walked over to Frankie and headbutted her shoulder. Moving to her neck, he began to nuzzle and emanate a low, happy hum. She shoved him back and looked up as the alpaca batted his big, thick lashes her way.

"Flirting doesn't work with me, dude. Hard to charm your way into to my panties of steel."

"Well, then you should consider some lace," a weathered voice came from behind. "Lace likes to be charmed. Perhaps silk."

"We should take her to The Boulder Holder, Lucinda," added a voice that sounded like the queen of England, only with an Italian accent. "They're having a Harvest sale on all their autumn colored unmentionables."

Frankie shot the last nail in the board and turned around. Standing at the bottom of the walkway, in overalls and holding shovels, was Aunt Lucinda, her two sidekicks, ChiChi Ryo and Pricilla Moreau, and her cat. Okay, so ChiChi was dressed in a tan pantsuit and wearing gem encrusted gardening gloves, Aunt Luce was holding a pickax, and Mr. Puffins was wearing a sunbonnet, but they were all ready to do some serious manual labor.

"Maybe my panties don't want to be charmed," Frankie said, dusting off her hands and hating that that uptight DeLuca flashed in her mind and she couldn't help but wonder if he was more of a silk or lace kind of man.

Mittens followed closely behind her, sniffing Mr. Puffins before taking an experimental nibble of the silk flower on the cat's hat. Mr. Puffins narrowed his eyes but allowed the welcome.

"Then you haven't met the right charmer, dear," Pricilla, world renowned baker and Napa County's coupon poker champion—senior and otherwise—said with a grin that made Frankie want to cover her eyes.

"Yeah, I remember what happened last time you said that." Frankie had spent the night sucking face with a biker named Wreck, before her three wide-eyed grannies had gotten them all permanently banned from Anaconda, a strip joint in Reno.

"Aren't you going to invite us in?" Aunt Luce asked.

"I thought you were here to work." Frankie looked at her freshly cut boards, the setting sun, and back to the grannies. It was too late to start on anything now. They all knew it, which was why they smiled expectantly up at her. Even Mittens seemed to be grinning. "You aren't going to go away until you come in and see the place, huh?"

"Nope," they said in unison.

Frankie crossed her arms and took in a deep breath. She loved her aunt and surrogate grannies, she really did. But she knew why they were here. And she did *not* want to talk about the judge's ruling, Charles's stubborn pride, or how she was sharing land with a freaking DeLuca.

"Not one word about idiotic men," Frankie muttered and Mittens bared his teeth.

"I just brought over dinner." Pricilla held up a to-go bag from Sweet and Savory Bistro, the new local's hot spot eatery that Pricilla and her granddaughter opened last month. "Lexi's special pork loin."

It wasn't an answer, she noticed. And she knew better than to believe the innocent blinking behind those bifocals. Frankie also knew better than anyone in town how much trouble these three could cause. She spent more time with them than people her own age. But Lexi's pork loin smelled amazing and Frankie was starved. She'd split her last Pop Tart with Mittens before she'd left for court.

Frankie gave them all a stern look for several long seconds before turning and walking into the house. "Watch your step." She walked through the front room, silently cringing as three sets of orthopedic shoes squeaked on the wooden floor behind her. She knew what they saw. Nothing about the house was impressive. The building itself was sound, but the furniture was outdated, the wallpaper covered in grapes, and everything was coated in a fine layer of dust.

Saul and Glow hadn't lived in the house in years. When their kids went away to college they had moved closer to town. So, in addition to prepping for the upcoming harvest and planting her soon to be vineyard, Frankie had a decade of grime to deal with.

They walked into a large farm style kitchen, with more grapes, and Frankie grabbed a bottle of her Cab off the table and four wine glasses. Pricilla pulled a sanitizing wipe from somewhere inside her crocheted purse and went about wiping the table down.

ChiChi opened and closed every last cupboard and shook her head. "Child, how long have you been living here?"

"Since Monday," Frankie admitted.

"How have you managed to eat when you don't have a single plate, cup, or fork in the entire house?"

Frankie looked at Luce who was stroking Mr. Puffins and rolled her eyes at ChiChi's outrage over Frankie's lack of homemaking skills. Luce was the one person who completely understood Frankie. They were two peas in an extremely screwed up pod.

"I have cups." Frankie held up her wine glasses and smiled.

"You've got a set of shot glasses too. The ones I brought you as a housewarming present," Luce added with a grin.

"Yeah, but no water to wash them. I guess Saul had the same tank working both the house and the vineyard."

"I already called Walt," Luce said. "He'll be over first thing Monday to check out the water tank and see if he can get the water running, at least to the property."

"Shot glasses. No indoor plumbing," ChiChi chided as though she didn't, on occasion, sip homemade Angelica, aka fancy people's moonshine, from teacups. "You two are as bad as my grandson, Trey. Boy doesn't even have a place of his own and he's coming on thirty."

"Lexi sent paper plates and plasticware," Pricilla said. "So stop harassing the poor girl and help me serve before it gets cold. And Trey would get himself a place if you all didn't pamper him."

ChiChi harrumphed but took her seat. In minutes, supper was being spooned up, plates were being passed, and a comforting hum of chatter filled the room. Frankie looked around the table at three incredible women whose friendship had outlasted wars, marriages, funerals, and feuds and found herself smiling. What would she give to belong to something as special as what they'd created?

Oh, she had friends. There were Jordan Schultz and Regan Martin—well, Regan DeLuca now—but for whatever reason, Frankie had never been able to fully open up. Not the way these women did. There was nothing hidden between them. Even when ChiChi had married Geno DeLuca, breaking Charles's heart and starting a feud that would forever change the shape of St. Helena, never once had their friendship waivered.

The humbling part: They'd always made room for Frankie in their group, especially after the divorce. Going out of their way to include her in all of their plans, their crazy and sometimes illegal schemes, to make her feel a part of something. Which was why, when Frankie looked up from her nearly devoured dinner to find the grannies' plates virtually untouched and all bifocals on her, she stopped, fork in midair. "What?"

They exchanged worried looks, then Luce spoke. "How are you doing? After today?"

"Great," she lied, taking another forkful of green. Usually she hated anything green on her plate, but Lexi always managed to make it taste just like bacon. And Frankie loved bacon.

"Stubby seemed concerned with your money flow," Luce said, referring to Judge Pricket. After a very brief and, according to Luce, unsatisfying affair during the Nixon administration, she'd resorted to calling him Stubby.

Frankie almost reminded them that there was to be no stupid men talk, then decided it was a waste of breath. If they wanted to talk about the land or Charles, they were going to talk. And talk. And talk. Until Frankie answered.

"Besides the small issue with the water tank and sharing soil with a DeLuca"—she looked at ChiChi—"no offense".

ChiChi waved a dismissive hand. "None taken. I know how rigid my Nathaniel can be."

"Which is why I need to know if you can do this," Luce said. "You two have been at each other since high school when he won first in the science fair for his studies on Motzart's effect on Merlot."

"It was rigged," Frankie insisted. And the biased science fair wasn't the issue. It was that Nate had felt Frankie up on a Friday night in Saul's vineyard, ignited civil war within her family on Sunday, and asked Sasha Dupree to prom the follow-ing Tuesday—in front of everyone. "His dad was a judge."

"So was yours," ChiChi countered, forgetting that having her father on a committee in a contest that he felt should be a man's challenge wasn't the same thing.

"And you both want this land," Luce went on. "But Stubby was serious. If you two can't make this work he's going to re-zone the land to residential."

Frankie stopped chewing. "Rezone it? He didn't say any-thing about rezoning it in court."

God, if he did that then there would be a big ugly tract of identical taupe boxes stinking up the land between the Baudouin and DeLuca vineyards. Talk about running the prop-erty value into the ground.

"He can't do that. The traffic, the noise, the everything." Her heart started thrashing in her chest. "It would ruin every-thing."

"I know, dear." Luce reached out and uncharacteristi-cally squeezed Frankie's hand. Which was weird because, like Frankie, Aunt Luce wasn't one for public displays of affection. "That's why he said he'd do it. And I think if you two make even one wrong move, he will send in the bulldozers and we all lose."

No kidding. If the judge rezoned the land as residential, put it back on the market, and blocked the DeLucas from mak-ing another bid, there was no way she could afford to buy the other parcel. Then her dream, not to mention the beautiful vineyard next door that she grew up loving, would be ruined.

Talk about pressure. Frankie looked out the kitchen win-dow, past the fence, and felt her breath catch at the never ending rows of vines, heavy with grapes, their leaves already turning the color of fire were swaying in the breeze. She'd spent her life working that land and even though her grandpa didn't think she belonged there anymore, a part of her would die to see it ruined by a bunch of yuppies with their hybrid kids and entitled SUVs.

More importantly, that vineyard meant everything to her aunt. Luce didn't have kids or grandkids or a husband. Her life's work had been preserving the land and traditions that her father had handed down to her and Charles. Frankie didn't know what Luce would do if neighbors moved in and ruined what she'd worked so hard to create.

"Don't worry, Auntie. I'll make it work with Nate. Pricket won't get the chance to put any McMansions up. And neither of your vineyards will be ruined."

Luce shifted in her seat, ChiChi cleared her throat, Pricilla started pulling out truffles from her bag, and Mr. Puffins' ears went back. And suddenly Frankie knew her day was about to get worse—if that was even possible.

"That's good to hear because we were wondering just how things with you and my grandson are . . . progressing?" ChiChi asked, waggling her eyebrows suggestively.

Luce puckered her lips and made kissy noises.

And Pricilla, hand over heart, pretended to swoon.

Frankie was glad she'd already swallowed her wine or she would have choked. "He kissed me! End of story. No progression."

"Is that right," Pricilla said, a blatant *liar liar* in her tone. "Because that looked like some kiss. I mean your hands were—"

"Trying to push him away," she cut in. "And it doesn't matter anyway, I'm not his type."

"Rubbish," Luce snapped and Mr. Puffins growled, low and throaty. "You are a strong, independent, beautiful young woman." All of the adjectives *not* associated with what a man like Nate was looking for. Not that she cared, but Nate tended to date willowy, elegant Soccer Moms in training. They were highly qualified, highly respected, and high maintenance.

"Child, you have—" ChiChi made billowing gestures toward her chest region. "You're his type."

"Yeah, well, he's not mine." Which was true. Even if she could ignore the fact that the man wore loafers—which was a big *if*—she knew stoic, starched, analytical types weren't her thing. Even though that guy had more pent up passion than an Italian army, with a butt that made most women weep . . .

Walking sex god or not, Nate DeLuca was not what Frankie was looking for.

"If you say so, dear," Pricilla said as she glanced at the other grannies, clearly not believing her at all.

❧

Sorrento Ranch's house was an old Victorian built back in the late eighteen hundreds. Even with its olive clapboard siding, steeply pitched roof, and massive stained glass windows, the only descriptor that stood out was *old*. As a kid Nate had thought the house was impressive. As its newest owner, he had to admit it looked more like a terrifying theme park ride than a piece of prime real estate.

And it was all his. Well, half his.

After the disaster of a verdict, Nate had spent Friday and the better part of the weekend trying to get a handle on how much power Judge Pricket really held—apparently quite a lot. And how close to empty Frankie's bank account was—bad but not dire. Now he wanted nothing more than to spend his

Sunday evening sprawled out in bed, reading a book, in the blessed silence of his sprawling, modern, and mothball-free house. Only every time he'd turned the page, instead of words, all he saw were Frankie's lips, full and luscious, mouthing *Bite me!* Which was why he decided to pack up a few weeks of clothing, hop in his car, drive over to his other house, and change the rules—unannounced.

When he arrived, the curtains were pulled, the lights dialed to *go away*, and the door locked. He was pretty sure Frankie was out, but just to be safe, he knocked. Twice. Then let himself in. He couldn't wait to see the look on her face when she came home to find him in *her* bed—screwing up *her* weekend.

He kicked the front door shut, flicked on the light switch and

"Do you have a death wish or are you really this stupid?" Frankie asked.

Stupid. He must be. Because one glance at her and he felt his inner Neanderthal, the testosterone driven idiot who grunted gibberish and only seemed to come out around Frankie, raised his nasty head.

She was wearing a tank top again, although it wasn't black or wet. No, tonight she'd gone for white and thin and impossibly tight. She also wasn't wearing a bra, thank you, and had the cutest case of bed head he'd ever seen. Her black hair was sticking up in the back while her bangs and, what looked like sheet prints, were plastered to the right side of her face. But what had him panting like a dog was what she had on below.

Or what she didn't have on. Pants. There was a serious lack of cotton and flannel going on down there. And way too much pink. Pink boy shorts to be exact. Which made a whole lot of goings-on happen in his own shorts.

The silky fabric rode high on her thighs and aggressively low on her hipbones, hugging her skin and screaming to be caressed. It wasn't a loud pink or even an angry pink. Frankie was sporting soft pastel pink that was delicate and surprisingly feminine. She was also holding a very dangerous wooden bat, and he knew for a fact she had one hell of a swing.

"What, no gun?" Nate said, dropping his duffle bag to the floor and crossing to the couch, where he leisurely took a seat. A decade of dust bunnies and lint flickered in the light.

"And risk Judge Pricket turning this place into a strip mall, or worse, Stepford Lane?"

"You heard about that too?" Nate leaned back and swung his feet up on the coffee table.

Frankie choked up on her grip. "Plus a bat works just as well. So I suggest you crawl back into whatever hole you crawled out of before I show you my award-winning swing."

"As long as you promise to show me your award-winning backside, I'm game."

She looked down, blinked. She opened her mouth to say something then closed it, all the while her eyes wide with confusion and—fluster?

The bat drooped slightly.

Yup, she was definitely flustered. So Nate folded his hands behind his head and sent her a wink.

After a practice swing—man, she did have a great arm—Frankie took a step forward. "Get the hell out!"

Hands in the universal gesture for *I come in peace*, Nate said, "No need to pull out the fancy welcome mat, sweet cheeks. I don't expect you to wait on me. Although I'd love a beer if you have one."

Another swing. This time it was aimed at his head.

Nate ducked and rolled to the other side of the couch, pushing to his feet. "But I can see that you're busy so I'll get it myself."

Narrowly missing the swinging bat, Nate started for the kitchen. He opened the fridge and laughed. Frankie lived like a bachelor. Nothing but takeout, a half-empty bottle of Riesling—Baudouin, of course—enough pudding cups to amp up a kindergarten class, soy milk and, *ah*, beer.

"You break in and now you want to steal my beer?"

"Hard to break in," he said reaching past the paper to-go box and grabbing the bottle by the neck, "when you own the house."

"Half the house."

"Yeah," he smiled. "I remember."

She rolled her eyes and snagged the beer back, which was all right with him since he didn't really want the beer so much as to annoy her, and because she'd lost the bat somewhere between the living room and kitchen.

"You already have a house. A big, obnoxious overcompensation on the other side of town." She twisted off the beer cap— on her arm—and flicked it at his head. "Where people actually like you."

He caught the cap and tossed it in the trash can.

"House, yes. But roommate, no." He hopped up on the counter, waiting for his words to settle. Her eyes went wide, then fuming mad. God, she was hot when she was riled. "I know this is a little weird. I mean, I haven't had a roomie since college, so I wasn't sure what to expect, but I got to say, sweet cheeks," he purposely let his gaze drop and he flashed her a wicked smile, "this is blowing away all my expectations. Talk about a welcome home."

She paused for a moment, as though trying to figure out if he was messing with her or being serious.

It was both. Not that he'd tell her that.

He'd come here ready to throw her off balance, but one look at her in her tank and itty bitty undies and his brain had been scrambled.

It was her amazing rack, he decided. A powerful weapon he'd have to steer clear of.

"Ha ha. Nice try, DeLuca." She hopped up on the island facing him, exposing what seemed to be a mile of the most incredible legs he'd ever seen. "Whatever your game is, it won't work. We both know you and your golden boy loafers won't make it here. There's no cable, no housekeeper, and no pansy-ass Frappuccino maker. You're just here to irritate me."

"Although irritating you is a surprise bonus, I'm actually here to prove to Judge Pricket that I am serious about this land and serious about making this work. We only have thirty days to change his mind or we both lose."

"*You* lose," she reminded him, tipping back the beer and taking a long pull. He watched her throat work. Her eyes locked on his over the rim of the bottle and he found himself thinking that thirty days was a hell of a long time to keep his hands to himself. Especially if this was her usual nighttime attire.

As if reading his dirty mind, Frankie's face flushed and she shifted on the counter.

Interesting. She was as uncomfortable with the sexual heat that seemed to sizzle between them as he was.

"I lose and we all lose, Frankie," he said hopping down and slowly making his way toward her, sliding between her legs and taking the beer out of her hand. Noticing she kept her gaze on his mouth, he took a sip and continued, "So unless you want to explain to your family how we let a bunch of Joe Dot Coms move in with their trophy wives and designer dogs, then you had better get used to me and my golden boy loafers, because we're moving in."

He didn't mention that his pansy-ass Frappuccino maker was in his trunk. Or that his plan to mess with her somehow backfired, because he couldn't seem to stop looking at her lips.

"Oh, yeah?" A totally cool, almost bored expression crossed her face as she casually leaned back on her hands. The movement made her legs open a little wider, slide a little closer to home. "And just how do you think this will work?"

Damn it. Now she was screwing with him, trying to pretend she wasn't the least bit affected. Too bad her breathing was just as labored, her eyes just as dilated.

Nate rested his palms on the counter, leaning in until their mouths were just a breath apart. "Do you need a diagram or would you prefer a demonstration?"

His voice came out totally unaffected, an effect that would be ruined if she scooted herself any closer because his southern region was already manning up.

"Dream on," she said and Nate smiled because there was a small stutter in her normally tough voice. "Because in the end, that tab and slot you're talking about would still belong to you and me."

His gaze slid down to the base of her neck. For several long seconds he watched as a pulse leapt beneath her creamy skin. Oh yeah, Miss Untouchable was aware of him, hyper aware of him. And suddenly Nate knew that making this work wasn't the problem. He was more concerned about what happened if it did. Because she was right. Come tomorrow morning, they would be staring at each other across the kitchen table, a legal pad full of new emotions to add to the already complicated list.

They both had a lot on the line, him even more so. And doing something as stupid as following through on this, whatever it was, would only backfire. He needed to focus on getting those other ten acres.

Giving her this one win, he pushed off the counter and stepped back—away from temptation. Ignoring the victorious smile on her pretty lips, he made his way into the front room, grabbed his bag, and walked to the front door.

"Leaving so soon?" she asked. He could hear the confusion in her voice, disbelief he had caved so easily.

"Nope, just locking the door. Wouldn't want to get any unwanted visitors." Swinging the duffle over his shoulder, he strode past a very pissed off Frankie, narrowly missing an elbow to the ribs, and headed down the hallway. "If you don't have a preference, I'll take the master."

"Too bad, DeLuca. I'm already in the master," Frankie said, shuffling past, her feet slapping on the hardwood floor and the lace cupping that backside shifting higher with each step, before she slammed the door.

He turned the knob and, no surprise there, it was already locked. The shuffling of furniture sounded as Frankie barricaded the door.

"I hope that bed is a king," he laughed outside the door. "Since this happens to be on the north half of the property, tomorrow night that bed is mine, sweet cheeks."

CHAPTER 5

"The water tank's only part of your problem," Walt Larson, the hardware half of St. Helena Hardware and Refurbish Rescue, said as he took in the disaster that used to be Frankie's well. "In fact, I'd say that llama of yours did you a favor."

An odd keening sound followed by a belligerent "*Wark*" echoed across the property moments before a low rustling came from the general direction of the tool shed. Mittens peeked his little Rastafarian head out, ears peeled back, dentures bared.

The second Walt had arrived, truck tires crunching down the gravel drive, Mittens, afraid he was about to be tranquilized and carted off to Alpaca Paradise, had hightailed it across the property and taken up residence behind Saul's old rusted-out tractor.

"Alpaca," Frankie corrected Walt, and Mittens snorted, then went back to chewing on the tractor seat. He was a nervous eater. "And I know that the property needs a lot of love, but right now I can only afford the water tank."

"Well, first you need a new water pump," Walt said, whacking the metal pipe that was connected to the wellhead with a wrench. "The motor's working too hard just to supply the house and few vines you have."

Poppycock.

"How long do you think this one will last?" Frankie mentally estimated how much a new motor would cost and then doubled it because that was how her luck seemed to be going. They hadn't even started the water tank portion of the visit and already she was out of money.

"It won't."

"What do you mean it won't?" she asked, suddenly wondering if the old man was taking her for a ride. "You haven't even pulled it out to look."

"Don't need to. You hear that clanking noise?" Walt yelled over the awful grinding, as though to prove his point. "That's the motor, struggling. Telling me it needs to be replaced."

"What are you? The well whisperer?"

"Nope, but I hear whispers all the same." He raised a disappointed brow. "People coming in the store are talking about how you and that DeLuca are shacking up."

"We aren't shacking up, so much as living under the same roof."

"And how come spring you two are going to plant this whole lot with vines. Together."

Frankie rolled her eyes. Walt was built like a tree stump, smelled like cooked cabbage, and had a penchant for prattle—which was how he'd managed to keep his hardware store open when one of the big DIY stores opened up in Napa. Knowing everybody else's business was good for business in a town like St. Helena.

And although his last name wasn't Baudouin, he was Frankie's third cousin on her grandmother's side—she even called him uncle—so, being a good and loyal relative, he harbored the appropriate amount of disdain for the DeLucas.

But what had his lips pursing was that his biggest competition was Tanner Construction, owned by former NFL running back and DeLuca Wine's newest business partner, Jack Tanner. So if they were developing the land together, Nate would insist on using his guy. Who was cheaper—and faster, Frankie thought as she watched Walt stick a welding rod to his ear, then rested the other end on the pipe like it was some kind of well-stethoscope.

"You and your store have been serving Baudouin Vineyards since before I was born," Frankie assured him. "So even though we are going to plant all twenty acres, DeLuca will plant his half and I will plant mine. Both using our own chosen suppliers."

"Good to hear. After the Showdown, there was all that talk about you and the buttoned-up brother necking, then when Charles . . ."

"Fired me?" Frankie added, but what she wanted to say was *disowned*. Because that's how it had felt. Still felt. She was within throwing distance from her childhood home, from her grandfather's land, and yet he hadn't dropped by once to see her. Hadn't even returned a single one of her phone calls.

"Connie and I were just worried is all. But you should be proud of yourself, hon. Half or not, you did more than sixty years of Baudouin griping accomplished." Walt gave her a pat on the shoulder, his eyes flickering to the imposing French chateau, which sat on the other side of the fence. "Your grandpa isn't going to be happy about his grapes sharing soil with the DeLucas."

"Yeah well, they're not his vines, they're mine. So is this soil. And I'm going to make this work," Frankie said and a heavy pressure started low in her belly at the reminder of Nate's suggestion for how things between them could work. Not that they would work, because she wasn't going there. She could if she wanted to, that much was obvious by the bulge in his jeans. All it would take was one well-placed look from her and he'd be game.

And then what? Wake to find his loafers sitting next to her motorcycle boots under her bed?

No. Nate was one of those guys who liked bed-sex. Not that there was anything wrong with bed-sex. But she'd dated enough to know that bed-sex usually led to talking, which somehow progressed into commitment. And Frankie learned long ago that she wasn't the type who guys felt committable about.

Sure, she'd had boyfriends over the years, but none of them had any staying power. She was careful about that. Always dating men who, come morning, she had no problem walking away from. Which was fine by her, because she knew that the walking away easily went both ways.

"Well, even if you decide to deny him access to the well, there is no way this pump can handle ten acres," Walt said, pulling her from her thoughts. "You need a commercial grade pump and triple the tank if you're going to make a go at this. Otherwise, this time next year, you're going to have a bunch of planted saplings and a broken pump."

Frankie braced her hands on her lower back and looked up at the sky. "How much are we talking?"

Walt took off his driver's cap and scratched his bald head. "I'd have to check on some pricing, see what kind of deal I can get you, but I bet we're talking about twelve grand."

"Jesus, Walt." She didn't have that kind of money. Okay, she had the money, but it was budgeted for other things she'd need in the upcoming year. "What if we just start with the pump?"

"That was for the pump." Yeah, she'd thought so, but was hoping otherwise. "For the tank, I recommend a coated steel fifty-gallon horizontal tank. I know a guy in Sonoma who would give you a good deal on one, but we're still talking thirty grand."

A distressed "*Wark*" sounded and it may have come from Frankie. This was the moment she had been waiting for. The court hearing had gone relatively well—for her—so she'd been waiting for the bottom to fall out.

A gentle nudge came from behind and a wet nose pressed into the side of her neck.

With a resigned sigh, Frankie reached back and gave Mittens a scratch behind the ear. She stared past the broken pump, past the flattened sheets of plastic, and took in the overgrown pasture and gnarled oak trees whose leaves, one by one, let go of the branch and floated the ground.

"That going to be a problem?" Walt asked as though she had fifty grand sitting in the cookie jar on top of the freezer.

"Nope, no problem," she said, hoping it was true. This was a once in a lifetime opportunity. Not just to prove to her family she could do this—that she was a talented enologist—but to finally make her dream a reality.

"You guys do, what," she said, thinking back to the cooling units she'd ordered for her grandfather's aging cellar last summer, "a ninety day billing cycle, right?"

"You'd need to come in and see Connie to set up an account in your name before we ordered anything."

"Sure, great. I can come down this afternoon."

"We require a proof of collateral from the bank for purchases this big," Walt said, taking off his hat and studying the brim like it was a matter of national security.

"I'm good for the money, Walt."

"I know that, hon, but wine is a tricky industry and my company can't front a purchase this big. Not to mention the matter of my marriage. Connie would have my ass, excuse the language, if she heard I extended a line this big to someone with no collateral or track record."

Connie Larson was Walt's wife, the town's resident furniture doctor, and a woman who had a spending problem as wide as the valley. So when it came to the family business, she held a tight purse string.

"Come on, Walt. Help me out here. How can we make this work?"

"Hell, Frankie. We're talking fifty grand and we aren't even adding in all the costs for irrigating the land properly, which you'll have to do before you plant."

"I know." It was what Frankie had allotted the majority of the money in her account for. Irrigation for her saplings. She had a five step plan to plant the land over the next five years; two acres and eighteen hundred vines at a time.

Walt looked up at the sky and sighed. "All right, I bet I can convince Connie to look past you being green and put everything on the company's tab if Charles agrees."

Frankie snorted. "First off, I'm not green. I've been making wine longer than most people in this valley."

"I know that, but you were working Charles's land, taking risks on his dime. Running your own vineyard is different."

It would be freeing, just like Jonah had said. For the first time in her career, Frankie would be able to make the decisions, take risks, and follow her gut without having to convince her grandpa.

"And I can tell by your scowl that things between the two of you are still rocky and that even if he'd be willing to spot you the credit—"

"He won't and nope."

Walt's eyes lit. "Hey I know, maybe one of your brothers or Lucinda would be willing—"

"Again, nope." Not going to happen. She'd made this mess, along with her alpaca, and she would figure out how to fix it. Getting her grandpa involved would be like admitting what a stupid decision buying the land had been. He'd remind her how, once again, she'd acted without thinking things through. Worse, he'd tell her that if she had come to him in the beginning with the deal, none of this would have happened.

Even worse yet, her brothers would find out and, even though she'd beg them not to, they'd get involved. Frankie would unintentionally force them to choose sides—something she swore she'd never do again.

She didn't need her grandpa's credit or her brothers' handouts. What she needed was a plan.

"I can't plant until late spring anyway," Frankie reasoned aloud. "So between now and then, the pump will take about the same beating as it has for the past sixty years. If I bought a new ten thousand gallon-tank"—still expensive, but it wouldn't break her—"do you think you could give this pump a little loving so it could get me through until next crush?"

By then, she'd have hopefully sold her futures and have some cash coming in. She was still waiting to hear back from Susan Jance who was interested in purchasing four barrels of Frankie's wine, Red Steel, at thirty thousand a barrel. If she liked it, which Frankie knew she would, she was going to give Susan the opportunity to offer her other clients a great deal on the prepurchase of future barrels.

That meant money upfront on grapes that were not even harvested yet. With most of the two planted acres falling on Frankie's side of the line, she was estimating a total of sixteen barrels next harvest. A profit that would put her well on her way to breaking even.

"I can try," Walt said, sucking in a breath through his teeth and making a whistling sound. "But you're going to have to replace it at some point and doing this in two separate steps is going to cost you a whole lot more money in the long run. And you'll have to get that irrigation going soon if you want to plant this spring."

That was what Frankie was afraid of. "Can I have a few days to think it over?"

Even though she knew it was most likely going to be the "long run" plan, she still had to run it by Nate. It was, after all, half his water—and half his responsibility.

"Sure, it will give me time to call around and see what kind of a deal I can get you," Walt said, picking up his toolbox and heading toward his truck. "Don't take too long though, we're expecting another scorcher this week and you've got a lot of grapes over there."

"I won't," she said, following behind. Mittens, on the other hand, took off, his little hooves pounding some serious dirt. As though Frankie had the time right now to hog-tie him and toss him in the back of Walt's truck. Nope, she'd give him another few days to get settled, let his guard down and then she'd drag his fuzzy butt to Paradise.

Walt hopped in his truck and, instead of starting the engine, rested his forearm on the open window and leaned out. "Last year my oldest granddaughter got into some fancy art school in Paris. The store was struggling because of that damn DIY megastore and the bank turned us down for a loan, so Connie and I met with Kenneth's wife, what's her name . . . "

"Shady . . . um, Katie?"

"Yeah, she gave us a line of credit on the hardware store, as a favor since we're family and all. She even looked past the hit we had taken in the past year and said the bank was investing in us because we had invested so much in the town over the years." Walt reached out and patted her hand. "Maybe she'd let you do the same, only using your grapes and reputation. Because you and I both know that besides the quality of the plant, there's nothing more important than proper irrigation. I'd hate to see you bet the vineyard on a pump that's older than dirt and lose it all."

Frankie considered that—for all of two seconds. "I won't lose these grapes."

He watched her for a long moment and offered her a concerned smile. "You're awfully sure of yourself, that's clear."

What was more than clear by the look on Walt's face and the way he was holding her hand—something that a smart person would avoid at all cost—was that he thought she'd be making a huge mistake not to blow her entire wad on the new pump and water tank. Although Frankie agreed with his assessment, she couldn't help but see the good with the bad.

The good news was that Nate was equally responsible in coughing up the bills to pay for this unforeseen cost. If he wanted to plant this spring, which she knew he did, then he'd need water too, which cut her overwhelming tally to a mere twenty-five thousand and change.

The bad part was that, unlike her, Nate could simply snap his entitled fingers and poof, a personal check covering his half of the costs would magically appear. Whereas Frankie would have to go down to St. Helena Federal and sit in front of her cousin's wife and bare her financial soul. The bearing would go through the loan officer first, then Shady Katie to sign off, and then—because Katie always had her eye on the prize—finally Charles, who would then write her off completely.

"Maybe." She tried not to laugh. She must have really done something to piss off the universe if her saving grace was Shady Katie. "Thanks for coming out on such short notice. And tell Aunt Connie I say hi."

"I will." He reached for the starter and stalled again. "You're going to be without water for a little while longer. You okay with that?"

"I'll manage," she said smiling.

Between Regan's and her best friend Jordan's house, she'd be fine. Although going to Jordan's house meant dealing with her brooding teenage daughter Ava, and Regan's meant listening to her new baby wail until Frankie's ears started to bleed, it wasn't so bad. She kind of liked watching all the fuss and commotion that goes on with families. Sometime when it got really crazy, and everyone was running around, she could almost feel a part of it all.

But no water was going to drive golden boy crazy.

"Take as long as you need, Walt," she said patting the hood when he fired up the engine. "The grapes and I will be just fine."

Frankie waved as Walt made his way down the gravel drive and went to find Mittens. It took twenty minutes, a bag of apples, and a solemn promise that he wasn't going to Alberta's Paradise Alpaca Farm and Pet Sanctuary to persuade the poor alpaca to come out from behind the tool shed.

~

"Are you going to marry my Uncle Nate?" Holly asked, her little girl eyes wide with wonder.

Frankie's hand, in the process of carefully folding over the top of yet another maple leaf, froze and then tightened, cracking the leaf in half and spearing her finger with the pushpin. A drop of blood beaded and Frankie, not wanting to stain Regan's rug, grabbed the box of Band-Aids, which still sat directly to her right from the last puncture-emergency, and wrapped her ring finger. Great, now she had a set of four matching fingers on her right hand.

"Cuz if you are, I'd like to let you know that I'm a really good flower girl and my daddy says I look like an angel in blue."

Holly was Regan's kid. She was cute, seven, and annoying as hell. She was also a DeLuca, which explained the annoying part, and the self-appointed head of the Maple Leaf Rose Committee for Baby Sofie's one month birthday. As if being forced to make hundreds of roses out of dead leaves wasn't bad enough, Frankie had been banished to the kids' table for improper use of a glue gun and a bad attitude.

The roses and lack of weapons weren't the worst part. Frankie always felt awkward around kids. Always. It wasn't that she didn't like them; she just never knew what to do with them.

Being the youngest in her family by five years, she was never around young kids growing up—never babysat, never coached little league, and besides Jordan and Regan she didn't have any friends with kids. Okay, besides Jordan and Regan she didn't have any friends. At least not ones that didn't qualify for a senior discount at The Grapevine Prune and Clip.

Frankie froze. Maybe it wasn't kids. Maybe she was just awkward around people, period.

"I could even help you pick out a dress. I'm real good at picking out princess gowns and tiaras," Holly said, sounding so excited Frankie hated to burst her little joy bubble. Or make her cry.

Frankie studied Holly's face for quivering lips or misty eyes. The kid sounded so excited, she really hoped she didn't cry.

"I bet you are," Frankie clarified as gently as possible, tossing the ruined leaf into the "Whoops" pile, as Holly had so adequately named it. Frankie's contribution to the "Whoops" pile was bigger than Holly's. "But Nate and I aren't getting married."

"You're not?" Holly's eyes narrowed in confusion. "But when Femi Lewis tried to hold my hand at recess, Daddy said it was against the rules for boys and girls to hold hands unless they were dating. And since he says I can't date until I'm married, I can't hold his hand."

Frankie snorted. "You fell for that?" Mini-Einstein just blinked up innocently and Frankie sucked her lips in to keep from laughing. Right. Kid and all. "Maybe your dad didn't want you to hold his hand because his name is Femi."

"Making fun of people's names isn't funny," Holly said, defiantly not laughing. "But I bet if me holding Femi's—" she paused, looking up at Frankie and waiting for her to snicker. Frankie bit her lip. "—hand is against the rules, then I bet that you living with Nate and not being married is super bad."

No, Nate invading her space was super bad.

"People should only get married when they love each other, right?" Frankie said.

Holly considered that. "I guess so."

"Well, then Nate and I can't get married," Frankie said, pleased at her deductive reasoning with a toddler. Or was she a tween? Frankie wasn't really sure. Usually by now she'd be sweating just being this close to peanut butter breath and thinking up some reason to leave.

"Why not?" Holly rested her chin on her knees, her lips pursing with confusion.

"Because I don't even like Nate."

Holly gasped, pulling out a pocket sized notebook and marking down a tally to the never ending marks on the page. "Saying you don't like someone is mean, Miss Francesca. Especially when it's their favorite uncle."

Miss Francesca tried not to roll her eyes. Holly was a big control freak stuck in a pint sized body with bouncy brown curls and cherub cheeks. But Frankie wasn't fooled because, like her *favorite uncle*, Holly fancied herself the all supreme hall monitor of the world, which explained the notebook entitled FRANKIE'S DIRTY JAR RECORD. It was three-quarters full and meticulously kept. Every questionable word uttered or bad attitude observed by her highness resulted in a twenty-five-cent fine.

Frankie paid the girl fifty bucks upfront, hoping to win her over and praying it would last her a year. That was only four months ago. And she was no closer to the first and almost of out credits.

"You're right," Frankie said, blaming Nate for her piss-poor attitude. Being mad at him didn't mean she had the right to make a little girl upset. "I'm sorry."

"That's okay." Holly plucked another leaf from the pile. Fold. Press. Tuck. Fold. Press. Tuck. "I'd be mad too if Mommy had taken away my glue gun and made me do baby crafts."

Well, now Frankie just felt petty.

Deep concentration creased Holly's little face and her tongue peeked out the side of her mouth. Her fingers moved with graceful ease over the leaf, efficiently folding and tucking until it resembled—a rose.

Huh? Frankie picked up a new leaf and tried again. Fold, press, tuck, fold, press—

"Crap."

Holly finished her rose, placed it on her massive "Perfect" pile and jotted down another tally. Then she picked up two leaves, scooted across the carpet, and took up residence next to Frankie.

"Like this," she said, slowly folding and pressing and tucking, patiently walking Frankie through the steps. Every few folds, her little fingers would smooth down one of Frankie's creases or tighten her last tuck. Finally, Holly handed her the floral tape and let Frankie wrap the wire that made up the stem. And with the tape secure she speared it with a pushpin and—

"I did it!"

"This is the bestest rose ever," Holly squealed and, bouncing on the carpet, clapped her hands in front of her face. Finally, Frankie could see the appeal. The kid was kind of cute when she wasn't lecturing. "Here, try another."

The two worked in silence, making one rose after another. Frankie was barely able to keep up with Holly's pace. Not only was the girl faster, but she didn't have to throw away every third rose. *Baby crafts my ass.*

"If you change your mind about the wedding—"

"I won't."

"Okay," Holly sighed, obviously disappointed that she wouldn't get to wear a princess gown. "Can I tell you a secret?"

Frankie secured a pushpin. "Um, sure."

"When my baby sister moved in with my family, she cried all the time. Even at night when we're supposed to be eyes tight, lights out," Holly began quietly, focus tightly glued to her rose. "I was sad cuz I didn't like her and I wanted to send her back."

"I imagine that it's hard to like a screaming baby." Frankie thought of her new roommate and felt an immediate bond form with the girl.

"Yeah." Holly slid her a worried look. "Mommy told me that I didn't have to like somebody to love them."

"Yeah," Frankie laughed. "And it's not like you can send a baby back."

Holly raised a condemning brow.

"Sorry, girl talk makes me nervous." And she was really nervous right now. Her hands were kind of clammy and her head felt a little light.

"I bet if you asked Mommy about marrying Nate, she'd say that same thing. Maybe you should use your words when he comes back with ice cream. He's buying Rocky Road," Holly said rubbing her belly. "And whipped cream. You can have some of mine if you want."

Frankie didn't hear anything past *marrying Nate* and *when he comes back*. Because that was it. Girl talk was officially over. Frankie shot to her feet and, knocking the "Perfects" into the "Whoops," effectively mixing the two piles, looked at the front door.

Holly stood also, blocking the exit, her little pigtails bouncing. "What's wrong, Miss Francesca?"

"I want to go home," Frankie blurted out and knew it was true. She didn't want to go to her little 1920's bungalow right off Main Street that she'd sold last month, or her grandfather's house. No, Frankie wanted to go to her beat up old Victorian with all of its creaks and dust bunnies and hug her alpaca.

"That's okay. Mommy says it's normal on playdates to get scared," Holly reasoned.

"This isn't a playdate. And I'm not scared. *Regan*," Frankie shouted down the hall, dragging out both syllables of her friend's name. "Your daughter's psychoanalyzing me again."

"Holly," a stern voice came from the doorway. It was way too low and way too amused to be Regan, and way too sexy to be anyone but—

"Uncle Nate," Holly squealed, rushing past Frankie.

"Hey there, kiddo," he laughed.

Frankie turned around and, *whoa*, go easy indeed. Golden boy leaned against the doorframe of the kitchen entry with Holly shrink-wrapped to his legs. He was covered in saw dust, a sweaty tee, and that DeLuca charm Frankie had seen at work more times than she could count on the local public at large. He cradled a squirming pink bundle of ten fingers and toes in one hand and enough testosterone to melt Frankie's panties in the other.

She knew that she was supposed to be mad at him. He'd kissed her, taken her to court, and then invaded her space, but she found herself melting at the sight of him and his two nieces. Who knew men and kids were such a potent combination? Frankie wondered if they were as good of a chick magnet as a Frisbee and dog.

"You taking it easy on Frankie?"

Holly lifted her right hand, no Band-Aids present, as though giving an oath. "Yes, sir."

Nate raised a disbelieving brow.

"She wants to go home," Holly said, swishing back and forth, blinking up at her uncle while innocently ratting Frankie out.

"I'm just tired," Frankie lied, fumbling for her motorcycle keys and helmet. "Plus I already made a dozen roses so that paid for the water I used. If you can tell Regan thanks." She turned and knocked her helmet off the corner of the couch and it went rolling.

"Holly, it's time to get in your PJs anyway," Nate said, his amused eyes firmly on Frankie. "Say goodnight and go wash up. After I walk Frankie to her car, we can have ice cream."

The girl did and after Nate ruffled her little fountains of curls as she ran by, her bare feet sounding like a charging herd of alpacas on the hardwood floor, Frankie grabbed her helmet and made a move for the door.

Nate pushed off the doorframe and stepped in front of her. "Unless you want to stay?"

"Nope."

"I know you can't eat ice cream. If I had known you'd be here I would have brought something nondairy," Nate said, adjusting the bundle like a football. Frankie froze. "But I bet Regan has some left over pie. It's fig. Hey, are you okay?"

Frankie nodded, and wasn't she a big fat liar. The truth was she was thrown, knocked over by something as small as him noticing that she didn't drink milk. She was tempted to forgive him of everything, take him up on his sweet offer and start over. Which made her not only a liar but pathetic.

"Have you met Sofie yet?" Nate asked, walking toward her.

Frankie, knowing what she'd see, a cute little bundle of poop and tears, took a huge step back. "Yup."

Nate raised a brow and took another step closer, boxing her in. "Had the chance to hold her?"

Frankie either had to look at the baby, and risk sending it into tears, or jump out the window. A glance behind her and a quick calculation of how far the drop was, and if the grass below would act as a cushion, later she was moving toward the window, ready to take her chances. Then she saw the screen and knew she was screwed.

Hugging her helmet to her chest, she explained, "Babies and I don't mix all that well."

"Ah, come on. She's got a fresh diaper and was just fed, she'll be an angel." Now he was teasing her. He had to be. Otherwise he was just being mean because it was obvious that she was rattled.

"I'm not good with babies." But when Frankie put her hands out in what she thought was clearly the universal sign for *hell no*, he took a step closer. Either it was a misunderstanding or Nate wanted to make her sweat, because instead of cuddling the wiggling poop-maker back to his chest, he grabbed her helmet and replaced it with Baby Sofie.

Frankie looked down to make sure the baby was actually in the bundle of pink cotton because it felt so light and, wow, the kid was knocked out. Dark little lashes rested on her chubby cheeks, her tiny chest rose and fell with each steady breath, and she smelled like baby powder and new car. Peaceful, cute, not so bad.

Frankie looked up at Nate and smiled. He wasn't smiling back. The good news what that it was his turn to be rattled. His gaze dropped to sleeping Sofie and back to Frankie and all of a sudden the room felt like it was getting smaller. The sexual energy that always seemed to buzz between them, heightened to the point of being palpable, surrounding them as though it was just her and Nate and—

It wiggled. The kid made some grunting noise and her eyes snapped open, hazy and milky at first, and then—*boom*—locked on to Frankie and wouldn't let go. It was as though Sofie was trying to incinerate Frankie with her gaze. Her face went from peaceful to tomato in two seconds flat, getting redder and redder as her lips puckered tighter and tighter, until—she exploded.

It wasn't just a cry. Frankie could handle a cry. It was more like a demonic screech, pulled up from the depths of Hell and released on the room.

"See," Frankie said extending the very pissed off package back to Nate. "She doesn't like me."

"Sweetheart, she's a baby, she doesn't like anyone," Nate said, sticking out his finger and fitting it in the tiny hand.

Only she *really* didn't like Frankie. Her screeching became wails and the kid's face was so purple Frankie wouldn't put it past her to stop breathing all together. How could she explain to one of her two best friends that she'd broken her baby? Just by holding her?

"Really, I can't," she said, a bubble of panic rising up. "I told you I'm not good with kids and"—*breathe, Frankie, breathe*—"I can't do this."

Nate must have realized that she wasn't screwing around, that she was about to reach DEFCON 1 and lose it, because his smile vanished and suddenly he was behind her, his strong arms around her, supporting Baby Sofie from underneath.

"It's okay," he soothed. For Sofie's or Frankie's sake, she couldn't be sure, but Sofie dropped the theatrics to a steady wet-sniffle and Frankie felt her breathing return to somewhat normal. "She just needs to be reassured that you've got her."

"But I don't have her," Frankie whispered. She'd never had a maternal touch. And it had never bothered her. Until now.

"Sure you do. Just put your hand here. Good. Now the other hand under her head." Nate deftly repositioned Frankie's hands to where the sniffles continued but didn't elevate, and tightened his arms around hers, firmly holding her against his body. He gently swayed back and forth. "She likes to be held tight and rocked."

Frankie realized that she liked to be held tight and rocked too. It was soothing and kind of nice. Like being wrapped up in a warm, snuggly, man-cocoon.

She turned her head to say thank you, thank you for not laughing when he easily could have, and thank you for letting her know that regardless of what was going on between them, in that one moment, he had her. Only she froze.

Nate, who had rested his chin on her shoulder to watch Sofie, was inches from her mouth. All she had to do was move a smidge to the right and up and they would be kissing. He seemed to be reading her mind because his gaze dropped to her lips and his hands, no longer on the baby, slid around her stomach.

"Frankie," he whispered, his pinkies dipped beneath the hem of her jeans, and she saw it coming.

He was going to kiss her.

And she was going to let him.

She should have tossed him the bundle and burned rubber out of there, but she couldn't. All the oxygen left her lungs in a single whoosh, her legs felt like she'd just harvested an entire vineyard, and instead of pulling away she felt herself leaning back, further pressing into Nate's hard chest, and tilting her head so that—

"Whoa, hey there," Gabe said.

Frankie jumped forward as though all the lying had finally caught up with her and her butt was on fire. Nate did some fancy footwork of his own, moving him a safe three feet in the other direction.

"Sorry about that. Didn't mean to interrupt," Gabe said, all smiles and no sorry.

"I was just showing Frankie how to hold a baby," Nate said, taking Sofie back and handing Frankie her helmet.

"That was some lesson. Looked like you were about to get to the part about making one of your own—"

"Do you have a point?" Nate asked. "For being in here?"

"You mean in my own home?" Gabe smiled at Nate even bigger. "I just came to check on things. Holly's worried that Frankie doesn't like you and she wanted to make sure you were using your words. But I can see that that isn't a problem. Well, maybe the using your words part was, but—"

"I gotta go," Frankie said, picking up her keys. Bad enough that she was in a DeLucas house helping make decorations. But now she'd been caught fraternizing with the enemy. And she'd liked it.

CHAPTER 6

Nate swung hard. Pain exploded, starting in his left thumb and shooting up his arm at the same pace and volume as the long list of choice words he rattled off. When he ran out of original phrases he started repeating. Even that didn't help.

"You might want to put ice on that."

Nate popped out his ear buds and turned around to see Frankie, standing on the back porch, nibbling on one of those toaster pastries she seemed so fond of. Mittens was dining on the other half.

"How long have you been standing there?" Nate asked, pretending his thumb wasn't about to fall off.

"Since you started singing to Skynard," she said around bits of dough. "Figured you for more of a classical kind of guy."

"Skynard is a classic."

She jammed the rest of the pastry into her mouth—whole— and shrugged. "I was thinking Mozart, but whatever."

She skipped down the steps and walked toward him through the ankle-high mustard weed, those hips of hers moving with quiet confidence. Today she wore her usual uniform of a tank top, ripped jeans, and boots—black and badass—but instead of the ball buster attitude she normally favored, she looked a little unsure. Untouchable, yes, but unsure all the same.

Nate knew it was because of the almost-kiss and never-going-to-happen conversation last night. Afraid she'd take him up on his threat to share the master and, idiotically hoping they'd pick up where they left off, Nate had chosen to sleep at his other house. Not that he'd slept. Even after a shower and a beer—both ice cold—he'd spent the night thinking about Frankie and how incredible she felt.

She stopped next to the pile of new cedar planks that Tanner had dropped off earlier that morning and looked at his hammer sticking out of the dirt. "You want to use my nail gun? Goes faster and less chance of splitting the wood." She looked at his hand. "Or your finger."

For about six-tenths of a second, Nate considered bringing up the kiss. Considered just getting it out there in the open and having a mature, matter-of-fact discussion about the insane sexual zing between them—and how acting on it would be a mistake. They both had a lot riding on this land, and getting distracted in something that would never, in a million years, work was just plain stupid. But he couldn't do it.

Because motorcycle boots or not, Frankie didn't look like Frankie. For the first time since, well, since they were kids, that tough girl attitude etching her face, shoving back her shoulders, or shooting that pert nose of hers in the air was gone. She looked vulnerable and tired, the kind that went bone-deep. And quite possibly a little nervous.

"You got one?"

"Yup, but not sure I should let you use it. A mistake like that with real tools could cost you a hand," she said, trying for smug, but he could tell she was relieved. They were avoiding the sex in the room, so to speak, at least for now. "What are you building anyway?"

"A bed for Mittens, since the hood of my car is no longer an option." He eyed the alpaca, who'd waited until he'd safely maneuvered himself behind Frankie before making a raspberry sound in Nate's direction.

After his first night here, Nate had welcomed the morning with hoof scratches on the front bumper of his BMW and a Mittens sized dent on the hood.

Frankie reached around Nate—a sweet flowery scent sucker punched him, catching him completely off guard—and grabbed the folded up blueprints out of his back pocket. She waved it in front of his face. "And you think that this is the answer?"

He grabbed for it, but she was quicker, spinning away and unfolding the paper.

"I found a place online that sells blueprints for camelidae friendly, green-habitats." Nate had spent most of last night trying to distract himself from the taste of her on his lips by surfing the net for the perfect solution to Mittens.

He knew that, although Frankie acted as though she couldn't care less if the alpaca went AWOL, she wouldn't get rid of the miniature camel. And Nate couldn't risk the thing eating what little vines there were. He needed those grapes and was determined to strike a deal with Frankie when the time came, but two well-placed bites and a headbutt later and Mittens would scale the only thing keeping him from an afternoon snack.

"Camelidae habitat? Is that educated people's talk for an alpaca barn?" Frankie asked, amusement tilting up the side of those pretty lips.

And there was the familiar battle. The one that had been raging between them for a decade. While Nate had opted for college, majoring in enology, Frankie had taken the hands-on approach, working the vineyard as her grandfather's apprentice. Which meant that she thought he was a starched sellout, and he thought she was shortsighted to place her entire career at the mercy of a fickle man. He agreed with her that wine came from the heart, but what she refused to acknowledge was that at the heart of winemaking was science.

"No. It's a smart man's solution to a complicated problem."

"Complicated, huh?" She flipped through the blueprints and that grin went full force. "You bought cedar siding, top quality redwood, and a floor plan fit for a Kentucky Derby champion. Christ, DeLuca, is that a skylight?"

Mittens made a snorting sound that sounded suspiciously like a laugh.

Faster this time, Nate snatched back the blueprints. "You'll thank me later when you still have something to harvest. Now, were you serious about having a nail gun or are you going to just stand there wasting air?"

"Yeah, but I've got something better."

Better, Nate thought, was the impressive view he had as she walked across the property toward the tool shed. Man, the woman knew how to fill out a pair of jeans.

A minute later, he heard some clanking as Mittens scurried out of the way, and Frankie muttered a few choice words of her own.

Finally, she was headed back his way, the front view just as appealing, and Mittens followed her like a lovesick dog. Nate could relate. Only Frankie wasn't bringing back a nail gun, she was rolling a tire that came up to her shoulders, was wider than the front door, and had the circumference of a Pinto. She rolled it right past Nate, past the habitat, and to the back steps where she tipped it over on its side.

His turn to be amused, he leaned against the porch rail. "And what is that? Mittens's breakfast?"

"Nope." She walked up the steps to the wide back porch and pulled an old towel off the railing, tossing it inside the tire. "It's a simple solution to a simple problem. Mittens. In."

And just like that, the damn mule hopped inside of the overturned tire and curled up, tucking his little hooves underneath so he resembled the sphinx. Humming with glee, he rested his head on the tire wall and blinked his big lashes up at Frankie.

"Traitor," Nate mumbled. He'd been feeding Mittens apples and carrot stems all day. Giving him chin scratches while reaffirming that he was loved. But the second Frankie came into the picture Nate was regulated to back-up friend. "You think he's just going to sit there peacefully and not wander around eating the grapes? This isn't a dog. You can't crate train him."

"Says the man with a cedar-lined crate."

"At least my way will keep him contained. Your way isn't a long term solution. Watch." Nate pulled out a handful of carrot tops. Mittens's lashes fluttered and his big nose started working time-and-a-half. "Come here, boy."

Mittens hummed louder and then cantered to his feet. He took a big whiff, an even bigger step and—

"No," Frankie said, inspecting her cuticle. "Sit."

Mittens sat.

"Plus, we don't need long term, he's not staying," Frankie said and Mittens let out a distressed nicker. She looked at the animal. "You're not. We've had this discussion. I don't do animals. Or roommates."

"Yeah, well, looks like you've got both, at least for a while. So we might as well build him a bed or the second you turn around he's going to start nibbling his way to a stomachache." Nate held out the carrot tops. "Come here, boy."

Mittens looked from Nate to Frankie, contemplating.

"Stay," she said and walked away. And the alpaca stayed. Even when Nate set an apple slice on the edge of the tire.

"How did you do that?" Nate asked when Frankie reached the back door.

"Get him to listen?" She laughed and turned to face him. "He's isn't a kid, he's an animal, which means outside of food and water, he needs discipline and affection. In that order. And you have to make him work and earn the second by following the first so he knows where he stands."

"Since he's the unsure one here, wouldn't it just be easier to give the guy a little scratch under the chin and an apple every morning so he knows he's not going to be shipped off?"

"Maybe." She gazed out at the barn and gave a little shrug. There was a vulnerability to the set of her shoulders as she shrugged that he hadn't expected.

A gentle breeze picked up, and she wrapped her arms around herself. Man, when she stood like that, emotion pushing its way through, she appeared so soft and fragile and Nate wondered how he ever bought the unaffected, nothing-gets-to-me act.

"But boundaries are good. It clarifies the rules and eliminates the chance for confusion."

Nate's heart about broke for the scared woman in the tough-girl package standing in front of him. What a way to grow up. To constantly work at earning things that should be freely given. As though no matter how much she loved, the only way she expected love in return was with conditions so that when the bottom fell out there was a rational reason to explain away the hurt and pain.

Both Frankie's dad and grandfather had made it clear to her, and to everyone who watched her grow up, that she had to work twice as hard to receive half of what they so readily gave to her brothers. And every time Nate was around, he managed to create more ridiculous conditions for her to overcome.

"What is that?" Frankie raised a hand and shielded her eyes from the sun. The sudden tension in her body didn't bode well for their growing ease with each other. Especially when she said, "Damn it, I told Walt that I wasn't ready to order the tank."

"I ordered it," Nate said, feeling his gut sink even lower. He was about to set her up again just so she could crash into a pile of more unattainable expectations.

"You ordered it?" She sounded mad, which was not how he pictured this moment. He'd expected her to be, hell, he didn't know, grateful. Instead, things got serious real fast. "This is *my* property."

"It's my property too," he said, not wanting to have this discussion now. Not when they were finally finding common ground after the near-kiss last night and the one three months ago.

"Yeah, too, as in two of us have a say." Frankie hopped over the railing and charged toward the truck. Before Tanner even unsnapped his seatbelt, she was standing on the running board, firmly planted in the man's face.

"Oh, no you don't," she said, projecting enough fuck-you vibes to have the crew who'd pulled up behind Tanner shutting their doors and barricading themselves in the cab of the truck. "I didn't order that. I don't want that. And if you don't start up your truck and drive out of here I will—"

"Morning, Frankie. You look nice," Tanner said, resting his forearm on the doorframe and leaning out the window and, with his easygoing smile in place, cutting her off.

Her mouth opened and closed, her face an adorable combination of confusion and irritation. Nate made a mental note of Tanner's Frankie-silencing method. Who knew being nice could silence the ball-buster?

"Are you fucking with me?" she asked. When he just smiled and tapped the front of his ball cap, she turned to Nate, jabbing her thumb over her shoulder at the construction truck. "Is he fucking with me? Because I swear to God the next man who screws with my life is going to find himself short one tool in the toolbox."

"Morning, Tanner," Nate said, walking toward Frankie.

"Nate, how's it going?"

"It's going." Nate rounded the truck and didn't stop.

"Hello?" she yelled, proving that she could be the biggest pain in his ass. Arguing about a water tank was not on his *To Do List*, but he could tell by the stubborn set of her shoulders that she would grab the shotgun if necessary. "Am I not standing right here? Is this some kind of lame game, ignore the—"

He didn't let her finish, didn't let her prepare. He kissed her. Just like that. No warning, no chance for her to knee him in the sac. He just put his mouth to hers and, man, he kissed the argument right out of her. At first she didn't respond, her mouth firm and resistant, but then he felt her lips soften, slowly give way and part beneath his, and he knew she was as gone as he was.

Her arms slid around his neck, and she melted into him. The taste of her filled his head, as she opened her mouth to him, taking it from a simple kiss to an invitation to get hot and sweaty. An invitation he wanted to accept, badly. And would have, had it not been for Tanner and his crew two feet away.

When they were both breathing heavy, he eased back and watched with a smile as Frankie's eyes slowly fluttered open. She was looking up at him like she had no words. Which was his goal.

"Wow, when you kiss me like that, I forget that I'm supposed to hate you," she whispered, her eyes still on his lips and her hands, he noticed, dangling from his belt.

"You don't hate me," he whispered back.

"Yes. I do." Finally her eyes met his. Hooded and heated and eating a hole right through his normally infallible restraint. "Was that to calm me down?"

"No. That was to shut you up. *This* is to calm you down." And he went back for seconds. And man oh man, had there not been an audience, he would have picked her up and taken her to that master bedroom so they could see just how big the bed was.

But they did have an audience. And sleeping with Frankie was a bad idea. So he gave one final tug of her lower lip and pulled back.

Without breaking eye contact, he took Frankie's hand and said to Tanner. "Can you give us a second?"

"Take all the time you need," Tanner said, and Nate didn't have to look up to know that the guy was laughing his ass off. "I'm on the clock."

Ignoring the crew all but high-fiving him across the field, Nate pulled a very pliant and very flustered Frankie toward the back porch. Mittens, surprisingly, was still in his tire.

He considered taking her to the kitchen, but decided to have their little discussion on the back steps, since the kitchen was closer to the bedroom. It also had lots of countertops, six if Nate remembered correctly—not including the table.

"Look, Frankie," he started, but she put a hand over his mouth. Her eyes narrowed and the look on her face was anything but flustered or pliant. Frankie was back.

"You kissed me!" She smacked his chest.

He caught her hand, holding it there. "You kissed me back."

"To shut me up," she accused. Incredible. Zero to irate in two seconds flat.

"No, that was just a surprise bonus," Nate joked. Not even a chuckle from her. He released a breath and decided he'd have to ride this one out.

"You bought a water tank." She jabbed a finger in his chest—hard. "Without asking me."

"Were you going to ask me?"

"Yes, I was. I needed time to sort through all the options and then I was going to talk to you, which was why I told Walt I'd get back to him later this week," she explained and he felt like crap. "And we can't buy this tank, I have to order through Walt. He's my uncle."

"It would have taken Walt at least a week to get this tank. Tanner got it in a day, and sold it to us at wholesale," Nate explained. "And you're right, if we're going to make this work then we need to make decisions together. I'm sorry."

He was. He should have talked to her. It was just that he wasn't used to running decisions by anyone with regards to the operational side of the vineyards. Especially when the decision was a no-brainer.

"I should have checked with you, but we need water. And that means we need a water tower. Fast."

"I know," she said, all her bluster from earlier replaced with straight up exhaustion. "How did you get it so fast?"

"I had to pull a few strings."

"I don't even want to know how much those strings cost," she mumbled under her breath. "We also need a new pump and a tank about five times that size to water both parcels when planted."

"Which is why a fifty-thousand gallon tank is being delivered and installed, with a new pump, next week."

"What?" She shot to her feet.

She was already nervous about cash flow, he could tell, and they hadn't even talked about the irrigation system that had to go in.

"See?" Lifting his bottom from the porch step, Nate pulled out the designs and bid that he and Tanner had agreed on last night. She took the packet, which was only a few pages long but extremely detailed.

Her face grew more taut with every page she read. He saw her mind working, watched as she thought through every possible scenario. Finally she looked up, panic in her eyes. "This isn't just tanks, Nate. It's a complete irrigation plan. For all twenty acres."

"I designed it so that even though we share the water source, everything else will be divided so it can function as two separate vineyards feeding off the same well. The great thing about the pumps Tanner found is they have dual zones that will allow the pumps to work independently of each other, so we can water simultaneously, set up our own cycles. It is a great solution to our situation."

"And you want to install this in one shot?" She flipped through the bid again, her eyes assessing every page.

"I was going to wait until spring, but since Tanner already has to rework the pump and the well, I figured it would be better to do it all now. By the time he places the orders and everything comes in, crush will be over and he'll just need a few weeks. It will be done, all before the winter hits so everything will be ready to go come spring."

She held up the paper. "I can't afford all this, Nate. Not right now."

"Relax, I am paying for half." He reached for her hand to tug her back down beside him, but she moved away and began pacing.

"Yeah, well I don't have that kind of money for the other half. Unlike you I don't have a magic checkbook that I can use at will."

And that just pissed him off. "Neither do I. In fact, since I have screwed this deal up from the beginning, I am paying for this out of pocket. My own, in case that was your next question."

He could see the shock in her expression.

"Sit," he requested. And to his surprise she did. Then he got to thinking about Mittens and suddenly regretted his request. "You and I both know that waiting to install the new pump and larger tank is not a smart business move. If we wait, it will cost us double in the long run and neither of us can risk this pump giving out in the spring when we plant."

"I get that. I do. But I don't have that kind of money."

"No, but you've got your grapes."

"And let me guess, you want me to sell them to you. No way."

"I was going to say you have them as collateral."

Frankie blew out a ragged breath. "I already tried that. Walt said it wasn't enough to secure the credit."

"I wasn't talking about Walt."

"Are you saying you'll loan me the money, using my grapes as—"

Nate stood, wrapped one hand around the back of her neck and brought her inches from his lips. "You going to let me finish or you want to make out? Because I'm open to either or both. But arguing. That isn't an option right now."

She studied his lips, licking hers in the process, and he could tell she was tempted. Hell, he was tempted. But before he could lean in, she stepped back. "Fine. Talk."

"I'm not offering you a loan. I'm suggesting we use my standing with Tanner's company to our advantage. Tanner always bills about sixty days out from start date, which gives you time to figure out your finances. When it comes in, we split it down the middle. You pay yours and I pay mine" he clarified, hoping it saved her damn pride.

"Walt offers ninety-days."

"Walt isn't the one offering to float the costs with his vendors." Not that he and his brothers needed Tanner to float anything. They could pay cash today, but Tanner always worked on a sixty-day billing cycle. And he knew that Frankie needed water and the time to come up with the money. That she chose not to see logic drove him nuts.

"He's my uncle."

So then why wasn't he here, doing whatever it took to make this work with Frankie, figuring out a way to get her what she needed at a price she could afford? Anyone who spent two seconds with Frankie would know she'd never flake on a deal. A sip of her wine would tell even the most amateur of wine connoisseurs that she was beyond talented. Her only downfall was she led with her heart.

"I understand about family, Frankie, but this bid and these prices are from Tanner Constructions not St. Helena Hardware. And contractually I have to use Tanner for everything. He's not only good, he's the best."

"I know." Frankie hooked the heels of her work boots one step below. Resting her elbows on her knees she dropped her head. "They've just had a rough year. Walt and Connie."

He wanted to run a hand down her back, massage away all the work and tension that was rolling off of her in waves. Frankie was one of the most loyal people he knew, and being in this position, forced to choose between her business and her family, was obviously tearing her apart.

Which was the only reason Nate could come up with for offering, "If you think Walt could match these prices, have him write up a bid. I'll work it out so that we would buy the supplies from him and have Tanner do the labor."

Head still in her hands, she turned it so she could look up at him. And wow, maybe that opposites attract bullshit Gabe and Marc were always spouting had some validity, because the smart-ass glare mixed with the small smile she was giving slayed him.

"You going soft on me, golden boy?"

"No, just trying to make this work. Give you a way to say yes."

She studied him, almost as if trying to figure out if he was telling the truth, if there was any hidden agenda that she was missing.

With a defeated sigh she said, "We both know that Walt can't come anywhere near those prices. If he sells to us wholesale then he makes nothing."

"Then have him send me the bid," Nate suggested. "I will reject it if the prices aren't competitive and since the whole town knows that Judge Pricket is looking for any reason to screw this up, he can't blame you and you are off the hook."

"I don't need you to fight my battles and—"

And they were back to arguing.

"—I don't do sneaky ever."

"Never said you did."

"And you telling my uncle some lame story is sneaky," she continued as though he hadn't spoken.

How did she do that? One minute he felt as if she was letting him in, the next she was ripping him a new one—when all he was trying to do was help.

Nate stared silently at her lips, listening to her rant about men this and controlling that. Less than a foot separated their mouths, separated him from silence, from trouble. He realized the second she knew he was going to kiss her quiet. She stopped talking and the air practically crackled between them.

Eyes wide, Frankie slapped her hand over her mouth.

Better. Now, "Making the smart decision when your heart is involved would be difficult for anyone. And you've had a hard time with your family lately, partly because of me, so let me help you."

"Fine," she drew out. "Tell Tanner to go ahead with the ten-thousand gallon tank and I'll call Walt about the rest. But if he can't match Tanner's price I'll be the one to tell him we are going with another bid." Of course she would. It would break her heart, but she would rather tell her uncle herself than have him feel embarrassed that his company was too small to compete. "We do it on your credit, but when the bill comes we split it like you said. And I don't owe you anything?"

"Nope." He wondered what he'd do if she faulted on the debt and had to sell the grapes. Or the land. Both were distinct possibilities. Not that he was setting her up. They needed those tanks and she was a business owner now. Owning a winery and making wine on someone else's dime were two different things. She wanted to join the big boys, then she'd have to step up if she was ever going to make this work. And if she did default, he'd get what he wanted, right?

"The way this land deal worked out, it's almost like we are business partners so I doubt this will be the only time we have to go in together on something. Today it's my connections and credit that secured the water, maybe next time it will be yours." He shrugged. "Who knows? But when it concerns the crop, we have to work together and make it happen. Deal?"

Frankie studied his extended hand. "Deal. But keep that DeLuca Jedi mind-kiss to yourself."

CHAPTER 7

O ne-hundred and fifty thousand dollars?"
 Katie Baudouin looked up from Frankie's loan application and pursed her lips. Her gaze was cold and bored, as
though Frankie was cutting into her lunch break, as though they
weren't really related, as though Frankie hadn't just spent the
most humiliating hour of her life listening to a risk assessment
that highlighted all of the 2,748 reasons her vineyard was des-
tined to fail.

 Number 2,749 was that Shady Katie was about to deny her
the loan. Right there. In front of every employee of St. Helena
Federal, who were all silently watching the situation unfold.
Frankie knew it. She could see it in the way Katie patted down
her helmet-hair and arranged the already meticulously arranged
papers on her desk so that Frankie could see just how pathetic
her debt-to-income ratio was. Even more pathetic was that it
was less depressing than the estimate Walt had handed her earlier that morning, which outlined just how expensive the new

irrigation system, trellises, and supplies would cost if they went through him.

It had taken him three days to put it together and two seconds for Frankie to realize that it wasn't going to work.

She had told Nate about it over breakfast. He had been more understanding than she'd expected, even offering to buy some of the smaller parts through Walt. But she couldn't. Even going with Tanner's vendors and his wholesale hook-up, she had to more than quadruple her loan request. There was no way she was going to be able to afford Walt's prices.

She planned on breaking the news to him later that afternoon. Not a conversation she was looking forward to.

"I know that the line I am asking for is two-fifths the value of the land as of now, but we both know that if I had the land reevaluated based on the recent sale of the parcel next door all of this would be a non-issue."

"A non-issue?" Katie said, her penciled eye brows disappearing into her hairline. "It would be a non-issue if you actually owned the land."

"I close escrow a week from tomorrow."

"And the land you are comparing yours to won't close for another three weeks," Katie said. "That is, if it closes at all."

"It will," Frankie said, almost laughing at the irony. She needed a DeLuca to close on the land that a year ago she would have run him over with her motorcycle to keep him from owning.

"Yes, well until it does, you'd have to pay for another evaluation of your land." Which would cost more money. "And I wouldn't recommend doing that until you have running water and a functioning well. With no way to water the vines you have, let alone the vines you still have to buy and plant, it will be a lower evaluation."

"Which kind of defeats the purpose of the loan, don't you think? As for the vines, I already have my saplings." The only thing that Charles still hadn't gone back on. And she hoped he wouldn't. Frankie had spent nearly every weekend and spare dollar over the past five years gathering cuttings from her family's vines after the pruning season and growing them on a small patch of soil behind Luce's lavender garden. The new crop of saplings in the greenhouse would be ready for planting this spring and slated for Red Steel Cellars. Frankie couldn't wait to get them in her ground.

"I heard," Katie said, and it was clear by her sour tone that she was not happy about Frankie taking vines from the family vineyard.

Well, too bad. They were hers, and she had just as much right to them as any of the other Baudouins. Actually, she had more rights, because she'd put in the time and sweat to splice the vines and nurture them to the beautiful saplings they'd become. They were hers.

"Have you considered entering that wine you are always fiddling with into the Cork Crawl?"

She had, but entry into the wine event was exclusive, by invite of the Wine Commissioner only. Most wineries selected family members to compete. This year Frankie had a winning wine, but no family and no sponsor-approved vineyard. Therefore no way to enter.

Which sucked poppycock. She had been waiting for this wine event all year, secretly working on a wine that, with its blend of two Cabernets and a touch of Syrah, tasted like the king of the king of wines. Red Steel Reserve was bold, fruity, and the best blend she'd ever crafted. Hell, it might even be the best blend ever made in the valley. It was perfect poetry in a bottle. And it was a shoe-in to be crowned the Cork King—a title that succeeded in elevating the price of the winner's wine considerably.

Only Charles had fired her.

She had originally entered her wine in the Summer Wine Showdown, her way of trying to find the silver lining in a full septic tank after her grandpa had publically given her rightful seat on the tasting tribunal to his stupid-as-shit dog, Simon. But when Simon was pulled and they were short a judge, Nate had, once again accidently messing with her life, asked her to sit on the Tasting Tribunal. She agreed and, because judging a contest where you are also an entry was a big no-no, been forced to quietly pull her wine from the competition.

Again with the poppycock because if she had won that Wine Showdown, which she was certain she would have, she would be negotiating with wine collectors right now instead of Shady Katie.

"I don't have a sponsor."

Katie picked up each piece of paper and stacked them in a nice, orderly pile. Although it looked nothing like Holly's "Whoops" pile, Frankie had a feeling it was headed there anyway.

"Can I be blunt?" Katie asked.

"Sure, because you've been so warm and nurturing up until now," Frankie mumbled.

"Even when you close escrow, you still have no verifiable income. No customers, no sales or even prospective buyers willing to give you a note of commit for your futures. So you are asking us to give you a loan on a piece of property that you haven't paid your first mortgage payment on."

"What about Walt?" Frankie said, that familiar feeling of ineptitude bubbling up. "You gave him a loan when their store was having problems."

"Yes, we did." Katie lowered her voice. "Although other people's loans have no bearing on your status." Voice tuned back to professional distance, she continued, "But Walt's family has over a hundred years of history in this town. A track record. You have nothing."

"I worked for grandpa for years," Frankie argued. "The last decade of Baudouin wine is all me and you know it."

"No, you worked for him. His land, his grapes, his reputation. As far as I know, you aren't even a shareholder," she told her, going for the soft underbelly and digging in. It worked.

"At least if I had shares I wouldn't have lost them on mail order kitty litter," Frankie said, rounding the reasons her vineyard was going to fail to an even 2,750. Although, insulting the loan officer who happened to have her lips permanently transplanted to Charles's butt might count double.

To be fair, this entire week had become one big, flaming ball of crap. Starting with an alpaca habitat and ending with baring her financial soul to the family devil. Oh, yeah, and there was a second never-going-to-happen-again kiss in there somewhere.

"Yes, well that's changing," Katie said and Frankie realized this was why her cousin, who was notoriously impossible to get face time with, had agreed last minute to forgo the usual chain of command and take over Frankie's appointment. This was what the entire conversation was building up to. "Charles is announcing at the Cork Crawl that he is taking on Kenneth as his apprentice. In fact, if all goes well, Kenneth will stand to inherit all of Charles's shares."

And just like that, Frankie was going to throw up. She'd forgone college, friends, her entire adult life to help him make Baudouin Vineyards what it was today. Yet her grandfather would rather leave her meat-head of a cousin everything than forgive Frankie one misstep. One misstep over fifteen years of loyalty.

It wasn't as though she had thought Charles would change his mind and forgive her just because she bought Sorrento Ranch. But she had hoped that over time her success with the land would prove to him that she was a damn fine winemaker, one worthy of taking over when he finally retired. And he was leaving it to Kenneth. A man-child who wouldn't recognize a good Cab if it bit him on the palette.

"If the Cork Crawl goes well?" Frankie asked.

"Yes, Kenneth is representing Baudouin Vineyards this year, and of course Charles is entering his latest reserve, so we have a real shot at winning."

Frankie rolled her eyes. The only reason they had lost was because Charles always entered his latest reserve. Well, the reserve that Frankie made as per his specifications. The man was so traditional he turned his nose up at anything remotely risky. In fact, he would rather lose to a DeLuca, year after year after year, than take a chance on something out of the box.

And that, Frankie thought with a sinking heart, was why Charles would have never left her the vineyard—ever. Even if she hadn't had the kiss-that-launched-a-thousand-ships with Nate. That was just his excuse.

All those years had been for nothing.

Setting her hands on the table, she leaned forward, getting eye level with her cousin. She refused to allow Charles's lack of faith in her to stop her. "So, you are going to stamp that big red 'deny' on my loan because I don't have the land yet or promise of an income, correct?"

"Correct," Katie said, victory swimming in her beady little eyes.

Frankie thought of Susan Jance and her client, and knew what she had to do. She leaned across the desk and snatched back her application. "Then, I am withdrawing my application." But before Katie could smile, Frankie added, "I'll be back next week when I close escrow. Oh, and with a signed letter of intent for all my barrels. So get that big black 'approved' stamp ready."

~

Frankie was mad. In fact, frustration and fury were two of the main reasons she wound up at the yoga studio Get Bent, drenched in spandex and sweat, joining the Mommy and Me Yoga class at the request of her friend Jordan. Oh, and Nate. Nate was the third part of that equation.

Even thinking about him—combined with her earlier meeting with Susan Jance and the woman's easy dismissal of Frankie's wine—made her stomach burn and every muscle in her body cord with tension. And here she thought things had been going so well between them. They'd managed to work side by side installing the new tank, to cohabitate for three days without a single argument—or kiss.

"Will you stop fidgeting?" Jordan hissed from the mat to her right. "This is supposed to be relaxing, and how can I relax when I can feel your inner confliction stinking up the entire room?"

"That stink is the unsanitary amount of dirty diapers." She turned her head and glared at Jordan. Her best friend, and the reason Frankie was currently surrounded by screaming ankle-biters in Gerber poses, glared back in a very un-zen-like way.

"I have thirty minutes. Thirty minutes to relax and enjoy today, so don't you dare ruin this," Jordan threatened, in a strained whisper. Yup, zen was definitely absent.

Properly chastised, Frankie looked out over the sea of yoga-clad backsides sticking up in the air and focused her attention on the instructor at the front of the room twisting herself into knots, and took a deep, cleansing breath.

It didn't help.

The kid directly in front of her let out a low, concentrated grunt and Frankie felt a rash break out on her arm. Death grip on the mat, legs stretched in some inhumane position, she lowered her head to the floor and averted her gaze.

Maybe if she focused on her breathing, she would forget that Susan Jance had all but shot down any chance Frankie had at saving her vineyard, forget that nearly every mat was taken, and forget that half the population was wearing diapers. She also wouldn't have to admit that the two-foot-tall-tot next to her, who had applesauce on her face and was in desperate need of a tissue, was better at yoga than Frankie.

"Why did you drag me here, again?" Frankie whispered to Jordan—the only other person in the room without an infant.

"You called me and threatened to light Nate on fire. I couldn't let you do that. Not today, because then I'd have to bail you out and I would miss Mommy and Me yoga." Jordan was toned, insanely flexible, and indeed a mother. "Ava and I have been looking forward to this for weeks, right honey?"

"Whatever," Ava mumbled, looking as though she'd rather light herself on fire than be in the same room with good old Mom. Today Frankie's goddaughter was sporting blue streaks in her red hair, white dance pants that barely covered her butt and finished off the proud-to-be-an-American look, and enough teenage angst to fuel a revolution.

"I heard you got another acceptance letter," Frankie said quietly, thankful they were in the next to last row, so as not to disturb the class. Although it was hard to disturb when half the students were gurgling, crying or chanting, "Binkie."

"Yup, NYU." Ava flashed a satisfied smile at Jordan before going into plank. "As in New York and Not Here."

For years, Jordan had overlooked Ava's bad attitude, her hoochie wear and body piercings, blaming her ex-husband for their daughter's less-than-sunny disposition and self-expression for her stripper-like persona. She'd put up with the below-average grades, the rolling of the eyes, even the constant use of words like "Whatever" and "Meh." But the moment she'd walked in on Ava and her study-buddy playing pirate and the fair maiden in the bathtub, Jordan had gone DEFCON-freak-the-fuck-out. She'd nearly castrated the kid, put Ava on house arrest, and became the founding member of the purity-for-eternity coalition.

Ava, realizing the only way she'd ever get to date was to move away, far away, spent her incarceration hitting the books and memorizing mathematical theory, resulting in straight As, a near perfect SAT score, and early admissions into every college she applied to—all conveniently located a cool three thousand miles from home, and her mom.

With graduation only a year away and acceptance letters piling up, Jordan, desperate to give her daughter the correct foundation for school, had signed up for every class and event that being a young, single mom hadn't allowed for.

"Which is why I was hoping you could talk to Jonah. See if he would give us a tour of the Sheriff's Station," Jordan asked.

Frankie looked at Ava, who rolled her eyes. But instead of her usually mopey mumble, she actually spoke. "My school went to the sheriff's station when I was a kid. Mom couldn't come because she was working, so she wants to recapture that precious family moment. And maybe if I'm lucky, she'll bring juice boxes and sliced oranges and we can all pretend that I'm not *sixteen*."

"Maybe if you stopped acting like a shit, she'd stop acting like some psycho helicopter mom," Frankie said, none too nicely. Too bad every mommy in a three foot radius skewered her with a glare for the profanity.

"Gee, and maybe you can even come along, like one big happy family, and show me what cell you were held in."

She got Ava. Understood why she was so angry. Her dad had walked out, married someone else and started family 2.0, forgetting that he had already had a kid who wanted nothing more than to be Daddy's little girl.

Only Ava wasn't a girl anymore, and even if Steve managed to pull his head out of his ass, which Frankie highly doubted, it was too late for Ava to be his little anything. And that had to hurt.

"Or maybe you can treat your godmother with some respect, go to the station with me and I'll consider letting her take you to the city on her motorcycle and pick out matching tattoos?" Jordan offered on an exhale.

Ava dropped her arms to her side and blinked. "Are you serious?"

"No way," Frankie blurted out at the same time.

"If you manage to make it to summer without giving me one more sleepless night or gray hair, I will let you get a tattoo for graduation," Jordan said. "It has to be small and able to be hidden underneath clothes. What?" Jordan said glaring at Frankie. Ava, who was diligently paying attention to the instructor as though she was in the running for Daughter of the Year, ignored them. "Don't look at me like that and don't you dare judge me."

Frankie put her hands up in surrender. A hard task when she was supposed to be balancing on one leg like a stork.

"No look. No judgment," she said loudly, then leaned in and whispered to Jordan. "Are you drunk? Is that what is going on? Jesus, first Mommy and Me, now a tattoo. Have you completely lost it?"

"Maybe, but at this point I am willing to do anything to make it to graduation without killing my child. Do you know how little sleep I get, how many nights I hide outside her window with my taser gun waiting for Mr. Sex on Wheels?"

"I thought Mr. Sex on Wheels had been effectively shut down."

"He was. But do you know how many horny high school boys have cars? Bikes? Scooters? Legs?" She practically shrieked the last word. "A limitless amount of possibilities to come to my house and impregnate my daughter? Possibilities that a 500-volt zap to the nuts eliminates." Frankie opened her mouth to say that maybe Jordan was being a wee bit paranoid, when she added, "I know what you're going to say and before you do, just take a look at the rack on my kid."

Frankie did and saw Jordan's point. Sixteen going on bombshell. When had that happened?

"And if the promise of a discrete tattoo and a ride on your bike will get me even a single night's peace, it will be worth it."

Jordan now studied her with the assessment of a worried mother-slash-best friend. Frankie leaned forward, reaching toward the front of the room, but couldn't help feeling that she too was another reason Jordan had lost sleep as of late. "Now, tell me why you were considering lighting Nate on fire."

"Not Nate, his car. And the rat fink cork-blocked me with Susan Jance."

"Oh," Jordan froze, leg in the air. "You were trying to land her new client that everyone is all abuzz over?" Frankie shrugged and Jordan's face went soft as she sat back on her knees. "Sweetie, Nate didn't cork block you, not on purpose."

Frankie willed her eyes not to roll. The DeLucas had taken Jordan and Ava in when Jordan had lost everything and she was to this day a loyal, if not misguided, advocate in her DeLuca support.

"Yeah, well purposely or not, he gets the added bonus of screwing with my life." *Again!* "Susan was so excited to talk about my wine last week and I was so sure that her client had already decided on me. Then Nate came in with his Italian swagger and impressive heritage and wooed her away."

"The man does know how to woo. You know what's impressive? His butt. Nate has the best backside in the Valley. I think it comes from all of the bending and squatting while he works his vineyard." Jordan smiled and Frankie could have sworn that she actually swooned a little. *Great.* "And to clarify, Susan came to him."

"I'll bet," Frankie mumbled. He probably flashed his Prince Charming smile and his even flashier credentials, and the woman came fluttering. They always did. Hell, even she had.

One kiss and she had sold him the farm.

"I can't believe I let him talk me into changing my planting schedule. If I had stuck to my original plan"—*instead of losing my mind over a stupid, calculated and totally incredible kiss*—"this wouldn't be so bad. But I was counting on that sale to pay for the tanks and irrigation that Tanner's already installing." Her stomach heated with anger. Anger at Nate for playing her, and herself once again being played. "God, it was like I walked right into Nate's trap."

"There's no trap, Frankie. Not with Nate, that isn't his style. Besides I took Susan's call." Which still didn't mean that Nate hadn't approached her first. Or that he hadn't known about Frankie. "She said that her client was looking for a name in the valley that had some history behind it."

"Yeah, she told me the same thing. Said that she needed a brand that had some heft, credentials as impressive as her black book." Frankie shrugged. "I just figured that after tasting my wine, which by the way she said was the best she'd had in years, she'd be willing to take a chance."

"Of course she said it was the best, because it is, which means the hard part's over. She has tons of clients, so you aren't the perfect fit for this particular one. So what?" Jordan shrugged. "All you need to do is give her a reason to recommend you and her clients a reason to say yes."

"Even if she could find another collector in time, I would face the same problem." That was why she had been banking on this client. He was the only collector who had shown interest in Frankie despite her winery's lack of heft. Without Susan's public stamp of approval she would have a hard time selling. No sale meant no loan, and it could quite possibly cost her the first few years of grapes.

"Collectors want credentials, right? Then give it to them." Jordan pulled her shoulder-length red hair into a haphazard knot at the back of her head and with the flick of the wrist managed to look effortlessly sexy. Frankie would need a stylist and a gallon of hair goop to get the same effect. "The Cork Crawl is two weeks away. Enter your wine."

"Already thought of that, but Charles is entering with Kenneth and Tom."

"Creepy Kenneth, your slug of a cousin?" Jordan made a sour face. "What about finding a sponsor?"

The Cork Crawl was established as a way to allow local wineries to shine in the presence of wholesalers and collectors. In order to keep the festival small and exclusive, the only way a new winery could participate was under a veteran vineyard's stamp of sponsorship approval. So in the event that a winery didn't have a team to enter or must, for whatever reason, forfeit their spot, the winery could use their entry to sponsor a new winery into the competition.

"Yup but since the opening ceremony is a week from Saturday, I doubt there are even any sponsorships left." Frankie tried to laugh, but lying flat on her stomach with her feet tucked behind her ears made it hard. Or maybe it was because she just couldn't seem to find any humor in the situation

"I know of one."

Frankie held her breath. "Really? Who?"

"I happen to know the exclusively female winery I sometimes work for is not competing this year."

"Are you serious?" Frankie said. Feet firmly back on the mat, heart lodged in her throat, she turned her head to look at Jordan.

She couldn't be serious. The only one-hundred-percent prochick winery in the Valley besides Frankie's was Ryo wines. Relatively new to the scene and already with awards up the wazoo, Ryo was owned and operated by none other than Nate's sister Abby and their grandmother. Which was too bad.

Being crowned king of the Cork Crawl was exactly what she needed. It would give her credentials, reputation, and something tangible for her to point at when looking for buyers—or a loan.

Competing under the DeLuca sponsorship, however, was just what Frankie needed to avoid. Another tie to the DeLucas was one other surefire way to piss off her grandpa and give him another reason to never speak to her again.

Then again, she was already sharing toothbrush space with Nate, Charles had already given away the farm so to speak, and that kind of endorsement would prove to the town that Frankie got that sponsorship on her own merit. Because to convince Abigail, the DeLuca Darling, to sponsor her was going to be impossible—well, impossible for someone without Frankie's talent.

Jordan smiled and . . . no way, she was serious.

"ChiChi is already a fan," Jordan said, exhaling and going into a lotus position. "She was raving about your wine last week at the board meeting. Said it was better than Nate's."

Better than Nate's? Frankie couldn't help but share her own secret smile. She'd been trying to get her grandpa to change things up for over a decade. It was why year after year they lost the Cork Crawl to the DeLucas. Because Charles was determined to keep with tradition, which was fine, but sometimes the most beautiful things could come from shucking tradition and saying screw you to science and going with the unexpected. Sometimes it led to something really amazing. It was how she'd created her Red Steel Reserve.

"She did?" Not that it mattered. There was no way Abby would agree.

It wasn't as though Abby disliked Frankie and she certainly didn't care about the feud, but she and Frankie—they were just different. Growing up, Abby was a cheerleader, prom princess, and hugged her friends like seventeen times every passing period. Frankie didn't like cheerleaders on design alone, never went to prom, and hugging gave her chest pains. Whereas Abby couldn't take a step without one of her brothers dutifully by her side, Frankie was always one step away from her brothers dutifully strangling her.

Frankie shook her head. "Abby would never do it. Sponsoring my winery would piss off her brothers."

"Which is exactly why she would agree," a peppy and princessy voice said from behind.

Frankie turned, and there, two mats to the right and one back, balancing on her forearms with her body completely vertical and her feet flexed, in some pose the instructor called the feathered peacock was Abigail DeLuca.

The woman was an odd combination of magical pixy meets Vegas showgirl next door. When she wasn't "being the pretzel" and stood upright, she came in at maybe five-one with big chocolate curls and even bigger chocolate brown eyes.

"I didn't know you were, um," Frankie zeroed in on Abby's zero-fat waistline, "qualified to be in this class or I wouldn't have openly admitted to wanting to dismember Nate."

"I thought it was torch, but no biggie." Abby untwined herself and went into lotus. "Hey, if you do decide to, you know, dismember one of my brothers, can you go after Trey? Or at least wait until after next week? If all goes well, Thursday will be my last wedding anniversary before I am officially a divorcée and Nate promised to come bearing tequila."

Abby looked at Frankie expectantly, as though waiting for her to say the right thing. A confirmation of some kind, maybe a heartfelt word. But the only thing Frankie felt was her hands go clammy. "Oh, I'm, uh . . . "

This was the part of the conversation where most women knew what to do, where the topic required a certain kind of finesse, a firm understanding of female subtext. Three skills that Frankie had never mastered. Because tequila straight from the bottle with a lemon would imply a sob-fest. But served frothy with Cointreau, lime juice, and one of those little umbrellas, could be a happy thing, right?

God, Abby was looking at her. Waiting for her to— what?—give a high-five because her soon-to-be-ex was a total douche? Or should Frankie lie and say she was sorry when, again, said husband was a total douche?

She settled on, "I'm sorry." But when Abby's lips pursed, she quickly added, "If you are."

Abby laughed and Frankie felt herself smile. "Sorry it took this long? Yes. That it is finally going to be over? Nope. That's why Nate's bringing the SUV and the pre-party. He's the designated driver, so Lexi and I can get trashed."

Of course he was. Nate was the sweet, stand-up kind of guy who went out of his way to make other people's lives easier. Well, other people except for Frankie.

"And I'm not in this class," Abby went on. "Jordan called me this morning and invited me. Right after ChiChi explained that your wine—how did she put it?—was a spiritual experience."

Frankie shot a look at her friend who was breathing deeply and innocently studying the instructor as though it was the most important pose of her life. They'd set her up.

"Then Regan called two minutes later, imagine that, just *begging* me to check out this class to see if it would be good for her and the girls," Abby mused. "Only to find you here. And why is that again?"

"Okay," the instructor called out, cutting off Abby with two sharp claps. "Hydrate time. Then onto Doggie Disco."

"I'm going to fill up my bottle. You guys need anything?" Jordan asked.

Frankie turned her head to say that, no she was an adult capable of handling her own shit when Jordan not-so-slyly jerked her head at Abby and mouthed *Ask her!*

No!

Chicken. Bock. Bock!

Fine! "So, I was——"

"Yes," Abby said with a perfectly sweet smile. "Ryo Wines would love to sponsor Red Steel Cellars for the Cork Crawl."

"Really?" Frankie blinked. Then reeled back in her excitement. This was a DeLuca. "Why?"

"Why would I sponsor you?" Abby's tone implied that Frankie was being a tad bit paranoid. And maybe she was, but she'd been burned enough to know to always proceed with caution. "ChiChi believes your wine will win and I do love winning. Plus, we sold out of inventory two days after being crowned Cork Queen last year, allowing Ryo Wines to pre-sell the next five seasons of futures before we'd even had our official grand opening. No product, therefore no reason to enter in the Cork Crawl. So if my nonna is set on you as our flagship, I have no choice but to be supportive." She raised a brow. "But shouldn't you be selling yourself to me, making me feel confident in my decision?"

"Not when you could be messing with me." Frankie eyed her skeptically. Selling five years of futures sounded too good to be true—which in her world meant that it was. "And especially not when I know how it would piss off your brothers."

"That's the best reason for me to sponsor you," Abby said, her mouth curving with mischief. "Did I forget to say that *my brothers* were crowned King to my Queen? A fact that I am reminded of often."

"Yeah, that would suck." Frankie hated it when, at every family get-together, Dax brought up the *one* time he managed to beat Frankie in a game of quarters.

"They know I can't enter and since Trey will be in Monaco for some wine conference, they are down a member for the Pick Till You Punt. But did they ask me to fill out their DeLuca team of four? Nope," Abby said, popping the last syllable hard. "They asked Jack Tanner."

The Pick Till You Punt was a pre-qualifier for the Cork Crawl. It pitted wineries against each other in a cut and carry relay race, which determined booth locations for the Cork Crawl. And in a crowded festival, with hundreds of wineries all vying for the attention of buyers, table location could make a difference—hundreds of thousands of them in fact—when it came to selling.

Frankie sighed. Ridiculous or not, she had always wanted to compete for her family, but her grandfather had opted to use her brothers or vineyard hands. She had always manned the Cork Crawl booth.

"I thought only family and vineyard employees could compete."

"Apparently Tanner isn't just our exclusive contractor, now he's Head of New Development, which in Italian means he's practically family. Nonna even makes him lunches on days when he's at the vineyard." Abby's lips went thin. "The worst part is that my brothers didn't even call to say, 'Hey we're making a deal that totally affects your business and your life. Oh, and it's with the biggest tool in the Valley. What's your stance on that?'"

Frankie bet by Abby's tone that her stance was closer to *Hell no* than *Where do I sign?*

"Now, not only am I giving that jerk Tanner piano lessons three times a week, but I am forced to see him every time I go to the office or my family gets together. So yeah, I might be helping you out, but you'd be doing me a huge favor."

"Brothers can suck." Frankie couldn't believe she was relating to Abby. Maybe the DeLuca Darling's life wasn't so perfect after all.

"Yeah, sometimes they can. And if we aren't careful they'll bulldoze right over us, which is when we have to draw the line, give them a little reminder of just where they stand. Which is why part of the deal is I get to be on your Pick Till You Punt team."

"Are you serious?" Frankie didn't mean to sound shocked, but Abby weighed less than Frankie's leg, and although she did have dainty, nimble hands—perfect for picking without bruising the grapes—Frankie doubted she'd spent much time in the fields.

"Dead." Abby gave a decisive nod. Just one. But it was enough to convince Frankie that Abby was fierce when effed with. "Don't let my size fool you. Nonno Geno bought me my first set of secateurs when I was four. By seven I was faster than Gabe with those clippers."

"Count me in, I'm on Ryo's board," Jordan said, tightening the cap to her water bottle and flashing her meticulously manicured hands. "And no, I have never cut a vine in my life, but when I was married to that rat bastard, I kept one of the best rose gardens in Napa County."

"Great. Now all we need is hired muscle. You think one of your brothers would do it? Oh, I know," Abby said with a smile, and she no longer resembled anything close to darling. Frankie made a mental note never to screw with Abigail DeLuca. "The hot firefighter one who was in the calendar last year."

"Adam?" Frankie blinked. Abby hadn't dated, shown interest, or even looked at a man since her soon-to-be-ex walked out on her. "Um, I could ask?"

"Good, because we have to win. I'm still burned that I lost out to them by eleven corks. Eleven lousy votes. And the only thing better than my brothers losing to a girl will be the look on Tanner's face when we beat his arrogant, over-muscled, egotistical backside." Abby wrinkled her pert nose. "Teach them to stick their nose in my life and screw things up."

"So, you're really offering to sponsor me?" Frankie asked dumbfounded.

"Only if you promise we'll kick my brothers' butts."

"Consider them kicked," Frankie said over the kiddy pop music that erupted from the speakers.

"Good," Abby said. Then with a smile added, "Now take a deep breath and bend over."

CHAPTER 8

Nate pulled a little pink ticket from the dispenser and took his place in line at Picker's Produce, Meats, and More if one could call a single person standing in front of him a line. But since that person happened to be Mrs. Craver, co-owner of the store, and she was arguing with Mr. Craver, Nate figured it could take a while.

Not that he was in any rush. In fact, Nate was in such a great mood, not even one of the Cravers' notorious blowouts could ruin his day. The sun was shining. There was a crisp autumn breeze. He'd snagged a parking spot two strides from the front door. His cart was full of groceries—ones that didn't come in a box and have a red dye number five warning on the back. He had some kind of fancy dessert, which Marc's fiancée had whipped up on special request, waiting at the bakery. And he'd managed to check off nearly every item on his *DAILY TO DO LIST*. One more errand and he was free for the weekend.

Yes, sir. Nate was in the mood to celebrate. It had taken three days—three long, hot, sweaty days—but the water tank was installed, the pump was up and working, and Tanner and his crew were finally gone. Gone as in, Nate and Frankie would have the entire place to themselves. They'd managed to go an entire seventy-two hours without a single fight and, even though there'd been enough chemistry sparking between them to toast s'mores, they'd also gone an entire seventy-two hours without kissing again.

Something he was seriously considering changing tonight. If he ever got his steaks.

Marilee Craver stood a good three feet from the butcher counter, waving some kind of legal document in Biff's direction. Her voice was hushed, but it bounced off the glass of the display case, making every word crystal clear and nearly impossible to ignore. Although Biff didn't seem to have a hard time tuning her out. He diligently rearranged the rounds of deli meat as though this were an everyday occurrence. The only sign that the man was even listening was that sweat had started to bead on the top of his bald head when Marilee starting talking divorce and papers.

Nate grabbed the handle of his cart, ready to come back later when Biff skewered him with a look. Nate knew that look. Gabe had sent him that look many times as of late.

Right, never leave a man behind. So he distracted himself watching Biff restack the pork ribs right through Marilee's division of assets lecture, watched him place the new cuts of ribeye in the correct case when she claimed full custody of their potbellied pig, Boss Hog. Even watched as Biff sucked in a big breath and closed his eyes as she threatened to shove his meatgrinder where the sun don't shine while taking an aggressive step forward.

One step and Biff straightened on an exhale that seemed to originate from his feet. He took in where his wife's shoes had ventured and his brows shot up in reprimand, wrinkling his cue-ball head. "Watch yourself, Mari-girl. You know what happens when you cross that line."

That was all it took. A few simple words, spoken calmly and directly and delivered with a weighted wink, and the woman who was rumored to take out a shoplifter with a casaba melon and a bag of fava beans from fifty feet away covered her mouth with a pudgy hand.

Now there was nothing but silence, and Nate decided that was worse than the arguing. At least the bickering was driven from frustration and anger. Silence, well, that held all kids of emotions that Nate didn't want to witness. It felt too private, as though he were somehow intruding. But to walk away now would be awkward, so he just stood there, staring at the smoked pig's head in the display case.

"I'm sorry, Biff," Marilee finally said. "I didn't notice. I was so busy . . . " But it wasn't her husband, though he was built like a slab of beef, who had her hands trembling or her words trailing off. It was the big white line painted down the middle of the floor that she had, in her state of fury, crossed.

"That's all right, honey. No harm," Biff said, maneuvering his massive body around the counter so he could take his wife's hand. After a little kiss on her cheek, he took the papers from her fingers and set them on top of the display case next to the cocktail sauce. "How about you let me help our customer and then I'll take a look at the papers?"

Marilee nodded and—holy Christ—the woman was actually blushing. All the way up to her curly grey roots. "You promise you'll sign them?"

"Never going to happen. But I promise I'll look at them. You can even cook us up one of your pot pies I love so much, and while we eat, you can point out every clause if you want to. Then after you're done showing me how hard you worked, I'll give you every reason why I'll never sign," he said, smiling, and Marilee smiled back.

"You're a stubborn old fool," Marilee whispered, sounding all twitterpated.

"Only for you. Now, go on," Biff said and Nate turned— too soon. Because Mr. Craver was goosing Mrs. Craver and she was batting her lashes and playfully swatting at his hand.

"Make sure you save some of the chicken thighs." Marilee said over her shoulder. "The free range kind."

"Already have them packaged."

Biff watched his wife waddle away, not taking his eyes off her until she had rounded the produce department and situated herself behind the register. Marilee turned her checker-three light on and gave Biff a sweet little wave, and damn if the man didn't flush.

Biff cleared his throat. "Sorry about that. Today's our anniversary and she always gets a little excited." He shook his head in wonder and when he spoke, his voice was rough with emotion. "Fifty years. Can you believe it?"

"You've been married fifty years?" Nate knew the Cravers were old as dirt, but to live with *that* for half a century, Nate wondered if the man was a masochist.

Biff laughed. "No, fifty years ago today was the first time she filed for divorce. I said no. And every year she comes back demanding her freedom, when really she's just trying to give me an out."

Nate wondered why the hell he didn't take it. Then he saw it, the way Biff looked at his wife, the way she looked back when they thought no one was watching. What everyone else in town saw as them bickering was their way of flirting. Of saying I love you.

"You ever hope she'll stop asking and accept that you aren't going anywhere?" Nate said, thinking of another stubborn woman.

"And miss getting the chance to tell her all the reasons why she's made me the luckiest son of a bitch on the planet?" Biff shook his head. "Now, what can I get for you?"

"I need a couple of steaks," Nate said. He crossed the white line and, making sure to keep an eye on Marilee's throwing arm, looked in the display case. "What's good today?"

"Let's see." The butcher took in Nate's cart. "You've got wine, candles. Strawberries? Looks like you're entertaining a lady friend."

"Just dinner. And she's just a friend."

"That Showdown picture Nora Kinkaid's got on the Facebook looked like a whole lot more than friends."

It felt like a whole lot more too. Truth was, Nate didn't know what Frankie and he were or even what he wanted them to be. She was unpredictable and stubborn and argumentative. And every time he thought about how her lips felt beneath his or the way she clung to him while moaning into his mouth, he seemed to forget that she was the last person in the world that he should be contemplating cooking for.

But after witnessing how two people who were so obviously mismatched could go from driving each other bat shit crazy to twitterpated in a single conversation, Nate began to wonder if maybe the Cravers were the ones who had figured it out.

"I was going to suggest a couple of private reserved porter-houses. Got them in this morning. Nice and marbled on one side, tender as veal on the other. But maybe something more delicate would be better." Biff lifted a rack of lamb and held it out for inspection.

Nate enjoyed good food almost as much as he enjoyed sex. As an eighteen year old college freshman interested in getting laid, Nate read a study in *Men's Health* that said women were sixty-six percent more likely to have sex with a man after a home-cooked meal, so he immediately enrolled in a culinary course for his elective. Over the years, he had impressed many a woman with his culinary prowess, and lamb always ranked high on the panty-dropping scale. But Nate had a hard time picturing Frankie, with her nail gun and work boots, nibbling on a little frenched lamb chop. "I think she's more of a porter-house kind of person."

"You sure? Because judging by the ball of fury headed your way, a sharp knife on the table might not be in your best interest."

Nate's gaze rose from Biff's beefy hand to the woman storming through the front door. He watched as she moved through the produce aisle at an alarming rate. Her hair was down and hung lose around her shoulders, just like it had been the night he broke in, and she was wearing her trademark black tank but with a pair of black stretchy pants that caressed every amazing curve of her body.

Nate hadn't seen her since this morning, where she'd appeared in a baggy men's shirt, those boy cut panties, and not much else. She'd eaten a Pop Tart while he'd sipped his coffee, she'd told him she still had to talk to Walt, he'd told her not to worry about it, she'd swallowed down her argument and promptly left.

Now with her body tense and ready to snap, Frankie rounded the cantaloupe barrels, her tennis shoes silent on the wide, wood planks of the floor, and past the artichoke display. Her head jerked right then left, scouring the dozens of patrons who made up the pre-dinner rush that filled the store, until those baby blues zeroed in on him.

"DeLuca," she yelled over the elevator music playing in the background.

"Yup, I'd go with the chops. Nothing says 'I'm sorry' like lamb," Biff advised and then went back to arranging the display case. Obviously the never-leave-a-man-behind pact was still in full effect.

The closer Frankie came, the less convinced Nate was that she'd stopped in to say she'd missed him or thanks for handling her uncle. The last thing he wanted to do right now was have a confrontation with her. By confrontation, he meant fight, which meant no round three of locking lips because based on the way her fists were flexing, the only lip action and heavy breathing he was looking at tonight was a verbal lashing.

Digging in for the duration, Nate leaned unconfrontationally against the glass display case and waited for her to start yelling.

"Do you have any idea what you are doing to me?"

He didn't need any clarification to know she clearly wasn't talking about their earlier kiss. He leaned forward, resting his arms on the handle of the shopping cart. "If it is half of what seeing you in those pants is doing to me, I think I have a pretty good idea."

"Not what I meant," she ground out, attracting attention from the one woman in town who could out-gossip his gossipy granny. Nora Kinkaid dropped her cantaloupe and shuffled over to study the avocados—which were a good five feet closer to the drama.

"You're looking nice in that dress, Mrs. Kinkaid. Is it new?" he asked. Nora harrumphed and went back to squeezing avocados, but not before he noticed her flush under that scowl.

When he was good and sure that Nora was at least giving off the pretense of minding her own business, Nate reached into the basket and picked up the soy milk. "And this? This is me getting us some groceries."

"There is no *us*!" Frankie grabbed the carton, marched her sweet ass over to the refrigerator section, slammed it on the correct shelf and marched back. Stopping so close he could smell her hair. She had really great smelling hair. "Got it?"

"Hey, Frankie," Biff cut in, his voice low as he rested his trunks for arms on the top of the counter and offered up one of his rare smiles. "I'm going to have to ask you to either lower your voice or take a step back."

Frankie looked down, saw the line was behind her and said, "Sorry, Biff. I was just—"

"I know. Not a problem. Just reminding you that only one woman is allowed to get all hot and bothered on that side of the line." He winked. "And never during business hours."

"Right. Sorry." She took a step back. Realizing the produce section wasn't buzzing with chatter anymore as everyone had stopped to see who would snap first, she grabbed his arm and tugged.

He could practically feel the anger vibrating though her body as she steered him, and in turn the cart, through the produce aisle, around the bakery where he was forced to say, "Excuse me," when he bumped into Peggy from The Paws and Claws Day Spa, who was also Judge Pricket's newest lady friend. A "Pardon me," two more, "Nope, all my fault," and a tour of the canned foods aisle later, Frankie pulled him to a stop next to the deli counter and spun to face him.

"There is no 'us'! There never will be an 'us,'" she said in hushed tones. Hushed, angry tones that made her breath heavy and managed to turned him on. "And stop staring at my mouth because we are never kissing again. Ever."

"That's a damn shame, sweet cheeks, because we're so good at it."

"Just stop." She held up a trembling hand.

"Frankie, what's going on?"

"That's what I'm trying to figure out. I mean, do you make a habit of ruining people's lives?"

"No." Nate actually thought he'd done a pretty good job of making people's lives easier.

His answer seemed to deflate her. All of the anger and spunk just vanished. "Then it's just me?"

"Frankie." He tried harnessing that same calm tone Biff used. "I have no idea what you're talking about."

"Of course you don't. You never do. That's the problem." She worried her lower lip, as though she was trying to hold it together. Not the response he was going for. "You know that Abby is more upset about the divorce than she's letting on, which is why you offered to be her designated driver next week. You know that Nora has been dieting and hasn't lost a pound, hence your line to her that she was wearing a nice dress. And that camel boy likes carrot tops, not the carrots just the tops."

"He's an alpaca."

"Whatever," Frankie drew out, stopping her eyes mid-roll as though horrified by the gesture. "What I am saying is that you pay attention to things, little things that everyone else is too busy to notice. And you say the right things, all the time, just to make people smile."

He didn't know whether to take that as a compliment. It sounded like a compliment, but he had a feeling that she didn't mean it as one.

"And yet everyone expects me to believe you had no idea I was in the middle of negotiating a deal with Susan Jance? Which her client passed on, by the way."

That was not what he wanted to hear. "I swear I didn't know, Frankie."

She made a disbelieving snort.

"Fine, I knew she was talking to other wineries. I even heard that your grandpa was trying to butt in on the deal, but I had no idea you were even in the running." Okay, once again, that was not the thing to say. "That came out wrong."

"You think?"

"What I meant was that you won't have a product for at least two years. She needs supply now."

"When did you become an expert on what I do or don't have?"

"I'm not. I just assumed—"

"Yeah, well, can you stop doing that?" She threw her hands up. "Because every time you assume, you make an ass out of me. Not you, me! Get it, golden boy?"

Yeah he got it. He got that the tornado of attitude she usually wore like armor was gone and that you-can't-touch-me thing she did so well with her eyes wasn't anger. Today it was hurt. Maybe it always had been and he was too busy being busy like everybody else in her life to tell the difference.

He also got that Frankie's life, although chaotic and complicated and not how he'd choose to live, had been going just fine until he photo-bombed it. Well, until he'd bullied her into sitting on the Tasting Tribunal. The kiss only made it worse.

And admitting that Trey had sold the woman Frankie's grapes, grapes which at the time of the sale they had assumed would be theirs, probably wouldn't help anything right now, except make him look even guiltier. But Nate was all about honesty in business and in life, and Frankie deserved to know the truth.

"The grapes Susan contracted are yours."

Frankie froze. "Excuse me?"

"When we bought the land, Saul led us to believe we were buying the entire twenty acres and all the grapes."

"Which you pre-sold to Susan," she finished for him and he saw his entire day turn to crap. "So the other day, the 'we're partners and we're in this together' bullshit, was that just a way to screw me out of my grapes? Make sure I have to sell them to pay off Tanner?"

"You know me better than that, Frankie. I don't work that way."

"I want to believe you, I really do. I want to believe you've always out-sold, out-performed, or out-shined me because it just wasn't my day or because I hadn't had my chance to show what I can really do yet. But now I am beginning to wonder if maybe I've been playing against a stacked hand this entire time."

No way was he letting her believe that. "I know how this looks but I'm not your grandpa."

It was as though he'd slapped her. Frankie took a step back, her eyes round with hurt, her face slack with humiliation. And his heart went out to her.

"I didn't say that to hurt you, I said it because it's the truth." He took her hands and laced their fingers, surprised when she let him. "Our situation is tricky. We're roommates, competitors, and I hope, after all of this, still friends. I am beyond sorry that you lost the contract with Susan, but I'm not going to pretend I'm not proud for landing it. That would be a lie and I would never lie to you. And I would never set you up to fail."

When she didn't speak, just stood there watching him, he tugged her closer. "I don't know what you want me to do here. Susan's client bought the DeLuca name, not those grapes. She wanted a brand with proven history and a winery with experience." And one that could provide enough wine to fill the client's cellar and his hotels', something Frankie could never do with her ten acres. "So even if I could call Susan and back out . . ."

Which he could not. Would not. This was about more than him and his wine. This was about his brother's belief in him, his dad's Opus—a whole lot more than chemistry and a pretty woman. Although, if he were being honest, and it was only him who would take the hit, Nate would walk away and give Frankie the deal. In a heartbeat.

"She what?" Frankie dropped his hands and shrugged. "She wouldn't want me?"

"Frankie, that's not—"

"Two reasons to zip it before I put my boot print on your ass." Frankie glared at him with pointed disregard and raised a finger. "I don't need *you* to do anything for *me*, especially since I can see your superman complex is sprouting another head.

"Second," she ticked off and there went another finger. It wasn't a coincidence that it was the middle one or that she dropped her index finger. "I don't need you to back out, Nate." Of course she didn't. Frankie never took anything freely offered. Not that he was actually offering. "Because I'm not selling my land or my grapes, so you might want to give good old Susan a call and let her know you may have the history, but you're about six tons of grapes shy of a deal."

She offered him a broad smile and turned to leave. "Oh, and Nate. Experience this."

Frankie pulled a ball cap out of the waistband of her pants and shoved it on her head. With a smart-ass salute she marched right out the front door. But not before Nate read the writing on her cap: RYO WINE'S FLAGSHIP CHAMPION. RED STEEL: CRUSHING THE COMPETITION.

The words wouldn't have hurt so bad had they not been surrounding a picture of a combat boots coming down on— Christ, was that a pair of testes or grapes?

CHAPTER 9

Frankie parked her bike in front of Bottles and Bottles, the local pharmacy and wine shop, and realized she still had to talk to Walt. She unclipped her helmet and, ignoring the urge to tell him that they'd decided to go with his bid and worry about finding the money later, focused on what was important—finding Charles.

She stepped off the curb and made her way across the street toward the hardwood store. Situated on the south end of Main Street, right next to Picker's Produce, Meats, and More, St. Helena Hardware and Refurbish Rescue had been in Uncle Walt's family since his great-great-grandfather first opened their doors back in 1874. Well, the hardware part had, and the refurbish rescue was Connie's addition to the family business. Although it had been renovated over the years, the clapboard building looked exactly like the photos that hung in town hall, only with a little extra harvest spirit.

Frankie shoved through the door, a cowbell clanking in her wake. The scent of sawdust, motor oil, and all things home repair greeted her. So did her Aunt Connie's voice.

"I'll be with you in a minute," she beamed from under-neath a purple feathered lampshade. "Just setting up my new display."

Her aunt loved to decorate, considered herself a decor doc-tor extraordinaire. What started out as a way to pass time by fixing flea market finds became an all-encompassing passion when her kids moved out. It didn't take long for her "projects" to overrun their home, so she sweet-talked Walt into selling her unique wares out of the shop. "Unique" was what she called her Dr. Seuss-meets-Tim Burton spin on interior decorating.

Connie's claim to fame was that there wasn't an abandoned piece of furniture she couldn't match with a forever home.

Apparently not the case, Frankie thought as she fingered the arm of a recliner, which was wedged between a zebra print couch and a dozen or more dressers. There wasn't a spare inch of room in the entire store.

"Isn't that a beaut?" Connie asked, making her way toward Frankie. She was short, squat and wore more velour than should be legal. "A couple special ordered that and then returned it. They said the color made their eyes bleed. Eyes bleed? Can you imagine someone saying that about such a unique piece?"

"I can't imagine why," Frankie said noncommittally. Connie was the gatekeeper, and there was no sense in offending her because tonight was Friday. And Friday nights were home to the Veteran Vintners of the Valley's Put up or Shut Up. Held in the basement of Walt's shop, entry by invitation only, it was a weekly game of high stakes poker where vineyard owners from St. Helena came together to settle their battles over a hand of Seven Card Stud. There were only three rules: no weapons, no women, no whining.

And Charles was down there.

A handful of people saw her storm out of Picker's wearing a Ryo Cork Crawl hat—a handful and one nosy Nora Kinkaid. A photo was already up on Facebook. She checked. It was accompanied by a poll asking who the town thought had the biggest grapes in the valley. Frankie was not only winning by a landslide, but they had also given her three-to-one odds that she'd crush what little grapes Nate DeLuca had left by the end of the Cork Crawl. It was good to know she had supporters.

What was not good was that the town gossip vine was already chattering, and even though Charles was technologically challenged, there was still a risk that he would find out before she had the chance to tell him. A mistake she did not want to repeat. If she was going to do this, she would do it like a Baudouin and face the consequences head on. Which was why she asked, "Is this shag carpet?"

"Faux shag," Connie said as though faux made it better. "I tried to take it home, but Walt said no, then he cut off my credit and won't let me buy anything else until I get rid of this eyesore. His words not mine. I've marked it down twice, but so far no takers." The older woman wedged herself behind the counter. "You in the market for a new reading chair? I bet it would look lovely looking out that bay window in the front of your new house."

"Sorry, redecorating isn't in my budget right now."

"Well, after what you did, I might just give it to you."

Did they already know? And if so, was the chair punishment for disloyalty?

Frankie fidgeted with the top of her helmet, feeling for the second time that day like she'd failed her family. She knew she should have come by yesterday, but after the bank Frankie had chickened out.

"Aunt Connie, I—"

"I already know."

Frankie swallowed. "You do?"

"Oh, yes." Connie looked around the store, her eyes wide and darting right then left, as if she were about to divulge a matter of national security. "Don't tell Walt I told you. I wasn't supposed to be eavesdropping, but I knew when I saw that sexy football player, the one who's set on running us out of business."

Frankie rolled her eyes. Tanner wasn't trying to run Walt and Connie out of business. He was just trying to get his customers the best deal. It wasn't his fault Walt ran his store like it was still the gold rush and he was the only hammer in town.

"He was asking for Walt, wanted a private meeting, so of course I showed him to the office and left, but not before clicking on the baby monitor I keep hidden behind Walt's garbage can."

Frankie felt her stomach clench. This was bad. "Oh, Aunt Connie, I was going to talk to Walt about his bid, but I got busy and—"

"Don't worry, dear, that's what I thought happened." Connie waved a dismissive hand and Frankie felt awful. Hearing the news from her would have been bad enough, but hearing it from Walt's competition must have been humiliating. Why would Nate do this?

"At first I thought I must have misunderstood. My hearing's been off ever since I went through the change, but when he started talking tanks, Walt went real quiet and then he placed your order. For. Every. Thing." Her voice elevated with every syllable.

"Did Walt come down on his pricing?" This made no sense. If Tanner had changed vendors, why hadn't he told Frankie? Or why hadn't Nate?

"Heavens, no. Walt gave you the best price he could," she said, her hand clutched her heaving chest. "So when that DeLuca boy told Walt the prices he had access to—" Connie's voice caught and her eyes got suspiciously glassy.

"Wait. What are you talking about? Which DeLuca?" Frankie asked, her own chest doing some heaving.

"Well, they all look the same, don't they? They sure seem to have that tall, dark, deliciously handsome part down pat, even if they do have a bit of a problem with accepting that they are the second best wine in the Valley. This one had a nice set of buns on him and a list of vendors."

Nice buns and carrying a list? Sounded like Nate.

"Oh, I know." Connie clapped her hands in front of her mouth. "It was the one you were playing tonsil hockey with at the Showdown."

Definitely Nate.

"The list," Frankie prompted.

"He had specific vendors matched to each item with a contact and pre-agreed price. A price that Walt gets to use when quoting folks now. But the sweetest part was that they sat there patiently, like they had all the time in the world, while Walt insisted on calling and introducing himself to each and every new vendor, then hand-wrote a separate order form for each transaction. The sexy ball player had to leave part way through, something about piano lessons, but the DeLuca stayed until Walt was done, well over an hour."

"When did this happen?"

"Well, around two." So after their run in at Pickers. Not that it made any difference, he still made it work with Walt, which meant a lot in her book. But did he do it because she guilted him into it? Or because he thought it would give him a better shot at buying her grapes? Not that she was selling. "But he called this morning to set up an appointment to make sure Walt was going to be around."

"This morning?" So he came down even after she had publically accused him of setting her up, stealing her account, and making her life difficult. All of which she knew weren't true. Nate was a good guy, a pain in her ass, but honest to a fault and so honorable it was charming. And she'd blown it.

Frankie looked up at the ceiling and let out a breath. This is why she didn't date. She tended to scare away the nice ones, leaving only the tools who were too dumb to run. But Nate hadn't run. He'd come here, to her uncle's shop and proved he had listened to her.

"At first I didn't understand. Tanner could have taken the sale for himself. He didn't need Walt. But then I heard the way that DeLuca boy worded it, claiming he and Tanner needed a local expert, someone who's been servicing the town's wells for as long as Walt to help them choose between this or that and saved my Walt's pride. And our business. And I knew that was your doing. You have always been so supportive and—" Connie's brows furrowed. "Why are you looking at me like I am as nutty as a fruitcake?"

"I didn't do it, Connie," Frankie admitted. "I wanted to use you guys, I really did, but I realized yesterday that even if I get that loan, I couldn't afford Walt's bid. I was going to break it to Walt tomorrow, but . . ." She shrugged. "What happened here today, that was all Nate."

"Well, either way, I know that boy wouldn't have even considered doing something like this without your encouragement." Connie patted Frankie's hand. "Which is why I'm going to find the perfect housewarming gift for you. As a thank you."

"Oh, that's okay." Frankie took an unconscious step back when Connie looked like she was going to force that chair on her. "No thanks necessary. It was really Nate—"

"Nonsense, I heard Nate tell Walt that it was you who convinced him to go local, give him the chance to get a bid in. I want to make you something pretty. As a token. I know it won't even come close to what you did for us but—"

"Actually you can help me. I need to deliver these to the mayor." Frankie set down the Cork Crawl application, noticing how her hands were shaking. Why had Nate done that? She'd been nothing but nasty to him and he'd been . . . wonderful.

Connie picked up Frankie's application and flipped through it. "Does he know?"

"I hope not," Frankie said, not pretending she didn't know who *he* referred to. Charles wasn't known for having a cool, even demeanor and the whole town would be speculating on how he would react to the news. "That's why I'm here. To give my application to the mayor, make it official, and tell Charles that I'm competing. I don't want him to hear it from anyone but me. I already blew it when I snuck around behind his back and sat on the tribunal."

"You did what was right for this town," Connie defended. "If you ask me, your grandpa is a stubborn old fool. You were the best thing that happened to that winery since your dad passed."

"Thanks, Aunt Connie, but I should have told him first. Instead I convinced myself that keeping it a secret was for the best. It wasn't. The truth was I didn't tell him because I was scared. Then I bought the land and never told him." Frankie paused to gather her breath. "I don't want to make the same mistake again."

"I don't want you to either, but if I let you down there, Walt will have my head. You know the rules: invite only. He's already going to blow his top when the executioner's chair I got for a steal on eBay is delivered tomorrow. I was going to cover it in toile and lace with Bubble Wrap accents. Wouldn't that have been lovely?" Connie looked around the cluttered store, her hand on her chest. "I think he might stick me in it to see if it works."

"I need to get in that poker game, so I'll make you a deal," Frankie said with a smile. "An invitation to the game for that chair."

"The eyesore?" Connie asked, so much hope in her voice Frankie wanted to hug her.

"Yup."

"The chenille shag I used on the reupholster is called, hang on . . . " Connie disappeared under the counter where there was a lot of clattering and shuffling. A few layers of dust heavier, she rose with a pink swatch of fabric in her hand and bright blue reading glasses perched on her nose. "Lacquer Up and Dye."

"Perfect. I'll take it." Frankie pulled a credit card out of her jacket pocket and dropped it next to a swatch of the most god-awful color she'd ever seen. It was pink, neon, and nauseating. And would look perfect in the master bedroom.

"You sure? Because I don't want to have the same piece brought back twice. People might start talking."

"With a sales pitch like that, I won't be bringing it back."

Convinced that Frankie wouldn't suffer from buyer's remorse and hurt the chair's feelings, her aunt agreed to give her the chair for free—if she were willing to have it delivered tonight. Never one to pass up a bargain, Frankie told her the door was unlocked and gave specific details of where she wanted the chair placed.

"I can't wait to see what your grandpa says when he discovers you're competing under a DeLuca sponsorship," Connie said, handing over the receipt of sale and one invitation to the Put Up or Shut Up. "Must be some pretty good wine to convince Abigail DeLuca to sponsor you."

"It's going to win."

"I never had a doubt. Which is why I bet next week's grocery money that you'd slaughter those DeLucas, so don't let me down."

"I won't," Frankie promised and made her way through the store to the back. As she passed a urinal that had been transformed into a planter and between a pair of matching bedazzled shoe racks, Frankie felt her confidence start to waiver. Because there, at the bottom of the stairs, smoking his pipe and calling out the mayor and Sheriff Bryant, sat Charles Baudouin.

Somewhere between seventy and prehistoric, Charles was a handsome man, short in stature with a full head of silver hair and a crooked posture. What he lacked in height he made up for in command. Her grandfather knew how to work a room and if he had been using his silver fox swagger for good instead of ego lately he would have the ladies lining up. Although the only lady he was interested in impressing was the one lady who had every reason to hate him.

Steeling herself against her grandpa's reaction, Frankie walked down the stairs, flashing her invitation to every stunned man she passed. But no matter how many times she told herself this was the right thing to do, that she would be okay, she knew it was a lie.

It wasn't Judge Pricket pinning her with a hostile glare that had her heart pounding through her chest, or that two of Nate's brothers were in the room. No, what had Frankie ready to say screw it and head home was that her grandpa, the person who had taught her everything she knew about wine, the man she'd spent her entire life trying to live up to, didn't do more than give her a brief glance before discarding half his hand and returning to the game at hand.

"Hey, grandpa." She walked over to his table and placed a kiss on his cheek. He didn't turn his head as usual for the double cheek-kiss, so she straightened.

"Francesca," he said so formally it hurt. It was the same way he greeted her mother after the divorce. He was making it clear to Frankie, and everyone in the room, he wasn't over her betrayal.

She cleared her throat. "I'm here to let you know I'm competing at the Cork Crawl."

"Team's already full," he said, his voice commanding as ever, eyes still on his hand. "I thought you knew I asked Tom and Kenneth to compete this year."

Frankie wanted to ask him how he assumed she would have known, since he hadn't bothered to talk to her in over two months. "Katie told me, but I wasn't talking about competing for Baudouin Vineyards. I'm here to give the mayor my application and wanted to tell you in person."

That got his attention. Charles set his cards down and watched the mayor flip through Frankie's paperwork. If Charles were even considering ending this three month standoff, then the next few minutes would probably cause him to add an additional six of withholding his approval and love.

"Everything appears to be in order," the mayor said, his expression one of sympathy. "But you do realize that if I approve this, you'd be competing against your grandpa."

"Nonsense," Charles said grabbing the application. "She would never—"

Frankie was tempted to resend the application in her grandfather's hand. She'd always fallen in line with his every whim
and wish, and she had learned a lot from shadowing one of the
best winemakers this valley had ever known. But she was tired
of hiding in his shadow, tired of seeking his approval, tired of
his love being conditional.

It had crushed her when he'd fired her, but in the end,
maybe he'd done her a favor. It gave her the courage to set out
on her own. And she'd made it this far.

With or without his stamp of approval, Frankie was ready
to go all in.

"No, sir," Frankie said to the mayor, then shifted her attention to her grandfather. "I am competing for myself this year.
Red Steel Cellars will be a flagship entry under the sponsorship
of Ryo Wines."

And if there was anything that could have silenced a room
full of men, that was it.

"Ryo! You're willing to align yourself with a DeLuca?"

"If that's what it takes to enter my wine, then yes."

"The one you've been playing with over at Lucinda's place?
That's what this is about? You're willing to pit family against
family over that wine?" Charles snorted as though he didn't
give her wine a snowball's chance in hell of winning.

"My wine will win." Frankie swallowed. "And I'm not placing anyone against anyone. You did that when you fired me."

"I did no such thing. You were fired because you took a direct action against the vineyard, which resulted in loss of business." Actually, his attempt to sabotage the fundraiser and
one-up the DeLucas had been what led to a sudden drop in
business and a surplus of grapes, but Frankie didn't want to get
into that. It wasn't why she was here. "And I have no intention

of allowing your immature and reckless nature to further impact this family."

"I didn't do this to hurt you or make you angry," Frankie whispered. "I did it because I wanted to make my wine. And because I thought I could make you proud."

Charles stood and, relying heavily on his cane, leaned in to look Frankie in the eye. At this distance the deep grooves around his mouth and pallor to his skin were clearly visible. Grandpa wasn't as unaffected by her leaving as he was letting on.

"Then stop this nonsense. Apologize and I will let you come back and work for me."

Apologize for what? she wanted to ask. If anyone should be apologizing it should be him. Not that she would go back even if he did, not now, not after realizing what it was like to work her own land. If she went back, nothing would change, he would want things done his way and she would be stuck making someone else's wine, spending her life trying to live up to his very difficult expectations.

"Don't you mean I'd work for you and Kenneth?"

"Better than working alongside a DeLuca." That he didn't deny it confirmed Frankie's worst fear: Charles truly was training Kenneth to take over the vineyard. "You're making a mistake, Francesca. You don't have the proper backing or connections. And trusting a DeLuca?" He shook his head in disgust. "I don't know what you think you will find with him, but mark my words, they are playing you and that means that in the end you, my dear, are nothing but expendable."

CHAPTER 10

Nate was screwed.

He stood outside his new bedroom door, staring down a bright pink monstrosity that looked more like a Muppet than a chair, and wondered how his life had gotten so out of control. Three months ago, he'd been living alone in a plush house off Main Street, dating a nice pediatrician from San Jose, riding the high that he was going to own Sorrento Ranch.

Now he lived on said ranch, which he still didn't own but was forced to share with an alpaca, a shag chair, and a roommate who he was going to kill or have the best sex of his life with—either way it was bound to get complicated and end messy as hell.

Which was why, instead of grabbing a few pre-family dinner drinks with his brothers, Nate had spent the last hour of sunlight working on Mittens's habitat. The foundation was finished and the framing started. He'd expected to finish the framing too, except Nate had a hard time focusing on anything other than Frankie.

That look on her face when he'd expressed surprise over Susan's interest in her wine still got to him. She'd been shocked, then confused, then hurt, which left Nate pissed—at himself. Sure, he'd had no idea she was pitching Susan on her wine, but he shouldn't have discounted her.

He'd meant what he'd said the other day: They were partners, the most unlikely of partners, but partners all the same.

"And friends," he said, reminding himself that it was time he started acting like it. Which was why he'd bought the lamb.

He grabbed a pair of jeans and a shirt that didn't smell like cedar and sweat, tossed them on the bed and made his way to the bathroom. Not bothering to let the shower heat up, a routine he'd become accustomed to since sharing breakfast space with Frankie and her sleepwear, he stepped under the spray and rested his head against the tile wall until his entire body was good and cold.

He'd just stepped out of the shower when he heard a knock at the door. Slinging a towel around his waist, he padded his way to the front door and opened it.

Standing on the other side of the threshold was Frankie. Even her combat boots and motorcycle jacket couldn't make up for the fact that she was nervous. Based on the dust on her boots and the amount of alpaca fur on her pants, Frankie had been home for a while, most likely brushing Mittens. Something he'd noticed she did when she was stressed.

"Forget your key?" he asked, even though the door had been unlocked.

"What?" She looked up, and blinked.

Interesting. She'd been checking him out. And—*Bingo!*— the spark in her eyes told him she liked what she saw.

"I asked if you forgot your key."

"No, and it was unlocked," she said as though he were the crazy one. "I thought I told you that I would handle Walt."

So that's what this was about. "I am guessing he called you?"

"No, I spoke to Connie, and she told me." Frankie crossed her arms under her chest, and what a great chest it was. "We had a deal."

"No, you said you were going to talk with him, but you were working on old information and—wait, did you knock on the door just to yell at me for giving you what you asked for?" Nate asked, folding his own arms across his chest, making sure to flex in the process.

Her eyes dipped briefly to his pecs. "No, I came here because I wanted to say that . . . about today, about how you handled . . . I mean, after what I said to you—Are you going to invite me in?"

He leaned causally against the doorjamb. "Are you going to yell at me?"

Frankie toed the porch with the steal tip of her boot. "I'll try not to yell, but I can't make any promises."

"Great." Nate pushed off the wall and walked into the house. "Then I'll try to keep my tongue to myself, but I can't make any promises."

He couldn't be sure, but he thought she mumbled something against his entire sex as she stepped inside and slammed the door behind her. Frankie followed him down the hall, dropping her helmet on the recently cleared coffee table, tracking dirt down the freshly swept floor, and stopping short when he went into the master.

"What are you doing?" she asked, looking at the threshold as though if she stepped over it, everything would change. And it would. And Nate, sick as he was, hoped she took the step.

"Getting dressed." He pulled on a grey t-shirt. "Is that a problem?"

She shook her head, but her gaze was riveted on his hand, which played with the rim of the towel.

"Great, then have a seat. You can be the first to use my new shag chair." He stopped and mulled over the name. "And tell me what you wanted to talk about so badly that you had to knock on your own door."

Frankie walked over to the chair and fingered it with a smug-ass smile. It was the first time she'd smiled since he'd answered the door. It was also the first time she didn't look like a gentle breeze would blow her over.

She sat down and pushed back, the footrest popping up, amusement sparkling in her eyes. "It's a thank you from Connie. I picked it out myself. Thought of you sitting here, writing your lists and plotting how to further butt your way into my life, and I said, 'That's the one.' You like it?"

He liked the way her hands were stroking the armrests.

"Yeah, it's not bad." Nate turned and headed toward the bathroom for the rest of his clothes, dropping his towel and giving her an eyeful in the process. "How about you? You like it?"

"Not bad," she said from the other room. "A little lumpy and kind of soft for my taste."

Lumpy, my ass. Nate knew he was in great shape. He also knew that women liked his body—they usually told him so. Not Frankie though. She liked his body all right, he'd caught

her several times checking out the goods when they were working on the well and she thought he wasn't looking.

Nate pulled on his boxer briefs and grabbed for his pants.
"You were saying?"

"Right," she hollered. "I knocked on the door because I
didn't want to come here as your roommate or business partner
or anything. I uh, wanted it to be clear that I was, you know,
here as a, uh . . . friend."

Pants midway up his thighs, Nate stopped. She sounded a
little vulnerable and a whole lot lost. Jerking up his pants, he
walked back to the bedroom. "Frankie, about earlier today, I
never—"

"Please." She held up a hand, bringing him to a stop. "Let
me finish, then you can talk. Okay?" The okay was tacked on.
Her way to change a direct command to a request. Something
was up.

"All right," he said, sitting on the edge of the bed, forcing
his body to relax.

"I thought about what I said earlier at Picker's, about how I
accused you of purposefully screwing with my life, and I wanted
to say that I was, um . . . I was . . ."

With a frustrated grunt, she pushed forward, releasing the
footrest, and stood. She dug in her pocket, pulled out her cell,
and seconds later his pinged.

He grabbed his cell phone off the night stand and read the
text. It had one word: *WRONG*

"I was," she gestured to his phone.

"Wrong," he filled in.

"Yeah, that, when I accused you of not listening to me, and
making my life harder, and being mad that you got Susan
Jance's client. I know you didn't go behind my back and that

you didn't mean anything by what you said. I was just so mad and frustrated."

She looked so adorable bumbling her way through what he assumed was the first apology she'd ever made. "Frankie, you don't need—"

"I'm not done." She took a deep breath, adding a forced, "Okay?"

"Okay." He couldn't help but smile.

She paced, stopping just a few feet from the end of the bed—and him. "I was embarrassed that she didn't think my wine was good enough to stand on its own because my grandpa told me the same thing, although I think they are both full of shit and wouldn't know a great wine from perfection, but it is still her choice what wine she goes with," she said it like she was reminding herself. "And it was—" Again with the gesturing.

"Wrong."

"Of me to drop the bomb on you about your sister sponsoring me the way I did. And I'm really—" She walked to the end of the bed, so close that their knees brushed. A simple touch, and pow, all he could think about were her lips.

How they felt.

How they tasted.

How he would do anything to taste them again.

If he made a list of all the reasons why kissing her was a bad idea, he'd spend the entire night in his shag chair. God, now he was thinking about shagging, and Frankie, and her breasts were at eye level, her legs were touching his and it felt really good. Too damn good.

She fiddled with her cell. "I'm really—"

His pinged.

"Sorry," he read the text quickly and looked up at her, but she wouldn't meet his gaze.

Why the hell was she apologizing? Here she was putting everything out there, laying it all on the line, and all he could think about was how to get her out of her clothes and into his bed.

"You're sorry?" he repeated.

"For not being a better friend."

Finally her eyes met his and everything he'd been contemplating over the past few minutes was obliterated. Complicated no longer seemed to fit this situation, because friend was the last thing he was feeling. And sex, well sex wasn't the first thing on his mind anymore. It was the second, right behind what an amazing woman Frankie was and how he wanted to take the sadness out of her eyes.

She swallowed. "What you did for Walt was probably the most noble thing I've ever seen. You're a good man, Nate."

Reaching out, he gently cupped her hip and drew her toward him, parting his legs to make room. He could smell the crisp autumn air on her skin with undertones of lavender. "I did that for you, Frankie."

"I know," she whispered, her hands fidgeting with the hem of her shirt. "But I don't understand why."

"Because of this—" he leaned up and brushed his mouth against hers. If he didn't push this too far, logic would step in, remind him that she'd had a hard day, hell, a hard few months, and that she was just feeling lonely and lost in the aftermath of being fired and losing her first major deal, and that it was wrong of him to take advantage.

But Christ, her mouth started working his and all the blood left his head and traveled south. He expected her kiss to be angry or challenging like it had been the other day—it was anything but. Instead her lips gently gave way on a single sweet rush of air.

Nate was a tall guy, used to bending down when kissing. So he never considered what a fucking turn-on it would be to sit on the bed with a walking fantasy between his legs, towering over him. Especially when she started teasing him, gently nipping his lower lip and then pulling it into her mouth.

As promised, he tried to keep his tongue to himself, but when she slipped hers inside of his mouth, he figured that rule was off the table. And when her fingers slid up his chest and into his hair all of his rules about mixing business with pleasure evaporated under the heat of her hands. There was something sexy and so damn feminine about those hands, soft and strong at the same time. But it was this new side of Frankie, the vulnerable side that wrapped her arms around his neck and just held on as though he were the only thing grounding her to this moment, which made all logic disappear.

Spanning his hands around her waist to the small of her back, he slid them lower, over the shape of her spectacular ass, which was even more incredible than he'd imagined—yeah, he'd been scoping her goods too—and down, stopping at her upper thigh. Needing more, he drew her closer.

She came willingly, using his lap as her own private seat, her knees straddling his thighs while that sweet backside of hers nestled against his legs. Cupping his face, she pressed closer and, hot damn, every inch of her breasts were smashed against his chest, and nothing had ever felt so right.

She pulled back, just enough to look down at him. The air between them hung thick, and without a word, Frankie raised her arms in invitation. No pretense, no guarded exterior, just Frankie stripped down to that sweet woman hidden beneath it all.

Nate eased his thumbs under the hem of her tank top and slowly started to push it up. The higher he tugged, the more silky, smooth skin he saw, the tighter his jeans became, until he was afraid he'd have some serious chafing issues.

"You sure?" he asked, his thumbs brushing the undersides of her breasts, and Christ he hoped she didn't change her mind.

"Don't you dare stop," she said and he had to smile when she added a breathy, "Okay?"

"Okay," he said and pulled her shirt over her head, then saw a flash of pink lace. "Jesus Christ, it was worth the wait."

She was perfect. Small tucked in waist, toned stomach, and the most incredible set of breasts—a full C, maybe even a D— encased in delicate pink lace with a little matching bow that was made to fuck with a man's mind. It sat there, nestled between her creamy swell of flesh like a bow on a present, implying that with just one pull he could unravel her completely.

"Pink, huh?"

"So I like pink," she said a little self-consciously, and a little defensive.

"Me too," he said grabbing her wrists before she could cover herself. What a travesty that would be. "Didn't you know that it's my all-time favorite color?"

Well, it was now. He'd become such a fan of the color that he wanted to declare September National Pink Month so Frankie could walk around in nothing but pink lace and skin. And the boots. Definitely those boots.

"You're staring," she whispered, a little unsure.

"Yeah, just give me a minute." Hell, he could stare at her for hours. He started by letting his eyes roam over her, taking in every single inch. "I've been dreaming about this moment for a while now."

Actually, he'd been dreaming about this moment ever since spring of senior year, when he made out with Frankie in Saul's vineyard. He'd kissed other girls, but with Frankie he'd gotten to second base—over her sweater, but second base all the same. He'd been smitten, she threatened to knee him in the nuts, and so their relationship began.

"Nate," she whispered.

It was hard, but he managed to drag his eyes north to meet hers. "You want to stop?" he asked.

She shook her head and he realized that her hair was down. He was one lucky SOB.

"I want to look at you too. It's only fair."

"I like fair," he teased, reaching behind with one arm and dragging his shirt off. Her eyes were glued to his chest and she bit that plump bottom lip. Yeah, he liked fair.

He cupped her by the neck and was about to drag her mouth to his when there was a loud slamming of the bedroom door, followed by Marc hollering, "For the record, I did knock!"

To Nate's surprise, Frankie didn't jerk away like she had the other night. Instead she buried her face in his neck and laughed. That laugh slid right through him, taking up residence in every cell of his body. Every muscle in his body shifted and goddamn it, the realization hit hard: Frankie didn't hide, because like him, there was no denying the truth.

"Thing about Italians is they never knock." The sound of the fridge closing and a beer popping came through the closed door. "They also don't know when to leave."

She pulled back and man, was she beautiful when she smiled. "I should probably shower anyway. I smell like Mittens."

Nate looked at her breasts one last time, imagined them wet and covered in suds and groaned. "I hate my brothers right now."

She climbed off him and tugged on her top. "I think it's sweet they're here to see your new place."

Something about the way she said it had him pausing. "Have your brothers been by?"

"Jonah saw it that day you were here. And Luce, Pricilla, and ChiChi brought me dinner last week." With a shrug, she crossed the hall and closed the bathroom door.

Message received loud and clear, talking about her family was off limits.

His family, however, was not off limits. And they were about to receive a message of their own with coordinating hand gestures.

They were still arguing.

Frankie lay on her kid-sized bed, in her kid-sized room. The one that she begrudgingly moved into last week when she'd come out of the shower to find Nate sprawled out across the master bed. His hands folded behind his head, sexy-man smile dialed to high—his underwear neatly folded and tucked in the dresser drawer.

With her feet propped up against the wall, head hanging off the end of the mattress, Frankie let out a frustrated sigh. She'd been there for a good fifteen minutes, staring at a dust bunny tumble back and forth across the floor as the breeze brushed through the open window.

After her shower, a cold one, which she had deliberately drawn out by washing her hair twice and meticulously shaving her legs, she heard heated words being thrown in the kitchen so she'd barricaded herself in her bedroom.

Not that it mattered. She was still so turned on that her breasts felt heavy against the cotton of her t-shirt and she could still taste him on her lips. To make matters worse, even through the closed door and hallway separating them, she could sense Nate, and hear every single word spoken.

"I was just about to hand Tanner his ass," Trey said. The youngest DeLuca was equal parts playboy and hothead, the worst combination in Frankie's book, which was why she usually wanted to punch him. "Then your girlfriend walked in—"

"Frankie's not my girlfriend, we're just living together. As friends," Nate clarified. In case anyone in the room still had concerns about their relationship, he added, "As in we're not sleeping together."

Someone cleared their throat.

"You know what I mean."

Frankie mentally shrugged.

He was right, they weren't dating. They hadn't even made it to the touching portion of the evening, but for some reason her stomach pinched a little at his dismissal. She gave it a rub and decided that she was only hungry.

"From what I saw, I can attest that there was no sleeping going on." Frankie strained her ears and then decided that it was Marc talking. Some sort of scuffle followed, glasses sliding, chairs scraping against the floor, a loud clank and then, "I wasn't done with that."

"Then learn how to use a coaster. Or better yet, go home and destroy your own house."

Frankie smothered a laugh. Nate, she'd come to realize over the past week, was as anal about his living space as he was about his loafers. She would find her books, receipts, dirty dishes, all magically organized and in their correct place. He'd even taken to folding her clothes. She was more of a toss the clean clothes in the basket and dig through as needed kind of girl. But yesterday she'd come home to find her basket not in its usual spot—the floor of the guest bathroom—but perched on the foot of her bed, her clothes neatly folded. Even her underwear had been organized by color.

Never one to turn her back on a friend in need, Frankie had made a habit of dropping her things at random just to give him something to do. So far, her dirty work boots on the hardwood floor seemed to get the biggest reaction.

"Well, welcome to it, bro," Gabe said. "This is why I stopped having you guys over all the time. You come, you eat, you leave a mess."

"Keep telling yourself that, Gabe," Trey said. "Because I give it one more week before you dig yourself out from the piles of diapers you're living in and start begging us to come over, smoke stogies, and throw back a few."

"Can you just get back to what happened at Walt's with Frankie?" Nate sounded frustrated and tired. "I thought he was strict on the 'men's only' policy."

"Yeah, tell that to the woman you're 'just living with.'" Frankie could almost hear Trey's air quotes cutting through the air. "She walked in like some leather-clad hottie in her black jacket and boots. Man, those boots give a guy—ow! What the hell?"

"Get to the point," Nate bit off.

"Sorry, I thought she wasn't your girlfriend," Trey challenged.

"She's not."

"So then it wouldn't bother you that when I think about her in all that leather, I get—ow!"

"Bottom line," Gabe said.

She heard a huff and assumed it came from Trey. "Frankie told Charles that she's competing under Ryo and entering her wine in the Cork Crawl."

"Which explains the alpaca fur," Nate said so low that Frankie almost missed it.

"Fur, what are you talking about?" Marc asked.

Yeah, Frankie thought, what was he talking about?

She sat up, felt all the blood rush to her feet, which was how she explained away the lightheadedness she felt when Nate said, "When she's upset she brushes Mittens and . . . What?"

"I just told you that Abby is sponsoring Frankie, with a wine that ChiChi claims is groundbreaking and you're babbling about an alpaca?" Even down the hallway Frankie could hear the low, lethal drawl in Trey's voice that time.

"Groundbreaking?" Nate asked. "She used the word groundbreaking?"

"We might lose everything we've worked for and you don't seem to give a damn," Trey said. "Do you not remember what happened to DeLuca Vineyards the first year we won?"

Frankie knew. It was why she wanted to enter. DeLuca Vineyards had been on the verge of bankruptcy when the brothers won their first Cork Crawl, and the win resurrected the DeLucas' reputation as the best wine in the Valley. Their next win gave them the title as the most respected name in wine. Period. And Frankie wanted that same chance to prove herself like Nate and Gabe had. And this was her year.

The DeLucas just didn't know it yet.

"I understand exactly what is at stake," Nate defended. "And we are not going to lose anything. Abby agreed to sponsor Frankie because she is still pissed over Tanner. And since when do we care who the hell else competes? *Our* wine is incredible, and it will win. Like it does every year. So how about you focus on your job—selling what I make."

There was a heavy silence. It stretched on for so long that Frankie stood. Even through the closed door she could feel the tension turn combustible, which explained her pacing. The funny ache in her chest, however, came from Nate implying that Frankie was a non-threat. That Abby was just extending the pity branch, but in the end it wouldn't matter, Frankie's wine would matter.

"Like the sale we had with Susan?" Trey accused, his tone growing harsher by the syllable. The frat boy persona was gone and in his place reared the hotheaded youngest brother who blasted through life with a chip on his shoulder and something to prove. "Christ, Nate do you know how hard I worked on that deal?"

"Yeah, I do because I was right there beside you," Nate said low and lethal. "I looked Susan in the eye and promised her grapes we don't happen to own. It was only right to come clean to both her and Frankie."

"But it was *my* deal and my reputation. I don't fly around the world selling 350 days a year for you to cut me out. You had no right to talk to either of them without me," Trey barked back. "What were you thinking?"

"That keeping secrets from stubborn women hasn't worked out so well for us in the past," Marc said, speaking from experience.

Last summer the DeLucas were involved in a distribution deal that centered around Lexi's grandmother's recipes. Lexi almost lost her grandmother's bakery, and Marc had almost lost Lexi—for good.

"Look, I get why you're upset, but this isn't a big deal," Nate said and Frankie knew he was lying. This was a big deal. He did the right thing even though it might have cost him a huge contract. "I called Susan earlier, explained the situation with the land and offered her client 400 cases of our Santa Barbara reserve at a discounted price."

"And she called me to say that Frankie's wine was good enough to give her pause. At least until after the Cork Crawl. She wants to make sure her client is getting the best."

"We are the best and she knows it." Frankie could almost hear Nate give one of his confident shrugs. The one that used to bug her but now she found kind of cute. "She either buys now at a reduced price or later. Eventually she'll come around and when she does, it will cost her double per case if she wants to play."

"*If* she plays. You're making a lot of assumptions here. Frankie doesn't have enough vines to offer the quantity Remington will require for his own needs let alone his hotels, but if she wins it could be a game changer. The price of her barrels would skyrocket and Charles could easily weasel his way in with Remington, and we'd have to find ourselves a new collector in a tight market."

Remington Hotel? No wonder Susan didn't even bother to entertain Frankie's wine as a fit. Wouldn't matter if Red Steel boasted a perfect hundred from *Wine Spectator*, there's no way her ten acres could support his hotels.

"What do you want me to do, Trey? Say I fucked up? Make Frankie sell us her grapes, tell her she can't compete, force Abby to take back her sponsorship? I blew it, okay? I should have dug deeper with Saul's deal, but I didn't. But Frankie has as much of a right to compete as anyone else."

"I'm not saying to hardball her into anything."

"Good, because I did that at the Showdown and I won't do it again," Nate said leaving no room for argument.

"So instead you sell us out." Frankie had never heard Trey sound so—deadly. "You trashed the deal I set up with Susan, put us all in a tight spot and for what? So you could play house with the competitor?" Frankie swallowed hard as that knot in her stomach twisted tighter. "If you weren't thinking with your dick you'd realize that maybe Old Man Charles is playing us and she is playing you."

"Not Frankie's style," Nate growled.

"Maybe not, but it's Charles's. For all we know he's using her and she just hasn't figured it out. Either way, we lose those grapes and this deal and we're ten acres short and three years behind on the game plan that cost us double what you estimated all so you could fuck around with a woman whose own family doesn't even support her."

"Shut the fuck up, Trey," Nate barked.

Frankie's chest constricted and she threw open the door and stomped down the hallway, hating how those words hit her like a blade to the ribcage.

Nate was the peacekeeper of his family, the rational arbitrator. His ability to remain calm in the shitstorm that was his family was something Frankie had always secretly admired. And though Nate's earlier words had stung, she didn't want them arguing—not about her. She'd had a lifetime of practice at dividing families. Adding Nate's to her count would only ruin what they'd both fought so hard to create.

Ignoring that she had on a pair of pajama shorts, pink with SWEET stitched across the butt, she walked into the kitchen where four tall, dark, and oh-so-Italian men stared back at her. Well, three sat at the table, one stood against the counter—a good five feet and one heated argument away, arms folded, scowl rigidly in place.

"Great, the DeLuca invasion has begun," she said, but made sure to send Nate a little smile.

Then all four men were standing, offering the traditional DeLuca chivalrous welcome, ChiChi would be so proud, but Frankie just wanted them to sit down. Formal manners made her feel all girly, and when issued by a DeLuca, they made her sweat.

All four DeLucas though, with their bedroom-eyes, alpha-male presence and super-boost, testosterone-loaded smiles, were enough to make a girl—even one who owned steel-reinforced, ball-buster boots—clamor. Marc was the biggest of the brothers but Gabe was easily the most intimidating. And Trey, well, he was just plain annoying. Hot, but annoying. And he knew it. Which is why he kept winking at her.

And, good Lord, why were they all still standing?

"You can put all the Prince Charming shit away," she said walking past the Italian trifecta to get to the one DeLuca who mattered. The only one who got under her skin and flustered her. Growing up with three older brothers, she knew that if she went in defending Nate, it would only make things worse—for him. "I'm just grabbing some dinner."

"I was going to cook us something as soon as I got rid of my brothers," Nate said, propping up the entire counter with his body and effectively blocking the only cabinet she needed to access. His smile said he knew it.

"Yeah," Marc snorted. "He was making Lexi's lamb recipe."

All three guys started laughing. Nate did not.

His was too busy taking in her tank top and shorts—which suddenly felt too low and too high—and her bare legs. Between Nate's inventory and the suffocating sexual tension, it was hard to move. Plus, it was more than obvious that her nipples were in full party mode. A fact that Nate addressed when he finally met her gaze, eyes hot—apologetic, but hot.

"I've already got dinner covered, but thanks."

When it became clear he wasn't going to move, she reached past him and silently cursed when the sensitive tips of her breasts brushed his chest and sent her lady parts into overdrive. Making a point not to make eye contact, she opened the cupboard and rolled on to the tips of her toes to grab a new box of Pop Tarts.

Nate, never one to miss a detail, tucked a finger under her chin, tilted her face to his, and said softly enough that only she could hear, "Are you blushing?"

"No. I'm probably still hot from my shower."

Nate wasn't buying it. "And this isn't dinner." He grabbed the box and started reading the ingredients. "It's not even food."

"You act as if I was offering to share. I'm not." She grabbed for the box but he held it above his head, so she crossed her arms and glared. "And for your information, it contains three of the major food groups." He raised a disbelieving brow. So she ticked them off. "Fruit, grains, and icing."

"Icing isn't a food group."

"It's the best food group." She lunged at him, stretching upright as he stepped even closer, close enough that their bodies brushed in all the right places. Close enough that all she could smell was sexy, fresh-from-the-shower man. It took everything she had not to lean in for a better whiff—and maybe even a little bite.

"Yup, definitely a blush."

"Ow," Trey said from behind, cutting off her reply. Which was for the best since she would have had to lie. "I was just try ing to read what her shorts said."

Frankie dropped to her heels and Nate handed her the box, but not before shooting a death glare over her shoulder—most likely at Trey.

"Well, I'll let you get back to boys' night." Frankie opened the fridge and grabbed a beer. Dinner in hand, one family dispute successfully avoided, she headed for her room. But just in case they thought to pick right back up when she left, she added, "Oh, and Nate, when you get a chance to sit in your new chair, pull out that home improvement checklist you've worked so hard on, the one that's itemized and prioritized, and add insulation to your red column. These walls are so thin, I can hear Mittens fart in the pasture."

CHAPTER 11

"What would it take to get in your pants?"

The probationary—aka rookie—firefighter, who looked about twelve, froze mid-demonstration with his pants around his ankles and visibly swallowed.

"I was just wondering if that was part of today's tour?" Ava innocently clarified and Frankie rolled her eyes.

"I bet he'd let you," a seven year old boy with freckles and a red stain down the front of his school uniform whispered loud enough for China to hear. "Last year I got to sit in the captain's seat."

"And I got to pull his bell," Holly said.

"His bell, huh?" Ava gave Probie a flirty shrug, sending the strap of her top sliding off her shoulder and him into a coughing fit.

St. Helena Fire Station #1 was giving a tour to the St. Vincent's Academy's second grade class, and Frankie had managed to get Jordan and Ava on the list. Something she was rapidly regretting.

"You aren't going to get any better at this if you won't go near them," Jordan whispered.

Frankie looked at the herd of ketchup-crusted ankle biters and shivered. "I am near them, just not close enough to interact."

Jordan shot her a humored look and Frankie huffed. "Fine. I'll go engage."

She watched an ankle biter with a dirty nose and glue stuck in his hair shove Holly aside as he screamed, "I want to pull the bell!"

Frankie palmed the kid's head and turned it to face her. "You shouldn't push people smaller than you or someday you'll be the small one and karma sucks, kid."

"Is there a problem?" a blonde soccer mom said, placing her hand on Kid's shoulder.

"Yeah, he pushed Holly," Frankie said, noticing that her soil-stained jeans and purple hands didn't really scream qualified chaperone.

"Linden, say you're sorry."

"But I want to pull the bell and wear his pants!"

Soccer Mom didn't even blink when she explained to Frankie, "He's working on his manners. Aren't you Lindy? Yes, you are."

Frankie actually felt sorry for the little bully. Being addressed like a purse-dog would give her rage issues too. "Well, since he's already mastered pushing girls, maybe he can figure out those manners before he takes on pulling hair."

"Excuse us," Jordan said, taking Frankie by the arm and pulling her away. Before Jordan could begin her lecture on what Frankie was positive would be inappropriate adult-child relations, her brother Adam came striding over.

"No dress-up today, kids," he said.

The kids booed.

Ava and every mother chaperone in the firehouse—expect Regan DeLuca, who was bouncing a burrito wrapped Baby Sofie—stared, not even bothering to hide their interest. He got that a lot.

Adam had the Baudouin swagger and beefcake build and was the leader of an elite smoke-jumper team. Which meant he was an expert at parachuting out of planes to get behind fire lines and sweet talking his way behind panty lines. Even dressed in a pair of dark blue work pants and matching SHFD t-shirt and ball cap, he looked pretty impressive. And the women took notice. But even though he was three years older and five inches taller than her five-ten, she could still whoop him in darts.

"But if you make your way out front, one lucky Scout can run the siren," he added and the kids cheered.

Arguing over who got to sit in the fire engine, the group followed Probie through the opened bay door toward the shiny red truck. It was as clean and charming as the rest of the station. Built in 1912, the only firehouse in the city limits was a historical brick-faced building with stone encasings framing the three massive arched doors. Situated at the end of Main Street, the St. Helena Garden Club took special care in tending to the rose-filled planter boxes and pansies filled wine barrels that lined the curb.

"Thanks for setting this up, Adam," Regan said in a soothing singsong voice, most likely to keep the demon spawn from waking up.

"Yeah, and thanks for letting Ava and me join in," Jordan said, offering up her best smile. "Now, if I could just ask one more favor."

Adam gave her a weary once-over. "Last time you asked me for a favor, I ended up in nothing but a scarf and underwear."

Jordan patted him on the arm. "And that calendar made my year as PTA President the largest grossing year ever. So thank you. Oh, and thanks in advance for this." Without giving Adam a chance to see what was coming, Jordan reached up, wrapped one hand around his neck and planted a fat kiss on his lips.

"What the hell was that?" Adam asked, wiping his lips with the back of his hand.

"Don't worry, Smoky, I remember what your underwear looked like when they had the red Power Ranger plastered across the crotch," Jordan said, not an ounce of interest in her eyes. "I was just making sure that you were so unappealing Ava wouldn't be tempted to sneak out and see if your bell needs ringing."

Adam frowned. "Ava is what, all of sixteen?"

Jordan looked over her shoulder at her daughter who, dressed in a strip of denim held together by a chain, glared back. Adam followed her gaze.

"Holy shit, when did she get so . . ." Adam trailed off, his hands making a *Ba-dow!* gesture.

"Do you know what I'd give to go back to the slobber and poop phase?" Jordan sent Baby Sofie a longing look, then stifled a yawn. Regan did the same and Frankie was pretty sure that both friends spent most of last night pacing outside their kids' doors.

And here Frankie was complaining because Mittens had gnawed through the porch rail.

"Baudouin," Captain Roman Brady hollered from the captain's office. "Get in here."

"Be right back." Adam skulked off, but not before sending Jordan a hard glare. And Frankie knew that her friend's kiss had a dual purpose: to gross out Ava and piss off Roman.

"And you wonder where Ava gets it," Frankie said.

"The man has been sniffing around my skirt for months and won't make a move. I was just giving him some inspiration."

Adam stopped at the door to whisper something in Probie's ear. Probie straightened, slack jawed, and took a ginormous step back. "Sixteen! I swear I thought she was a nanny or something."

"Or something," Adam said over his shoulder. He shut the captain's door, cutting off the grumpy grumbles of his boss.

"Oh, look what I picked up this morning." Jordan dug through her enormous purse and pulled out a card. It was black, glossy, professional, shaped like a wine label, and exactly what Frankie needed if she was going to sell her wine for top dollar.

"This is amazing." She turned the promotional card for her winery over several times, swallowing back the weird urge to hug her friend with each flip.

Last week, after she'd discovered that Susan was going in a different, more DeLuca, direction, Frankie sucked it up and did something that normally gave her hives. She asked for help.

If she was going to sell her futures to an elite clientele, she needed to put on a polished front and give them a reason to feel comfortable saying yes to a risk. For a girl who considered competitive darts as an effective way of networking, Frankie sought out the two most polished people she knew to give her winery a professional makeover.

"I don't know what to say," Frankie admitted. Actually, she knew what she was supposed to say to her best friends who had gone out of their way to make Frankie's dream that much more of a reality. But for some reason the words "Thank you" didn't seem enough, and anything remotely close to "I love you" made her palms sweat. So she settled on, "You guys rock."

"Well, the old logo promised a swift kick to the groin with every bottle," Jordan said. "And I would love to take all the credit, but since Regan is the resident marketing goddess and standing right here, it's probably best to admit that I had her do all the fancy stuff."

"Not fancy," Regan clarified, leaning in and pointing to the logo. She was so close that Frankie got a sniff of, well she didn't know what, but it reminded her of Mr. Puffins when he was a kitten. "I polished it a bit, reworked your logo and made the *t* in Red Steel resemble the sword you wanted."

"It's in my family's crest." Frankie traced a finger over the logo. It was professional and classy, and still somehow *her*.

Charles had made it clear that Frankie couldn't use the Baudouin name with connection to her wine. But he couldn't stop her from using elements of her heritage.

"I changed the font, went with matted onyx for the background and glossy, deep red for the accent color. I think it looks elegant, sophisticated with the appropriate amount of bad-assery."

There it was again. That powdery, fresh scent.

Frankie looked at Baby Sofie sleeping and leaned closer. "Do you Febreze her?" She inhaled deep through her nose. "The other kids smelled like a petting zoo and hot ketchup. And she smells like." Sniff. Sniff. "New car."

"It's baby powder," Regan said smiling. "Want to hold her?"

"Hell no." Frankie stuffed her free hand in her pocket. "Just wondering if it works on alpacas. Or would it mess up his fur?"

"Why don't you just get one of those pine-scented car fresheners and hang it around his neck," Jordan offered. She took the card and turned it over. "I ordered a thousand but don't worry. My supplier gave it to me at a huge discount and even threw in dual-sided for free, so I had them list your contact info, a little history about Sorrento Ranch, and some of the praise you've received over the years on the back."

Frankie looked down the list of quotes, stunned at what industry people had said about her wine. "Where did you get these quotes?"

"I made a few calls." Jordan shrugged as if it were no big deal. But to Frankie, it was huge. No one had ever done anything like this for her before. And suddenly she didn't feel so alone.

"Speaking of calls, have you talked to Nate since the almost bed-sex?" Jordan asked.

"We were on the bed, but trust me it was nowhere near bed-sex."

"If it wasn't bed-sex, then how come when I showed up to the studio for my seven a.m. Buddha Baby Yoga class, you were half asleep on the stoop?"

"Because I missed my best friend."

Jordan just looked at her.

"What?"

"Admit it, Nate gets to you. He always has and instead of talking about what happened, you got scared and hid."

"I'm not scared and I don't hide." Which was why, after the DeLcua three had left, she had specifically *told* Nate she was sleeping when he knocked on her door. When she'd heard his loafers squeak down the hall and away from her room, she thought she was in the clear. Until her phone buzzed with a text. It was the same text she'd been re-reading all week. The reason why she *had* woken up on Get Bent's stoop with yoga mat in hand:

SLEEPING HUH? *I CAN SMELL YOUR SHORTS ON FIRE FROM DOWN THE HALL. I'LL GIVE YOU TONIGHT, BUT WE WILL TALK IN THE MORNING.*

Closely followed by:

NIGHT, SWEET CHEEKS.

"Uh-huh. So why haven't you called him yet?"

Frankie shrugged. "I figure he's busy with their vineyard. Prepping it for the harvest."

Between yoga, lunch with Luce, checking on her saplings, and doing a few practice runs for the Pick Till You Punt with Jordan, Frankie had managed to keep herself busy until well into Saturday evening, where she had no option but to go home and face the sexy Italian in the room.

Only, when she'd arrived at the ranch, she found it shy one DeLuca. In his place was a note, perfectly folded and addressed to her, sitting on the kitchen counter. It explained that he had to take a last minute trip south to check on their Santa Barbara property and that he would be back Friday at the latest.

A dry Indian Summer combined with a couple of stupid campers in Los Padres National Forest had ignited a wildfire. The strong winds had quickly spread the flames north through the Santa Ynez Mountains, a range that butted up to Santa Barbara and Santa Ynez Valley, threatening some of the top vineyards outside Napa Valley. Including Charles's latest four-hundred acre noose.

When Luce told Frankie that Charles had already sent a few extra hands down to help prepare for the worst, if the worst came, her heart pinched. Their business would be sunk if anything happened to that land, and yet she wasn't allowed to help protect it—a job that a few months would have fallen under her purview.

So she wasn't surprised that Nate had taken the first flight out as well. The DeLuca's owned several premium vineyards in the Santa Barbara area, and if there was trouble, she knew he'd want to be in the thick of it.

What had surprise her though was that on the back of his note he'd written a *SWEET CHEEKS CHECK LIST*.

First item under the household category was to pick up carrots for Mittens but to make sure that they were, secondly, attached to the tops since, thirdly, Mittens only liked the green portion of the vegetable, and he needed to be, fourth, fed twice daily. As though Frankie didn't already know all of this.

The second column of the list addressed the business side of their partnership, clearly outlining that Tanner would be by Wednesday to measure for the new tank, which would be delivered sometime next week, marking the six remaining weeks she had to find one hundred and fifty thousand dollars or she would have to sell her grapes—most likely to the sexy Italian who at the end of his very detailed and incredibly annoying list told her to keep Friday clear for dinner and a long talk, which Frankie knew would lead to bed-sex.

The exact reason why she'd bailed Saturday morning in the first place. Because although she could lie to Jordan, she was never one to lie to herself. What happened between them four days ago might not have taken place while *lying* on the bed, but the way her heart melted when he'd touched her, the way it still stuttered when she thought of how he'd looked at her, Frankie knew that with Nate something was different. The kind of different that told her they could have been anywhere and it still would have been bed-sex worthy.

A dangerous place to be when there was no future for them outside of the bed.

A loud shrill of the sirens blared and the kids' screams of delight echoed throughout the empty engine bays.

"Yes, sir." Adam stalked out of the captain's office, frustration underlining his respectful tone.

He took off his hat and made his way across the bay. He let out a big breath and Frankie stilled. Something was wrong. She could see it in the way his face furrowed. Adam never furrowed; he was the easy going one of the family.

"Is everything all right?" Frankie met him halfway. "Is it grandpa?"

"No, nothing like that." Adam ran a hand though his spiky hat hair. "The Cachuma Fork fire jumped the fire lines and is headed toward the Santa Ynez Valley. Captain's sending me down as part of a task force situated at the base of the hills to cut a new line and wait for the fire to come to us, so we can knock it out before it reaches the vineyards."

"How bad is it?"

"I leave in an hour."

That bad. "If anything happens to the south county vineyard—" she started.

"I know." Adam shook his head. "Right now I'm more worried that I won't make it back in time to for the Pick Till You Punt."

"Oh." Frankie's heart sank because with Dax back overseas and Jonah working the event in an official capacity, she was out a team. But she brushed it off quickly. "Don't be. We're good."

"You're short one person, which is why I was going to talk to Jonah and ask to fill in for me," Adam said.

"No, don't do that. I'll work it out. You just focus on staying safe." She gave him a Baudouin family hug—which consisted of a swift punch to the shoulder. When Adam didn't punch back, or look even remotely convinced, she added, "Jonah's working that day anyway."

"But I'm not." Regan smiled.

"You can't," Frankie said, staring horrified at the wiggle that came from beneath the pink blanket. It was just a little quake, but enough to have her taking a small step back.

"Why not?" Regan argued. "I'm VP of marketing for Ryo Wines, sister-in-law to one of the owners, granddaughter-in-law to the other, and sleeping with the man who has fooled himself into believing he runs it. Plus, it could be a girl power team."

"Fine, but if I can't bring Mittens, you can't bring . . ." Frankie pointed to the—definitely moving—pile of cotton. Blue eyes latched onto Frankie and Baby Sofie took one look and let out a screech louder than the siren.

~

"We're going to lose." Tanner said, dropping an empty crate on Marc's foot. Both men were staring over the rows and rows of grape-covered trellises toward Main Street.

Squinting past a giant Pick Till You Punt banner, Nate stepped around Gabe and walked to the end of their row to see what everyone was gawking at. One look at the woman dismounting her motorcycle and stalking through the community park and he had to agree.

No truer words had ever been spoken.

Because headed their way were four beautiful women and a half pint, "Crushing the Competition" hats pulled low, ponytails swinging and attitude flying. They all wore matching bright pink t-shirts with "Crush This" written across the chest, black hip huggers and combat boots that, aside from having the steal reinforced toes, looked incredibly hot. And judging on the silent men beside him, he wasn't the only one appreciating the view.

But Nate was only interested in the five-foot ten, blue-eyed view who was leading the pack, ax in hand, which had no purpose in the contest other than to intimidate. Point to Frankie, it was working. She was composed, ready for battle, and so damn beautiful he knew he should just turn around and walk away.

The Pick Till You Punt was about to begin any minute, and he needed to focus. Not that he doubted Team DeLuca would win—they always won, but the one thing that Trey had been right about was that there was a lot riding on how the next few weeks played out. The smart thing to do would be to keep his mind on the goal and eyes off the way that t-shirt clung to Frankie like it had been painted on.

Which was why Nate found himself leaning against one of the stakes, waiting for her to approach. He was done with always doing the smart thing. Around Frankie all of the static about wine, his family, the direction of the company, the effect Sorrento Ranch had on the big picture faded and Nate found himself living in the moment. Found that the heaviness around his chest, which had started after his parents' died and made it impossible to breathe most times, disappeared and he could just relax without the expectation of what the next breath would require of him. Something he'd never allowed himself the luxury of doing.

"Have I ever told you how much I love pink?" Nate asked when Frankie was less than a foot away.

"Lexi picked it out. She sewed the words on it too." Frankie tugged her shirt taut to show him, unintentionally pulling the neckline down for his viewing pleasure.

Nate took a long, thorough look at everything Frankie had on display. He didn't feel the need to rush, which was a good thing considering he'd missed the hell out of her over the past week and because she was taking her sweet-ass time doing the same.

Her blue eyes zeroed in on his mouth, sending a shot of hot lust straight to his groin. He had it bad for the town's bad girl.

Face flushed, eyes dilated, Frankie wet her lips. If that wasn't hard evidence that she was as busy picturing him naked as he was her, the pretty peaks poking out, just above the top curve of the *U* and second *H*, did the trick.

"How was the trip? Is your property okay?" Okay, so she didn't want to talk about what happened between them last week, or what was happening between them right now.

"Yeah, the firefighters got it under control before the flames got too far north, so we were lucky. How's your grandpa's land?"

She shrugged and the fabric of her tee rode up and exposed a sliver of smooth skin. "Haven't heard anything yet. But if something happens, one of my brothers will call."

So Charles was still freezing her out of the family. Nate wanted to pull her into his arms and give her a hug. All Frankie ever wanted was to make her family proud, and her grandpa used that big heart of hers against her, used it as a way to control her, to get her to come back on his terms. The faint bruising under her eyes told him that Charles's plan was working—to a point.

He doubted that Frankie would give in, but he also doubted that she had slept much while he'd been gone. "How's everything at home?"

"Tanner started prepping for the big tank, the grapes are looking nice, and I followed your list to a tee, even cleared my schedule."

"I'm sorry I missed out on dinner. With the fire, planes couldn't take off, so I had to drive home and decided to leave early this morning."

"Yeah, I got your message." But she didn't call him back. "Mittens missed you."

"Yeah?"

Frankie nodded. Scooted a little closer. "He ate through the back porch rail and the tractor seat, and I can't find the weedeater."

Nate rested his hand on the stake next to her, crowding her body a little. God he missed her. "What about you?"

"I burned through nine boxes of Pop Tarts, three tanks of gas, and took up Yoga." Her eyes never left his. "It was a stressful week."

"Want to talk about it?"

Frankie frowned. "I thought we just did."

"Morning, ladies," Tanner said as he walked up—right into their moment. He looked at Abby, who looked like the other women, just shorter. "Abigail."

"Jack," Abby said, taking out her vine clippers and a sharpening stone.

"Didn't expect to see you here," NFL said with a smile—a smile that Nate did not like the look of. It was the same one he'd just given Frankie. "Figured you'd be over with your grandma, protecting those hands of yours."

"Just because my brothers subscribe to some sort of boy's club, doesn't mean that my talents should go to waste. Plus, these hands of mine—" She holstered her clippers in her tool belt and wiggled her fingers. "Lethal."

"I know," Jack said.

Oh, hell no. Old instinct kicked in and Nate took a huge step forward. So did Gabe and Marc. It wasn't just Tanner's tone; the guy was actually sizing up his baby sister. And business partner or not, Tanner held the team record for the most pass receptions, on and off the field. And Abby was still reeling from her impending divorce—an easy target for a guy whose nickname, Hard Hammer Tanner, was derived from how hard he nailed the opponent.

"What the hell, Tanner?" Marc said, pressing his size in Tanner's face, which was kind of ridiculous. Even though Marc was by far the biggest of the brothers, Tanner still had a good two inches and thirty pounds on him.

Then again, the DeLucas had two extra sets of fists and a combined ninety years of practice beating the crap out of anyone who messed with their sister.

"Oh. My. God." Abby leapt between them, swinging a set of clippers in one hand and shoving Tanner behind her with the other, like a referee at a WWE tournament trying to call a time out. Lucky for Tanner, none of the brothers wanted to tangle with Abby. She fought dirty when she was mad. "And you guys wonder why I never date?"

"Are you saying this is a date?" Tanner said, laying his fucking hand on Abby's shoulder.

Abby turned, pinched his nipple, and twisted, taking Tanner to his knees in one swoop. "No, I don't date my students. And because you're being a total idiot, you get to practice chopsticks all week."

"Better than Twinkle Twinkle Little Star," Tanner mumbled when Abby let loose of her death grip on the man's pecs.

"That's next week," she said then stormed off to take her place, second leg in. Great, she would be competing directly with Tanner.

"You going to blow this to impress my sister, or do I need to replace you?"

"We're good," Tanner said, but his eyes were on Abby's retreating backside.

"Uncle Nate!" Holly squealed and launched herself into his arms, saving Tanner from a fat lip.

"Hey, kiddo. I missed you."

"Guess what? Frankie gave me ten dollars this morning, all in dimes and pennies, and she is almost out of dirty credits," the "Crush This" mascot said. She was wearing a pink tank, dark jeans and mini combat-boots. A real ball-buster—just travel-sized.

"Dimes and pennies?" Nate said, looking at Frankie who just shrugged. But, he noticed, sadly, she was a whole lot farther away than she had been a second ago.

She continued to edge away as Gabe took Holly and by the time he'd tossed her in the air and delivered a big kiss to each flushed cheek, Frankie was standing on the outskirts of the group, checking and rechecking her tool belt.

"Where are my other kisses?" Gabe smiled at Regan, who was bouncing on her toes with Baby Sofie in a sling. Still holding one daughter, he kissed his other on the forehead, and then his wife until everyone looked away. "Did you come down here to wish me good luck?"

"No." Regan stepped back, proudly pointing to her shirt. "Team Frankie. I'm their ringer. And I have been given strict orders that there is to be no fraternizing with the enemy. So no more kissing until we kick your," Regan looked at Holly, who, eyes wide and lips parted, was waiting for the twenty-five cent fine to be spoken, "pants."

Holly sighed, deflated.

Gabe frowned, about as pleased by that comment as Nate was. "No way. You aren't going to be squatting down and cutting vines in your condition."

"It's called motherhood, not a condition." Regan gave Gabe a pat on the cheek.

"And she isn't bending or cutting. Frankie will be doing her leg of the race," Jordan said staring right at Nate. "Regan's just going to be pushing the grape cart."

"With the baby?" Marc said it as though they had this in the bag.

Gabe snorted. "Have you seen my wife juggling both kids while navigating a full cart at Costco? It's impressive." He reached down and, while smiling at his wife, pulled his daughter out of her sling and nuzzled her close. And Nate felt something unfamiliar stir in his chest—jealousy.

"I'm dropping the kids off with ChiChi in a second. Imagine how impressive I'll be then," Regan teased.

"What do you mean you're pulling two legs?" Nate asked Frankie after Regan took Holly by the hand and led his two nieces toward the stands. "It's the Pick Till You Punt. A relay race. Meaning you have to punt the baton."

"I am." Frankie stared up at him defiantly. "I'm passing to Abby who passes to Jordan who passes back to me. The rules say that the teams have to be comprised of four members. Nowhere does it state that they all have to cut or push."

Marc shot Nate a worried look. "Is that even legal?"

Not only was it legal, it was smart. Nate was ticked that he hadn't thought of it first. Frankie's team wouldn't lose any cutting time while running the crates up to the platform. He gave a terse nod. "Yup."

She must have seen the realization register on his face because she sent him a slow and downright sinful smile, and every dream he'd harbored over the past week came back with alarming accuracy.

"Well, see you at the finish line, golden boy." Frankie gave his arm a gentle nudge, and man, just her hand on his shoulder shot his concentration to hell. Or maybe it was the view he got as she walked toward her row of vines—which, wouldn't you know it, was right next to his—her jeans pulled tight, leaving a lasting impression and making him consider things. Stupid things, such as dragging her to the utility shed over by the back entrance to town hall and picking up where they had left off.

His dick showed support by pressing painfully against his jeans. His common sense told him that until they talked about last week, about what taking this further meant, conferences of any kind that were labeled "private" would be a bad idea.

CHAPTER 12

Eyes on the golden grapes in front of her, Frankie rolled on the tips of her toes, waiting for the sheriff to sound the bell while doing her best not to openly stare at Nate, who was one row over and three legs down. Apparently he was their closer, which meant they'd go head to head in the final sprint of the race. He was also staring right at her. She could see him out of the corner of her eye.

She could also see he was wearing a grey DeLuca t-shirt that clung like a second skin to his broad chest, a chest that she'd been within licking-distance just a week ago. His jeans were faded in the most impressive spots and hung low on his narrow hips. Today he had forgone the loafers, instead wearing a pair of worn work boots that had her sucking in a breath.

Gone was the starched scientist with the stick up his ass, and in his place was a let's-get-down-and-dirty grape grower with a butt that made her lady parts tingle.

Since staring ahead wasn't working, Frankie closed her eyes. Even though it was already late September, heat radiated off the ground and had begun to seep through her clothes. She swept the sweat off the back of her neck and wished she'd agreed with Abby on shorts rather than fighting for jeans.

The air was thick with the sweet scent of grapes as Frankie inhaled, blindly maneuvering the crate in her hand to shape and weigh it. It looked like it held ten pounds of grapes, but this year the committee had sloped in the bottom and, at best guess, it probably held nine to nine and a half pounds, which meant that she'd fill up three to four crates among her six vines. A good possibility since the vines were full and the grape clusters heavy.

Winning the Pick Till You Punt wasn't just about being the fastest cutter or having the strongest back. It would come down to the person who could accurately estimate how many grapes equated to one hundred pounds. Her hands, and gut, were telling her that her team needed eleven full-to-the-brim crates to win. With a few extra clusters thrown on top to be safe.

Frankie set the crate on the ground and placed it between her feet, scooting it back and forth down the line to get a feel for it and to create a smoother path for when the race started. When she got to the end of her row, she carried it back the other way, dropped the other three crates an appropriate distance apart and then positioned the arch of her boot in the perfect place on the lead crate.

"I can't believe you showed up."

Cracking her neck from side to side to release the sudden tension, Frankie looked over her shoulder and saw Kenneth. He was beanpole tall, dressed in Baudoiun colors, smarmy as ever, and in her face.

"I can't believe they let you hold a sharp object." She looked at the clippers in his hand and then to the Baudouin flag flapping three rows to her right. There were already three men in place, four of the fastest cutters her grandpa employed, including one imported all the way from France. "Plus, only industry professionals are allowed on the field. And since you don't know a grape from a prune, the only reason Grandpa is even considering you is to get back at me."

Kenneth shrugged, apparently unconcerned with how he inherited the vineyard, just that he did. "Says the girl whose future is going up in flames. You dug your hellhole with the old man, not me."

Yes, she had.

"Is he here?" Frankie hated knowing that she cared.

The last thing she wanted to feel today was that familiar pressure to make her grandpa proud. It ranked right up there with Nate telling her to clear her schedule for Friday and then not showing up. He'd called, sure, but she'd actually been looking forward to it. Looking forward to seeing him, spending time with him—and not just naked time either. Which was something Frankie never let herself feel for guys, so when she got his message canceling their date, even though she knew it wasn't a real date, it had felt as though dinner wasn't important to him.

"No," Kenneth said as though *she* were dimwitted. "He's still down in . . . holy shit, he didn't tell you." Kenneth smiled. "I guess my dad was right. Gramps really is done with you."

Frankie's heart dropped to her stomach at his comment, then to her toes at the realization. There were only two reasons her grandpa would miss today. And neither one of them were good. "Is he okay? Is he still at the South Ynez Vineyard?"

Kenneth shrugged one shoulder. "Nothing for you to worry about. Just family business."

Frankie was about to go "business" on him when the buzzer sounded. Chaos erupted around her, the sound of metal slicing and the scent of fresh cut vines swept through the air. Torn between donkey kicking her cousin in the throat and shoving his clippers someplace creative, Frankie faltered for a brief moment. She wanted to win, needed to win. But she also wanted to know where Charles was and if he was okay.

"Frankie," carried out over the crowd.

She jerked her head toward the voice and found Nate. He was big, bad, and barreling her way, ready to pounce on Kenneth if she gave him the go-ahead. It made her insides turn to mush and kicked her heart into high gear.

Noticing that Kenneth was already gone and the other teams were partway through filling their first crate, she sent Nate a got-this wink and shifted into high gear.

Head down, hands fluid, focus set to tunnel vision, Frankie fell easily into the zone. She cradled, swiped, dropped, and scooted—over and over—her fingers never hesitating, her feet judging the exact spacing to catch the falling cluster. She filled the first crate, then the third, a full fourth, and before she knew it her row was harvested, the grape cart loaded, and Reagan was rushing it toward their scale.

Not even breaking a sweat, Frankie whispered to Abby, who, true to her word, was incredible with a pair of shears, to go for a three full boxes. She jogged past Jordan with a high five and a direct order to just overflow one crate, and took her position at the fourth and final section, waiting for her final leg of the relay. Her plan, since she could cut twice as fast as Jordan, was to fill the final three.

Nate stood on the other side of the trellis, under a flapping DELUCA, REIGNING CORK KING sign, casually leaning against the flag post. Those intense eyes traveled over her entire body and back, but when they locked with her it took everything she had not to grip him by the front of the shirt and kiss him.

With each passing second, she felt her breath pick up. Filling four crates in just under two minutes didn't have her sweating, but one smoking hot look from Nate and she was ready to combust.

"That was the sexiest thing I have ever seen," Nate said. And even over the shouts of the crowd she could hear the huskiness in his voice. He wanted her. Bad. "Christ woman, you had a late start and still managed to smoke everyone. Poor Gabe is struggling to make up the time he lost gawking at you."

Frankie tore her eyes away and looked at the other teams. Gabe was making his way toward the platform with the cart, but most of the other teams, including Charles's, were only midway through their first set. In fact, her team was the only one on their second leg, and Abby was tearing it up.

"Abby's fast, but Jordan's your weak link." Nate said. "Putting her against Marc was a bad move. She'll get frustrated midway through and Marc will make up the lost time."

"That's why she's only filling one crate."

"So you're leaving the last three for yourself? Risky, since I bet your arms are taxed from the first four." So golden boy had done his homework.

"Not even breaking a sweat, DeLuca." Frankie shielded her eyes from the sun, watching Regan rush by with Abby's three boxes, full and overflowing. "Plus, three, seven, a dozen, doesn't matter, I can out-cut you."

"Is that right?"

"Yup, I've spent every harvest since I was five in the field." Something her grandfather had forced her to do. "Plus, I always close the deal."

At that, he flat out grinned. "With these?" He reached over the trellis, his finger skimming the top of her tool belt. To most people it would look like he was just checking out her clippers, but the way his fingers brushed back and forth over the handle of her secateurs—purposely dipping under the hem of her T-shirt to tease her skin—it was clear he was trying to get to her.

And it was working.

She stepped back and, crate in place, reached for her clippers. Jordan was filling her crate quickly and Frankie wanted to be ready. "Yup, and you might want to keep your eyes on the grapes or you're just going to end up watching my ass the whole way."

"Looking forward to it, sweet cheeks."

~

"What do you mean a tie?" Frankie shouted, mid-high five. All four women went from smiling and throwing around their cutting-prowess to utter confusion as they looked at the row of giant metal scales, which took up most of the community park's outdoor stage. "I was already at the scale while Nate was loading up his last crate on the cart."

"I was right behind you and I'm a faster loader." The jerk smiled.

"You both set the crates down at the same time," the mayor said, his mustache curling down.

"But I was the fastest cutter."

"Then how, if we finished at the same time, do I have six more pounds than you?" Nate said jerking his chin to the scales. His read one hundred and eight, whereas Frankie's team picked one hundred and two pounds.

"That just means you overestimated the size of the clusters and the crates." Frankie shrugged. "Amateur mistake."

"Since there's no precedent for this kind of thing, Mrs. Rose is getting the rule book out." The mayor shifted nervously on his feet.

Mrs. Rose was the current wine commissioner of St. Helena, and therefore the person appointed to settle this dispute. She was also built like an ox, had the personality of a pit bull, and was completely unpredictable.

"If you two could come to an agreement on which table you want, preferably different tables, we can finish up here and get on over to the Punt Luck before Mrs. Rose comes back," the mayor said, adding the last part only after he'd checked the surrounding area for Mrs. Rose.

"You're right, Mayor." Nate held his hands up and took a step back. "Ladies first."

"Why? So you can look like the good guy?" Frankie crossed her arms. If she won this it was going to be because she earned it, not because Nate was giving her some pity pick. This town already thought she'd made it on her grandfather's coattails. "Not going to happen."

"Why the hell not?"

Nate knew as well as Frankie did that for a company like DeLuca Vineyards or Baudouin Wines, location wasn't as crucial. They were the big guys of wine. People would seek out their booths, if only to brag that they'd rubbed shoulders with a wine tycoon. But to a fledgling winery like her own, who needed as many people as possible to taste, love, and vote for her wine, location could mean the difference between paying Tanner off and having to sell her grapes.

"Because I won this and you know it. And as soon as you're ready to admit it to me and everyone here, let me know so I can pick my table and everyone else can pick theirs."

Nate smiled, his whisky eyes dropping to her mouth. "Are we arguing?"

"I don't know, are we?" And to Frankie's horror she sounded breathy instead of angry—and she'd moved closer. The worst part was that she couldn't even remember what they had been arguing about.

"I sure as hell hope so," Nate whispered, the space between them quickly disappearing.

Before she could get out another word, or tilt her head up so he could reach her more easily, a shot rang out and juice splattered all over Frankie's top.

~

"Now, seeing as there are no rules for this kind of situation, I get to make the rules. Anyone got a problem with that?"

Nate sure as hell didn't. Not when Mrs. Rose stood— rule book in one hand and the starter's pistol in the other— with her teeth bared and her frosted bun glistening under the afternoon sun.

Frankie, however, had other ideas, and opened her mouth to speak when Mrs. Rose pointed her .45 with perfect accuracy at Frankie's scale. "Rule One: Another peep out of you and I start firing."

Frankie looked at Nate's scale. Dripping with juice and pulp, his needle now teetered between one hundred and five and one hundred and six pounds. With a sigh, she wisely closed her mouth, but not before letting loose a series of colorful opinions under her breath.

"Good. We're in agreement." Mrs. Rose went on. "Rule Two: You both have three minutes to decide who wants what table or I start shooting crates until you are both underweight, we have a new winner, and I get to go eat some of Pricilla's Chocolate or Die Cake. Understand?"

What Nate understood was that the starter pistol wasn't loaded with blanks, and if he and Frankie couldn't come to some kind of agreement, then Charles would win by default. Something he wasn't willing to let happen. Not after the look on Frankie's face when her cousin had approached her at the start of the race. He didn't know what had been said, but he knew that Kenneth had hit the intended target with painful accuracy.

Nate looked at Kenneth, who was preening, and back to Mrs. Rose. "Five minutes, no shooting, and I will buy you an entire Chocolate or Die cake. Deal?"

He didn't wait for an answer, didn't have the patience or the self-control. Instead he took Frankie's hand and pulled her toward town hall, surprised when she laced their fingers and followed without argument. Which was a damn shame, because he wouldn't mind a little verbal foreplay to get things sparking for the discussion they were about to have.

Weaving through the rows of vines, he took her around the back of town hall and out of sight of all the onlookers, to the utility shed. He pulled her inside and shut the door. And then his hands were on her. Gripping her hips, and backing her up against the door.

Her hands, however, were crossed over her breasts. Her full breasts. Her full, they've got to be Ds, breasts. What he wouldn't give to know if the lace matched the shirt, both up and downstairs. But he only had five minutes— well about four and some change and that wasn't enough time.

"I say we race the length of the park," she said. "Fastest one wins."

"I didn't bring you in here to talk about how to settle this."

"Then why are we in here?"

"Because last time I kissed you in public, you kneed me." He leaned in, he couldn't help it, and trailed little kissed over her jaw, her neck. God, she smelled good, like hot chick and Pop Tarts or something. All he knew was that she smelled good. Better than good. "And since I've been rock hard for a solid week, I didn't want to risk it."

Her hands fisted in his hair and she brought his face to hers. "Are you going to kiss me or do I need to start yelling?"

"Oh, I'm going to kiss you until you start yelling"—he smiled—"my name."

"We'll, see," she whispered before dragging his head down and crushing her mouth to his.

His body went haywire, with all of the emotions and pent-up tension from the past week tangling into one complicated, and really freaking hot ball that settled right in his groin. Especially when her hands smoothed down his chest, teased across his stomach, and—bingo—right over the front of his pants. Her fingers traced the hard ridge of him through his denim and before he could return the favor, his zipper was down, pants around his ankles, and her warm hands were firmly wrapped around him.

Her hands. Oh my god, her hands officially blew his mind. Which was the only excuse he had for bucking into them. Because they cradled him, while stroking from base to tip, tightening a little more every time the motion was repeated, driving him closer to the edge with each pass.

Nate's eyes rolled back into his head and he had to reevaluate his earlier statement. This was the sexiest thing he'd ever seen.

"Christ, Frankie, I already said we weren't racing, so slow down. You're killing me," he growled. And of course Frankie, who never listened to a damn thing he said, picked up the mind-blowing pace. A part of him died at the thought of her stopping. Another part of him knew that if she stroked him one more time with those hands, this would all be over. And he was, after all, a gentleman.

Grabbing her wrist, he stopped her and for several intense breaths he held perfectly still, afraid that if he moved, even an inch of friction would set him off.

"Slow down? We only have like a minute and you're almost there," she murmured, her mouth still working his.

Almost didn't even describe how close he was.

"Like it or not, sweet cheeks, I am a DeLuca and in my world, it is always ladies first," he whispered, then took her mouth in one hell of a hot kiss. A kiss that got a whole lot hotter when Frankie started using her teeth and tongue to nip and tease at his lips.

With a low growl, he pressed her to the wall, pinning her with his hips, and freeing up his hands to do some exploring of their own. He ran a palm down her breasts, over her stomach, and following her lead, right down her pants and—holy hell.

He felt her breath catch and his hands stopped when they met lace. Sexy, skimpy, and extremely wet lace.

"You're wet," he whispered against her neck while he kissed his way to the creamy swells pushing out from beneath her shirt. "What color are they?"

"Black," she moaned. Her hands were now fisted in his hair and, lucky guy that he was, holding him to her, so he buried his face into cleavage. "And yes, the bra matches."

Everything inside of him demanded that he rip off her clothes and check for himself, because he could tell she was lying and he wanted to know why. But she was right, time was running out. And there was no way she was going to beat him twice in one day. Oh, he knew she'd won—she'd out-cut every damn man there—but he wanted to rile her a little first.

And rile her, he had. Her body was so primed it was humming when he pulled the lace to the side and slid one finger in, meeting more of that sweet moisture. Her whole body tensed, so he slid in another, loving the throaty sounds she made and the way her body gave itself over to him.

"Christ you feel good," he rasped. And he meant it. Tight and hot. The way she closed around his fingers when he sank them even deeper was enough to drive a man insane.

Slowly, he started pumping and her hips shifted to deepen the friction. This was what he wanted, what she needed, a taste of what was to come. She pressed forward, her thigh rubbing against his dick and things got serious, real fast.

Breathing turned nonexistent, his chest felt too big for his skin and Frankie was so damn close.

"That's it," he whispered, curling his fingers and hitting the right spot.

He took her mouth right as she screamed out and her body exploded around his hand. And Jesus Christ the woman never did anything small or half assed.

Nate rode out her orgasm with her, slowly slipping his fingers out and delivering easy, languid kisses. Every time he thought to pull back, let her catch her breath, one or the other would prolong the kiss, tighten their grip, press closer.

So he didn't stop, not until he felt her body sag against his and her eyes start to flutter open.

"Better?" He gave her a little kiss.

She nodded.

"Are you going to admit that you missed me too?"

"Maybe." She shrugged, but she was smiling. That blissful smile that only comes from a great orgasm.

Nate let her lean against him while he zipped her pants back up and straightened her clothes as much as possible.

"You going to admit that I out-cut you?" she said, finally letting go and scooping up her hat off the floor. He had no idea when that had gone flying and by the confused look on her face, neither did she.

"Maybe," he laughed, bending over to get his pants, a difficult task since he was still painfully hard.

"Well, then." Shoving the hat on her head she said, "Go."

"God damn it, Frankie," he yelled after her, but she was already halfway across the park and he was still standing there fully loaded with his pants around his ankles. By the time he'd gotten himself calmed down enough to zip his fly, Frankie had picked out their two tables, the rest of the teams were selecting theirs, and his brothers were sending him shit-eating grins.

He flipped them the bird and walked up behind Frankie who was in a heated discussion with her cousin. Nate picked up the pace and Kenneth, smart man that he was, made himself scarce before Nate approached.

He placed his hands on her shoulders, which were so tense there was no give. "Everything okay?"

Frankie turned around, her face tight. She wasn't looking relaxed or like she'd just had a standing O in the utility shed.

"What's wrong?" he asked.

"I'm not sure."

Okay, not the answer or warm reception that he was expecting after what they'd just shared. Hell, he was still flying at half-mast and she was looking like someone had just told her that Pop Tarts filed for bankruptcy. "Why don't we go get a piece of Pricilla's cake or maybe a cold beer and talk about it?"

It was weird: She was looking at him, but she wasn't really looking *at* him. "Um, that sounds good, but I have to meet you there." She blinked and added, "Okay?"

She didn't even wait for his answer before she turned and walked through the crush of people headed toward Main Street. He watched her get on her bike and head north, leaving him wondering what the hell had just happened and with no option other than to wait. Which he did.

He waited through two helpings of Pricilla's burnt almond cake, Holly's explanation of how Baby Sofie grew on a vine, and through the entire Harvest Happy Hour Wine Rush at the Spigot. He waited until his brothers were on their second pitcher of beer, Lexi was practically sitting on Marc's lap, and that look on Frankie's face was so cemented in his memory, he couldn't wait any longer.

Dropping a twenty on the table, he said his good-byes and was gathering his coat when Jonah approached their table, expression dialed to extra-serious. "You seen Frankie?"

"You mean before or after she kicked my brothers' asses?" Abby said and the group laughed.

Nate shot them all a dark look. "She was actually supposed to meet me a couple hours ago, but never showed. Why?"

Jonah sighed. It was long, and tired, and not a good sign. "I've been trying to get ahold of her for the past hour and she's not answering my calls."

"She's not answering mine either," Jordan admitted, and that heavy feeling Nate had been carrying around the past few hours fell hard in his stomach.

The deputy pulled out the stool, his way of asking if he could join them. And if Nate weren't so worried about Frankie, he would have laughed—it was such a Frankie move.

Nate resumed his seat. "What's going on, Jonah?"

The sheriff looked longingly at the beer. If the guy wasn't on duty Nate was pretty sure he'd drink the entire pitcher. "This isn't widely known yet, so what I say here doesn't leave the table."

After a silent agreement passed among the table, Jonah spoke. "The fire reached our South Yenz Vineyard."

"Ah man, Jonah, I'm so sorry," Gabe said. "How bad is it?"

"Bad," Jonah said, his entire frame deflating. "Lost half the vines."

Silence fell. Fierce competitors, ridiculous feud, Baudouin or DeLuca, it didn't matter; when a fellow winemaker lost their vines it hit everyone hard. And this loss was enough to topple Charles's entire legacy.

"Does Frankie know?" Jordan asked.

"That's why I am trying to find her. Adam called me earlier this morning to fill me in and we both decided to wait and tell Frankie. We didn't want to stress her out before the competition. I just hope we didn't wait too long."

"Kenneth," Nate said, already on his feet. *Son of a bitch.* "Kenneth told her."

~

Frankie pulled a bottle out of her secret stash and popped the cork. Holding the wine opener in her teeth, she grabbed a spare, because it was that kind of night, and walked out to the front porch. The heat of the day had disappeared with the sun but despite the chill in the evening air, the wood slats remained warm under her bare feet.

She dropped down on the bottom step and, not bothering with a glass, took a long swig. Red Steel wasn't the kind of wine Frankie would normally pick when the sole purpose was to get as tanked as humanly possible, but tonight it felt fitting. Plus each swallow chased away the goosebumps on her bare legs.

"*Wark*," Mittens nickered as he ambled over.

"Wine gives you gas, remember? Plus, you already took out my lemon tree. My *new* lemon tree. A gift from Luce."

With another low, apologetic "*Wark*," he looked up at her through those thick dark lashes.

"Fine," she huffed.

Mittens took this as a sign of forgiveness and compacted his body to resemble the sphinx. Not having another fight in her tonight, she worked her fingers behind his ears. With a satisfied hum, he rested his head on Frankie's thigh.

She looked out across the field, toward her grandfather's

house and the single lit window, and any hopes that she had harbored on salvaging their strained relationship died. He'd made it more than clear earlier that evening exactly where Frankie stood in the family—firmly on the outside.

Placing the bottle to her lips, Frankie tipped it on back and, *damn*, even guzzling it like a brown bag special didn't diminish from what an incredible wine she'd created. Her dad would have been proud, Frankie thought, and had it not defeated the purpose of this evening, it would have been a sobering one.

After threatening Kenneth with bodily harm unless he told her where Charles was, her cousin dropped the bomb that the south half of the South Ynez Vineyard had burned through the night and was nothing but ash.

Frantic, and convinced that Kenneth was just being his usual lying sack of shit self, Frankie raced to her grandfather's house. She found him sitting on his favorite porch swing, smoking his pipe, and staring blindly at the gently rolling fields of golden vines. He smelled like cherry tobacco and fresh cut grass, and, when she laid her hand on his shoulder, he felt like home.

It became clear in the first two seconds that Kenneth had been telling the truth, and that Charles wasn't her home, not anymore.

"I suppose that you've come here to gloat about your win," he'd said.

Frankie didn't know what hurt more, that he wouldn't even look at her or that he believed she'd purposefully do something to hurt him—especially under the circumstances.

"I just came to see how you were holding up. See what I can do to help," she'd said and he laughed. It was low and bitter and filled with disgust.

"You could have helped by sharing the news that Susan Jance was looking to sign a deal that could have saved this winery, yet you didn't say a word."

Because it would have placed her between her family and Nate. A position that she'd officially given up. "We could have partnered up: your grapes, Baudouin's name and wine. We still can. We only lost half the harvest."

Frankie's heart had cracked, right then. She thought back to when Trey had implied that Charles was playing her, remembered how Nate had defended her to his family, and knew that no matter what happened she wouldn't let herself be thrown in the middle ever again.

"It wasn't my place to share and it isn't our deal to make, Grandpa. You can talk to Susan, but I already have plans for my grapes. And her collector isn't looking to fill his cellar with two buck chuck."

"Then your place is no longer here and the only way you can help is to leave."

So she had. Fighting back the tears with every step she took through the vineyard, which she had spent most of her life working.

Frankie heard the sound of approaching boots crunching the gravel, drawing her attention to the end of the walkway. She looked up and saw six-feet-plus of pure unadulterated male.

Nate stood just a few feet away, his hands shoved in his front pockets and his attitude set to protect and serve. He was wearing the same clothes from earlier, but for some reason he looked bigger, stronger, and, the way the moonlight played off of his olive skin and dark features, like a walking ad for sex.

"I've got a bottle of Wild Turkey that will get you there in half the time." Even his voice sounded like sex.

"Half the time, but not nearly as fun," she replied.

"You don't seem to be having much fun," Nate said gently.

"It hasn't been a very fun night."

Nate studied her for a long moment, so long that she forgot what they were talking about. Then with a sad smile he said, "Jonah told me about the fire."

Right. The fire. Her grandpa. And her crap of a night.

"Well, at least my brother bothered to tell somebody," she said and even to her own ears she sounded bitter.

"He's been trying to get ahold of you but you aren't answering your phone."

"It's in the house." Buried under a pile of dirty clothes where she'd shoved it after discovering that all three of her brothers had known about the fire since last night and hadn't notified her. Not even a call.

In her heart, she knew they were waiting until after the Pick Till You Punt so she wouldn't be distracted, but it still hurt that the entire family had a meeting to discuss the South Ynez Vineyard without her there.

According to Kenneth, even Dax had been Skyped in from some base in Germany while they all decided how to handle the latest blow to the Baudouin legacy. A blow that could very well be the end to the legacy that, as of two hours ago, she was no longer a part of.

"Want to talk about it?"

"Not really."

"You sure? Because sometimes letting it all out helps."

She frowned. "Are you asking me if I'm going to cry on you?"

"I could handle it if you did."

Yeah, well she couldn't. Which was why if he didn't stop looking at her like she was about to snot all over his shirt, she was going to lose it. In fact, the longer he stared at her, the hotter her eyes felt until when she tried to focus really hard on Mittens, he got all blurry.

"I don't cry. And I don't want to talk about this." But she also didn't want him to leave. So she held out the . . . whoa, how had that happened? She held the bottle up to the moonlight and frowned—half empty.

Nate sat on the step next to her. Leaning forward, he rested his elbows on his bent knees, bringing his face eye-level with hers and his thigh flush with her bare legs. She wasn't sure if it was the simple contact that was reassuring, or the idea that getting drunk with someone seemed less pathetic than drinking alone, but the panicky feeling that had been strangling her ever since Kenneth told her about the fire seemed to ease up. Not all the way, but enough so that every breath wasn't followed by a sharp pain.

Nate took the bottle from her hand and, looking at the new and improved label, sent her a sidelong smile. "This looks great."

"Regan designed it," she said. "And it tastes even better."

Nate raised an amused brow. His eyes never leaving hers, he made a big to do about smelling the wine and swirling it around in the bottle.

"No glass?"

"Not a glass kind of night. Or a glass kind of girl," she added just in case he needed that in a woman. "I also don't cook, clean, or fold laundry."

"I know," he said as though he didn't care. He sounded so convincing that she almost believed him. And if she hadn't paid witness to every Suzie Homemaker and pedigreed professional Nate had paraded around town with since college, she would have. But the kind of women Nate dated and the kind of woman Frankie was were polar opposites.

As though reading her mind, he smiled. But was it a you're-my-dream-woman kind of smile or a dream-on smile? She didn't know. And the fact she desperately wanted it to be the former didn't help.

Without clarifying, Nate took a final sharp sniff and eyed her over the rim of the bottle. "Lavender?"

"The Syrah grapes came from my little vineyard behind Luce's lavender garden."

"And the Cabernet Sauvignon?"

"Right over there." She pointed to Saul's gentleman's vineyard. When Nate sent her an impressed look she shifted on the step. "Glow has been selling me their grapes for the past three years. I took care of her vineyard and the house. In exchange she cut me a deal on the grapes that I could afford."

"And no one knew?"

She shook her head and couldn't keep the smile from her lips. "That was Glow's deal and I didn't want to lose the grapes."

"Smart," was all he said before tipping the bottle to his lips.

Her heart skipped a beat. Then three more as he took a small sip and let wine settle on his tongue. This was it, the real test. Everyone who had tried her wine had loved it, but none of that seemed to matter anymore. The only opinion she cared about was Nate's.

She watched closely as he rolled the liquid around in his mouth, swallowed and—

Hot damn.

There it was.

His eyes went heavy and then slid closed. His chest went perfectly still before sucking in a breath and, even though it was dark, Frankie could make out the way his face relaxed into a complete and utter state of bliss.

"Francesca," he murmured, taking another sip, as though to be sure he'd tasted what he thought he'd tasted. "This is . . . wow."

She pressed her hands between her knees to keep from reaching out. "Are you sure? Charles said it had the potential to endure time, but was too simple and not dense enough to really transform."

Nate's expression went soft as he considered what she'd said. Charles had been supportive of her "project" as he'd deemed it, until he had tasted Red Steel. His assessment of what Frankie believed in her gut to be something extraordinary had really shaken her confidence. If a wine didn't transform, didn't evoke a different experience over time, then there was no point in holding on to it.

He took another sip. "Your grandfather is a fool. For that comment and for letting you go. This is one of the best wines I've ever tasted." He went on to talk about the smooth, buttery texture of the wine, the perfect balance between classic currant and spice with a smoky note of tobacco at the end, but all Frankie could focus on was the wonder in his voice, the look in his eyes.

He tasted what she tasted. Realized and appreciated what she'd created. And he was proud of her.

"It's going to win?" She hadn't meant to put the question mark at the end but tonight, after Kenneth and Charles and her brothers, she needed someone to believe in her. Believe in what she was capable of.

Red Steel wasn't just a wine. It was her, in a bottle.

"Oh, it's going to win," he confirmed.

Maybe it was the crisp evening breeze, or the fact that she was sitting in the middle of Sorrento Ranch facing the realization that her family would never be the same, but suddenly Frankie felt unsure and nervous, like the scared girl who'd just discovered that her dad was gone and no matter how hard she tried, she might never be able to make things right.

"Remember the night of my dad's funeral?" she said, her voice getting lost in the air.

Only seventeen and staring at her dad's coffin, Frankie had realized that under the grief was an overwhelming sense of relief. Relief that she would never again have to sit, on rotating weekends, at her dad's table and pretend she didn't know how he felt about her. His will had made his feelings more than clear, so instead of going back to the house with a family she didn't know how to be a part of, she had hid in Saul's vineyard and tried to figure out where, in her family of yours, mine, and ours, she belonged.

Somewhere between crying and the sun rising, she had realized that she didn't, and no matter how hard she tried, she probably never would. That was when Nate had found her. Without a word he picked her up and silently held her. She told him everything about her dad, being left out of the will, about how he didn't love her. And in the end, he'd kissed her. It had been her first kiss and he'd been her first love. And as always, Frankie and love proved to be a toxic combination.

"You kissed me and then threatened to knee me in the nuts the next week," he said and she could hear a smile creep into his voice.

"*You* kissed *me* only to ask Sara Dupree to prom that next Tuesday."

"I asked her to prom *after* you threatened to publically emasculate me if I ever touched you again."

"I trusted you with my feelings and fears and you kissed me and then went right to my brother," she said, surprised at how, after all these years, there still could be so much raw emotion attached to that night.

Nate touched her, gently cupping her cheek and tilting it so she faced him. His thumb traced a line from her jaw to her lips, while he waited for her to look at him. Really look at him. The way he was looking at her, as though everything he needed was right there in front of him.

"You kissed me back," he whispered. "And I'm sorry I betrayed your trust and made things harder. That wasn't my intention. I was seventeen and scared, the girl I was crazy about was hurting and I couldn't fix it, so I did what I'd do in my family. I went to your brother."

"My family doesn't work that way."

"I know that now. Just like I know you threatened me because you let me in, let me see you cry, and you got scared."

She nodded because he was right. He'd terrified her. She may have only been seventeen, but she was old enough to know that what they'd shared wasn't your run of the mill teenage hormones at work. That the tightness in her heart wasn't in response to the emotional aftermath of her dad's death. Their connection was real and intense and something that she could— and no doubt would—eventually screw up. So before it got to that point, before he changed his mind, she'd ended things and did her best to avoid him.

What started out as a way to avert more pain, bypass the inevitable heartbreak, turned into a habit until Frankie found herself a grown woman and still avoiding Nate. But he was somehow always there, in her business, her life, lingering in the back of her mind. No matter how hard she tried, she couldn't seem to break free.

And she was tired of trying. At least for tonight. Tomorrow she would go back to surface flirting and serious arguing, but tonight she wanted to feel what it was like to be loved by a man who smelled like forever.

Not that he would be her forever or that he loved her, she didn't have the forever-gene. But for tonight, anyway, she could pretend.

"I came here because I know you must be hurting and I wanted to be a friend, to be here for you." Nate's words came out a husky whisper. "But when you look at me like that, all I can think about is kissing you."

"Then kiss me."

Nate's slow smile turned into a full on grin. "No please or okay?"

Her eyes fell to his lips. "Kiss me, okay?"

One minute his lips weren't anywhere near her mouth, then he leaned forward and there they were and—*Oh. My. God.* The man was a genius. Nate DeLuca, starched loafer-lover, was a woman-whisperer of the magical kind.

He gently caressed her, languidly exploring the seam when she opened her mouth to deepen the connection and something changed—this kiss was different, unexpected. All of the earlier lust and desperation that was present in the utility shed was gone, replaced with a softness that took her by surprise and a gentleness that made her feel as though she were precious.

Frankie didn't know how to respond. Hard, primal, surface—that's what she was used to. But this, this confused her. And scared her.

He didn't move closer, didn't smooth his palms over her body, or press into her. The only contact they had was his hands on her cheeks, his mouth on her lips, and the faintest pressure of their thighs brushing as she tilted her head to the side. It was sweet and erotic and felt so right that a small burst of hope welled up, making her believe that maybe she fit. That with him she could be this girl, and that together they would somehow equal right.

Ignoring the little warning bells going off in her head, Frankie gave herself over to the moment. Maybe this was a mistake, but she wasn't going to think about it right now. Right now she was going to savor every second of Nate, enjoy feeling connected to another person, and leave the worry and insecurities for tomorrow.

Nate must have felt the change because he groaned into her mouth and the kiss turned hot. So hot that her nipples tightened to painful peaks and her heart raced to keep up.

Nate's hands slid through her hair while hers fisted in his shirt. She wanted him, wanted this, badly. He seemed to be on the same page because kiss after mind blowing kiss came at her, so many and so fast she lost track of time, lost track of who she was, or what her body was doing.

"Frankie," he said against her lips breaking the kiss.

Breathing heavy, he rested his forehead to hers and she realized that she was straddling his lap, her thighs wrapped tightly around his middle, ankles locked in the back. His hands were smoothing up and down her bare thighs, his fingertips teasing under the hem of her pajama shorts. And Mittens was curled up in his tire a good twenty feet from them, his back turned for privacy.

"Why'd you stop?" she whispered, rolling her hips forward and pressing against the swollen ridge in his pants. He was hard. And enormous. And even through two layers of clothes, his heat was powerful enough to send aching need rushing to her core. "I don't want to stop."

"I don't either, but you've had a rough day and I want to make sure—"

"Oh, I'm sure. And to prove it, let's see what's behind door number one, shall we?" In one swoop she pulled her top off and—

"Christ," he hissed. "No bra."

She let him look for a minute, but when it became obvious that Nate was determined to take his damn time Frankie wrapped her arms around his neck and raised up a little, crushing her chest to his. The friction of his cotton rubbing against her sensitive skin fell heavy between her legs.

Tightening her grip, she rose up, giving a small inch of space between their bodies, and with a teasing glance down and back up, let him do the math.

"Are you telling me that behind door number two is a matching set?"

"You already saw the matching set." She smiled and so did he. "And if you liked door number one, I promise you that door number two will blow your mind."

Nate's hands moved up her naked thighs, under her shorts and kept going, leaving a trail of tingles in their path. Never a man to be rushed, he took his sweet time, teasing and exploring higher until he met heated skin and someone groaned. She thought it was Nate. But it could have been her. Either way, she knew she had him.

"Being a scientist, I know you only take calculated risks, and you like to have all the facts before you to make a decision. You know, to be sure." She gripped the hem of his t-shirt and pulled it up a few inches, exposing some really impressive abs. "Do you have enough facts now, Nathaniel? Because I'd really love to get naked and spend all night in your shag chair showing you what's behind door number three."

"As long as it's not an alpaca with a coat."

"It's even better than a boobie prize," she joked.

But he didn't laugh, didn't move, except for his eyes, which dropped and took in every inch of her not covered by clothing. Without a word, his hands tightened on her butt, cradling her against his erection and holding here there while he took her mouth.

This time the kisses weren't sweet or gentle, which was fine because Frankie wasn't feeling gentle or sweet. She was achy and wet from holding in every ounce of pent up tension that had grown since, well, probably since high school.

Then his mouth was on the move, nibbling her lips, down her throat, and everywhere he touched her skin tightened. "God, you taste good."

"Keep going, it gets better." She rested her hands on his thighs behind her, leaning back and bringing all their hot parts flush. It also gave him easier access to where else she wanted him to taste next.

A low, masculine chuckle came from his chest. He raised his head and, *fucking men*, the look in his eyes was hot enough to scorch. "Of that I have no doubt."

She rocked against him as his mouth found her breast. He drew her in, his lips creating an exquisite suction as his tongue flattened against her hard nipple.

Frankie's head fell back on a sigh, and she pressed harder into him, trying to ease the building ache but it only left her dizzy. So she ground again, harder, desperate for release. She felt him smile against her breast before moving on to the other one, but his hands stayed put on her ass.

Not that she didn't like foreplay, she did, but she was wound so tight that she was going to die if she didn't find some kind of release. And soon.

"Just tell me what you want, Frankie." Nate said, kissing his way back up to her mouth.

"You inside of me," she whispered. He raised a brow, so she added, "Okay?"

"Okay." His hand slid down the curve of her bottom, around the front, his finger sliding deep inside of her. "Like this?"

No, she had something else in mind, but she was too busy crying out, too busy taking pleasure in the smooth, intoxicating rhythm he created, to do anything other than gasp.

"Does that feel good?"

And if her panting and whimpering wasn't proof enough, the way she pressed down against his fingers, her hips jerking with need, answered the question. Because if he kept up that pace, put his mouth right—Frankie grabbed his head and lowered it to her breast—right there and then—

"Oh, God," she groaned. "Do that again."

And he did, his thumb rubbed back and forth along her and suddenly two fingers were inside of her. He circled slowly while his teeth gently sank into her hardened nipple. And

Frankie was startled to realize that she was two circles and one bite away from an orgasm.

"Like that?"

Yes, exactly like that.

She bit her lip, trying to hold out, but the pressure built, fast and hard. It started in her toes and before she could stop it, heat rushed up, shattering every single thought in her mind until all she saw was a vast blankness and the best post-orgasm glow known to woman.

"You okay?" Nate whispered against her shoulder. His palm glided up and down her back, making opening her eyes impossible.

"I think so," she said but couldn't figure how her head managed to fall on his shoulder. He smelled good. She wanted to just lie there, in his arms and nuzzle against him.

"I can see that," he chuckled and slid his hands under her butt. Frankie let out a sigh and cuddled closer into the yummy curve of his neck. Only instead of his pulling her to him, she felt gravity shift and heard his boots hit the deck.

"Where are we going?" She looked up to find them standing. Well, Nate was standing, she was still twisted around him like a pretzel. A very spent pretzel.

"Bed."

"I don't want to go to bed." Frankie felt panic well up. The reality of what she'd agreed to crashed in on her. Sure, she wanted to have sex with Nate. She even wanted to play the forever game for tonight. But bed-sex? She didn't know if she could come back from that. "Why can't we stay right here?"

"Because I still haven't gotten to door number three yet. And getting *there* out *here* would require some creative positioning. Positions that would no doubt lead to slivers in unwanted places since you're practically sliding out of my arms." He opened the front door and kicked it closed behind them.

"I'm not sliding out of your arms," she argued, having a really hard time getting a grip on his neck. "And I have to brush Mittens or his hair will knot and tangle. He gets angry if I forget."

"You promised me there was no alpaca behind that door. Now, lie back." She did and realized that she was on a soft mattress. His soft mattress. She squeezed her eyes shut, then opened them. Immaculately made bed. Matching sheets and pillowcases. God awful pink chair. Yup. Definitely his bed. Crap. "And if in five minutes you still want to go brush the alpaca, then we can revisit this argument."

"Five minutes? Is that all you got?"

"After today, that's a generous estimation. I'm two and O, sweet cheeks. Meaning after two attempts I still haven't gotten my O. So yeah, five minutes if we're lucky."

"Fine," she said, looking up into his amazing eyes. "Five minutes in that shag chair and I promise to up your average."

CHAPTER 13

Nate rested his weight on his arms, the mattress sagging under him as he looked down at Frankie, watching every emotion she was feeling cross over her face. He wanted her for more than a single night. And he wanted to see all of her, not just what was under those shorts. Although he wanted that too. Bad. But one wrong move and he could mess this whole thing up, and that was not an option. Not when he was finally penetrating that wall she'd so skillfully built and maintained.

His goal was to get so deep under her skin and into her heart that she wouldn't wake up tomorrow regretting tonight. But he could tell that, for whatever reason, once they'd entered the bedroom she'd freaked. To the point that she was actually considering bolting out of here in nothing but those soft, and minuscule, shorts she thought passed for pajamas. So he pushed off the bed, straightened, and in one move tossed her over his shoulder. With a smack on that incredible ass, he ignored her squeak and walked to the chair.

"What are you doing?" She smacked his butt so he smacked hers again then rubbed little circles on her thigh.

"Getting my shag on," he said, setting her in the chair and smiling when her boobs bounced. Yeah, he could get used to Frankie. Topless. In his chair. Her hair a tangle of curls hanging loose around her shoulders.

She picked up a yellow legal pad that sat on the end table and grinned. "Color coded?" She flipped the page, then the next, her grin widening.

"I have a lot on my mind."

"Do you have a list for me?" Did he ever. Only that one wasn't written down. It was meticulous, had sub-columns, and was dirty as hell. In fact, the majority of every night in this house had been spent adding, restructuring, and ranking that particular list. And his face must have shown it because she asked, "What's at the top?"

"Tonight?" He snagged the pad and tossed it on the bed. "You. Naked. Screaming out my name in that chair."

"Take this off," she ordered, tugging at his shirt. "And let's see what we can do about checking that off your list."

With a smile he pulled it over his head with one hand.

"But about upping that average, I think you have some catching up to do first." Frankie levered herself up so she sat on the edge of the seat. She reached for the buttons of his jeans and, zipper down, slid the Levis and briefs off his hips and to the floor. Her long legs parted to make room for him as she pulled him toward her.

He managed to step out of his boots and pants while her palm wrapped around the length of him, her fingers cool and sure, gently stroking and caressing him from base to tip and back down. Watching her hands, he was fascinated how one minute they could looks so strong and the next elegant. When her mouth joined the party, fascination didn't even begin to explain what he felt.

"Oh, God, Frankie." His fingers ended up in her hair, fisting tighter with each lick. Her hands were magic, and her mouth. *God, that mouth.* If he wanted this to last longer than two seconds, he couldn't even go there. She sucked him in hard and his hips bucked, driving him deeper.

"Any more of that and we won't make it to door three." He stepped back, and she released him.

He took her elbow and helped her stand. Grabbing a condom from the bedside table, he sank into the chair and ran his hands all the way down her arms, to her hips, hooking his thumbs in the waistband of her shorts. He pulled her to him and placed an openmouthed kiss right on her center, applying just enough tongue to make her gasp. Burying his face against the soft cotton, he did it again, only this time her hips shifted forward, and he could taste her arousal on his lips.

"More," she moaned.

People pleaser that he was, he tugged the hem of her shorts down, just below the V of her thighs and gave her more. Right up the middle. From the center to top in one swipe of the tongue. On the third pass he felt her stomach tremble and her legs began to give out.

He peeled her shorts down to the floor, kissing her knee, thigh, stomach, before pulling her onto his lap and kissing her lips.

Frankie straddled him and sank down, her wet, hot skin settling over his tip. She took the condom off the table and, after a whole lot of stroking and teasing, slid it home. Then with a smile, that if he were being honest scared him as much as it turned him on, she reached down and pulled the chair's lever.

The seat tilted back. Frankie tilted forward, her hands braced on either side of his head, and, Jesus, those incredible breasts were situated right in his face.

"Whoever invented this chair deserves an award," he said, because all he had to do was lean up and—oh, yeah. She smelled like wine, bold and spicy, and tasted even better. And she was definitely a D.

Nate had never considered himself a breast man—he usually went for legs, which Frankie had in spades—but there was something about her breasts, something that he hoped to spend days figuring out.

Frankie, however, had other plans, because she arched her back and sank down, and slowly pushed until he was all the way inside of her. They both stopped breathing, stopped moving, and for a second took in the moment. Then Frankie started moving.

She rose up only to sink deliciously back down, taking even more of him. Her hips moved faster, harder, and breathing seemed to piss off his chest so he gave up on it. She let out a low throaty moan and closed her eyes and all Nate could do was watch her. The way her hair tumbled around her shoulders, her mouth parted as she let loose sweet little moans of pleasure, how she was two seconds away from exploding in his arms.

She was so damn beautiful.

"I'm going to," she gasped. "I need to . . ."

"Me too."

Nate gripped her hips, and rose up, moving faster and deeper. He wanted to make this last, but then her thighs started squeezing his, and she started making these noises that drove him out of his fucking mind, and he started thrusting harder.

The pressure built, but he held himself in check, barely, determined for her to go over first. He slid his hand between their bodies, rubbing his thumb back and forth over where they were joined. He felt her stiffen, take in a breath and hold it.

"Come on, Francesca, let go."

And thank God she did. She arched back, pushed down as he was coming up and her breath exploded from her lungs. Her walls clenched around him, nearly strangling his dick until it throbbed and Nate gave one final thrust and felt all the blood rush south. Then everything went black and he collapsed against the chair, while Frankie collapsed against him.

After he was able to breathe without gasping, he grabbed a tissue from the side table and cleaned up. Placing a kiss to the top of her head, he whispered into her hair, "That was incredible. You were incredible."

Her face was pillowed into his chest and all he could hear was the steady rhythm of her breathing. He ran a hand down her back to cup her butt and gave it a gentle squeeze. "Frankie?"

Her answer was to burrow further into his chest and let out a soft, sleepy sigh. Nate gave a sigh of his own, grabbed the matching afghan off the back of the chair and, pulling her tightly to him, covered them.

After a while his legs started to go numb and his cheeks began to hurt. He was grinning. He knew it and yet he couldn't stop. Then Frankie shifted, her lean arms sliding around his middle and he decided he didn't care.

～

A pounding came from right outside Frankie's window followed by pounding in her head. She cracked open her eyes and winced; the sun was barely peeking through her window, yet managed to pierce her right through the retina. She rolled over and—

"Holy poppycock," she groaned, grabbing her forehead. But it didn't help. Her mouth felt as though she'd spent the evening grooming Mittens—with her tongue—and pain pushed through the top of her head right down to her toes, making the pink shag chair even more nauseating than ever.

Shag chair?

Her hands did a quick morning-after pat down and—yup. She was alone, in Nate's bed, totally naked.

She struggled to piece together last night. She had only managed to get to the part where Nate found her on the porch having a pity party for one, which turned into a sex party for two, which led to the shag chair, and somehow bed—his bed, which explained the allergic reaction she was currently experiencing—when another crash shot through the air.

This time it vibrated the entire house and was followed by a pissed off bleating and several hostile *warks*.

"No, Mittens!" In one motion Frankie was on her feet and headed for the front door. She grabbed a clean top and bottoms—both neatly folded in the basket on her bed—and slipped into her boots on the way. According to the clock it was nearly ten, which meant Mittens would be hungry. "Not this time."

Images of horse teeth chewing through the side of the new tank flashed as she raced down the hall, past the now re-organized pantry, snagging a box of Pop Tarts, and out the front door.

"Don't do it, Mittens," she hollered, but not angrily. Because it wasn't the alpaca's fault that he was forced to dine on plastic and vinyl for breakfast. He was a nervous eater, Frankie knew that, and yet last night she had kind of yelled at him for nibbling at her new lemon tree and then, in her hormone induced haze, forgot to brush him before bed, something that had become kind of a ritual. "I've got your breakfast."

But as Frankie stood there, on the porch, waiving the foil wrapped toaster pastry as though it were her kid's lunchbox, she realized that Mittens wasn't anywhere near the tank. Nope, her shy alpaca was nickering and prancing behind Nate, who stood by a semi that held the enormous water tank, although at fifty-thousand gallons it was more of a tower.

Nate turned around to look at her and, one hand on his hip while the other slid Mittens a carrot top, gave Frankie an amused grin. A ball cap was pulled low on his head, shading his eyes and the lower half of his face. Instead of his usual polo, khakis, and loafers, he wore a grey t-shirt and a pair of loose cargo shorts that hung from his lean hips. Sweet Jesus, the man was dirty, sweaty, and looked like your basic, sexy-grape-grower for hire.

"Morning, sweet cheeks," he drawled as he walked toward her, his stride slow and easy.

She wasn't sure if it was the casual clothes or the dirt under his nails or seeing him in his element yesterday and nothing but shag last night, but Nate, like this, all manly and undone, was a sight to behold.

He stopped at the bottom of the front stoop and, flipping the bill of his cap backward, his heated brown eyes traveled from her face to her mouth and down her chest where it hung for a long, intense moment. His gaze felt like a gentle caress of sheer male appreciation, skimming over her hips and down her legs, making her heart flutter a little—and leaving her feeling ridiculously feminine.

"You look like—"

"Shit?" Frankie said with a self-conscious laugh. Hating how hard it was to breathe. She didn't do feminine and she didn't do morning afters for a reason. She sucked at both of them.

He walked up the steps, not bothering to stop until he was all in her space. Sweaty from shoveling dirt, he looked so big and imposing and so—manly. Nate DeLuca, uptight, loafer owner, looked manly. God, he even smelled manly.

"I was going to say, half asleep. You can barely hold your eyes open." He reached out and tucked her hair behind her ear and she forgot how to breathe all together. "Long night?"

Feeling way too dainty and too vulnerable, she batted his hand away and leveled him with her most intimidating glare. Only he didn't look intimidated, or leveled. The jerk actually smiled. It was a slow, sexy tilting of the lips that had her nipples breaking out the party poppers. Nate noticed.

"Who says I'm tired?"

"Honey, you're standing on the front porch in nothing but an epic case of bedhead, my shirt, lace and—" He looked down and, party poppers in full effect, there went that smile and—when he looked up at her through his eyebrows—that annoying fluttering. "There is a crew of about ten guys who are all silently hoping you'll notice you forgot to tie your boots and bend over, making it a great morning."

Palms flat against his chest, she rolled up on her tiptoes, looked over his shoulder and—yup, a construction crew of ten, including Hard Hammer Tanner, stood silently watching. Smiling. A few of the guys tipped their hats in greeting. Tanner raised a hand and waved as though a half-naked client welcoming his crew was a normal occurrence in his line of work.

Frankie waved back. "Yeah, well I don't care."

Which was a lie. She totally cared, but he was making her feel all protected and girly and all she could think about was how she had slept in his bed. With him. All night. Hell, she'd almost cried in front of him. Talk about embarrassing.

Nate stepped closer, so close that she could smell his crisp, clean, sexy scent. It was a lethal combination. He molded his hands in the curve of her waist, his body crowding hers until she could feel his heat seep through the thin cotton of her, whoops, his shirt.

"Well, I do," he grumbled, his hands warm and possessive on her body as he backed her through the door.

Once inside, he kicked the door closed with his foot, but his hands never left her hips. And his eyes, serious and intense and heavy with lust, never left hers.

"Oh," she whispered. And there went that heavy feeling in her chest again.

"And I know what you're doing," he whispered back. But his whisper came out a smooth rumble. "It won't work."

"What am I doing?" Really, she wanted to know. Because whatever it was, it was driving him crazy. And she kind of liked it.

"This whole prickly, nothing gets to me thing you've got going on doesn't fool me, Francesca." She loved it when he called her that. "Not anymore. So you can be upset about last night, mad that your brothers are jerks, mad that your grandpa left early, mad that you've worked your ass off and no one in your family even noticed. But," his hands slid around to the small of her back—then lower, "don't be mad that I saw you last night, the real you, okay?"

Frankie didn't know what to say. She was upset, but not for the reasons Nate listed. Okay, so maybe she was a little disappointed that her brother Adam, executable excuse or not, flaked and that her grandpa was proving to be every bit the jackass that Nate accused him of being. But if she were being honest, it wasn't anger that had her heart pounding, it was fear.

She was scared. Because, although they hadn't had bed-sex, she felt all connected and weird around him now. Like he knew things about her that he could use against her. And when he looked at her, how he was now, all understanding and patience, something soft and vulnerable and totally off limits started swirling in her chest.

Bed-sex with an expiration date before sunrise would have been better, safer, she thought.

Then she woke up. In his bed. Alone, but in his bed all the same, which meant that he'd put her there—that he cared. And her knowing that Nate cared, that he had seen the real her last night and that he hadn't run screaming made her stomach pinch painfully. Because he would run eventually, and the longer he stayed around the harder it would hurt when he did.

He must have taken her long silence as agreement because his smile slid higher, while his palm slid lower, right over her silk panties to cup her bottom. His thumbs, however, teased up under the lacy edges, gently exploring. The warmth of his skin on hers sent tiny tingles scurrying everywhere, making the tingles in her heart less noticeable.

"Now, you've got about ten minutes before Tanner kills the water. So why don't you go shower off and get dressed because the longer I stand here," he pressed a quick kiss to her mouth, "smelling me on you, the less likely I am to let you take that shower alone. And then you and I will wind up naked and skip going out."

Out? She didn't want to go out, she wanted to stay in. With Nate. Having wild monkey-sex all day. On the couch. To remind herself that she can have fun and manage to stay unattached.

"Why don't you join me?" she whispered, her hands doing some exploring of their own. Down his impressive chest, over each muscle of his six-pack. This she could do. Lust, shower sex, things that didn't involve talking and feelings. Or the bed.

His body curled closer and he buried his face in her hair, and oh yeah, delivered a very wet, very hot openmouthed kiss to the sensitive spot behind her ear. She was just getting into it, tilting her head to give him better access, when he pulled back and delivered a friendly smack right to the ass.

"Since every guy out there will be so busy focusing on what we're doing in here instead of their job, I'm going to pass." He stepped back and gave Frankie one last heated look. "Ten minutes. And pack a bathing suit."

"A bathing suit?" Frankie asked, not liking the sound of it. "Where are we going?"

"On a date to celebrate your win."

⌒〜

Nate watched Frankie's toes glide across the water as they sat on the dock. The ripples moved under the lily pads at the middle of the lake, and he felt frustration and something significantly more noticeable swell. He could make a list of at least a dozen things that were the source of the growing problem but for now, he'd settle on listing the top three.

First of all, Frankie had become downright hostile when he'd offered to drive so he had agreed to ride with her, not wanting this day to end before it even got the chance to get good. Which meant that he'd spent the past hour riding bitch on her motorcycle with her rubbing up against his dick every time she turned, sped up, or slowed down. He hated motorcycles, almost as much as he hated driving through town on one while Frankie honked at Marc, who sent him a wave with his pinky while laughing his ass off through the window of the Sweet and Savory Bistro. But the rubbing part, he didn't mind that at all. Even though he knew the bike was just another way to avoid conversation.

Secondly, they were sitting on the dock, only a few inches separating them and yet he felt as though they were on opposite sides of the lake. He'd given her an opening to talk about what happened, but every time he even circled serious she clammed up, or took a walk, or inhaled another Pop Tart—her addition to the picnic they'd packed. It wasn't that he'd minded last night—in fact it had been unbelievably hot and sweet—but he wanted to take this past great sex.

And third, he was pretty sure she wasn't wearing a bra. Or a bathing suit. A curiosity he'd slyly tried to ease on the ride up the mountain, but the thick leather jacket she'd been wearing made it impossible to tell. And the wondering made it impossible to focus. And if he had any chance to make today about more than just chemistry then he'd need to have some kind of conscious thought process available to him. They needed to talk about the fire, last night, and where they were going. Because Nate wanted to get the first two out in the open so they could move on to the last, which he had strong opinions on.

Frankie rested forward on her hands, her feet making cute figure eights in the water. Between the white shorts, which left her legs mostly bare, and her soft lavender toe nails, Nate had a difficult time swallowing. Feminine and adorable and completely unexpected.

"I don't want to talk about it, so can you please stop thinking about it?" She nudged him with her shoulder and he nudged her back until she smiled. "You're scaring away the fish."

Nate tapped the fishing poles. "I didn't say a thing and nothing ever bites here."

Frankie shot him a glace, a penetrating flash of blue. "I know that look on your face, golden boy." And he knew *that* look. Great. She was positioning him squarely in the friends category. Well, now it would be the friends-with-benefits category. "I know what you're thinking."

Nate knew that Frankie liked him. There was no doubt of that in his mind. She was just jumpy when it came to emotions, and he couldn't blame her. Her parents' divorce had been one of the nastiest this town had seen, with six-year-old Frankie being the prized commodity in the negotiations. So even though her evasive tactics frustrated him, after a childhood filled with heartache and disappointment, it didn't surprise him.

Wanting to lighten the mood, he dropped his eyes to her cleavage. "Really? And what is that?"

After he'd had a long and thorough study—his money was on no bra—he finally shifted his gaze to meet hers, which was equally amused and turned on.

"You know, you could always just ask," she said, then leaned in and kissed him. It was sweet and slow and had a whole lot of tongue. Which definitely made the talking part difficult. It also made the swelling problem a hell of a lot more dire. Too bad he was so set on talking, because her mouth felt incredible and his hand was on her waist. All he had to do was slide it up, just a few more inches and that aching question would be solved. But then they'd be no closer to solving the real problem—how to move forward.

So he pulled back, resting his forehead to hers. "Okay, you don't want to talk about last night, the fire, or your family. Then let's talk about mine. Come with me to ChiChi's Saturday night."

"Isn't that Baby Sofie's thing?"

"Yes, her one month-day and, according to Regan, she is the official harvest baby. It will be casual, fun, and I'd like you to come."

"I saw the invitation. I promise you there is nothing causal about it. Plus I'm already invited and have to go. I tried to back out," she admitted. "But the kid started crying and showing her gums and Regan said it was because Baby Sofie knew I didn't want to go. So now I have to go."

"I know," he said casually, trying not to make this a big deal. Even though everything in his gut said that it was. "I was asking you to come *with* me."

She pulled her feet in cross-legged and sat back, looking every bit the scared girl she'd been when they were seventeen and he'd brought up prom. It would have been funny, except she was on the verge of bolting over a casual dinner. "Like I told Regan, I don't do family dinners. Not even my own. Well, not anymore. Just going seems stressful enough."

"My family is loud, nosy, and annoying as hell. It's like spending the evening with five of me." She smiled and he felt his chest relax a little. "At least if you go with me, I can help you navigate the noise."

"Going to the party together seems less friends and more . . . couple-y."

"Couple-y? You do realize that we have a house, share custody of an alpaca, and we eat at least one meal together a day. Oh." He kissed her again. Quick and hard. "And you've seen me naked."

"Doesn't mean I want to pick out a picket fence."

"Which reminds me. We need to add 'get fence' to the 'Mittens's Habitat List.'"

"Mittens needs a fence about as much as—"

"You need a stress free night of fun and good food with a charming Italian man and his crazy *famiglia.*"

"Charming, huh?"

"I was going to go with sexy," he said, playfully tugging at her ponytail. "Now, how about I pick you up at six? ChiChi gets pissy if we are late."

"We live together, roomie. So there will be no picking up. Plus, I'm going late."

"Late?"

"Yeah, I have to clean up after the Cork Crawl." Her hands fidgeted and he knew that they'd reached the heart of the issue. She wouldn't have a team like everyone else to help with the takedown

"No problem. I'll help you clean up then give you a ride." His eyes dropped to her cleavage. He couldn't help it. He couldn't take his eyes off of her. "Just say yes."

He watched her, sitting there, staring out at the lake as though he'd proposed marriage, seven kids, and a budding alpaca farm.

She reached out, reeled in her line, and then recast it. "Why did you bring me here, Nate?"

"Because the water tank was being delivered and—"

She looked at him. "No, I mean, here. Why did you bring me here?"

Nate looked out at the lake. About the size of a football field, it was surrounded by an outcropping of rolling vines that glistened in the afternoon sun, making shadows on the water. The dock moved under them as water lapped gently against the posts.

It was peaceful, they were completely isolated, and she couldn't run. Most importantly, this was one of Nate's favorite vineyards and he wanted to share this with her.

"One day a week during the summer, my dad would kidnap one of us kids. Each of us had our special place to go with him. He took Gabe to museums, Abby to the symphony, Trey was forced to take dance, and Marc, lucky son of a bitch that he was, got to go to a daddy-and-me team building camp." That always pissed Nate off. "On my days, he'd sneak in my room before anyone was awake. We'd pack up the car and spend the day here fishing. Sometimes we talked, sometimes we caught lunch, but we always fished and we always had a good time."

Nate smiled at her surprise. "I would think that Trey or Marc would have been the more obvious choice in a fishing companion. I mean, fishing is dirty and unpredictable and based on luck. You're all structure and starch."

He had to laugh. "To be honest I hated it. After three weeks of catching jack shit, I went to the library and checked out a book. I still remember the look on my dad's face when he was baiting his line, and instead of a pole, I pulled out *What Fish Don't Want You to Know: A Guide to Freshwater Fishing.*" Nate laughed. "I spent more time with my nose in that book than with my hook in the water."

"Did you catch anything?"

"Nope. And nothing I did mattered. No matter how perfect I baited the hook, how flawlessly I followed the instructions, I could never figure out the system." He looked over at her and she smiled. "What?"

"That must have been . . . frustrating," was all she said, but he could feel her laughing.

"Beyond." He'd hated it, especially when Trey started giving him pointers. "So one week I asked him why he didn't take Marc fishing, and he said that I needed it more. Going to the team building camp and problem solving would have been fun, but coming out here forced me slow down, realize that not everything makes sense."

"Did you ever catch a fish?"

"Yeah, my dad told me to put the book down and forget what I had read. And wouldn't you know it, I caught a fish." He'd only been ten, but that was the first time he remembered feeling like a man. "It was a guppy and we had to throw it back, but I had caught my first fish."

"I bet your dad was proud." To his surprise, her hand slid all the way down his arms to lace their fingers and then she dropped her head on his shoulder and her feet back into the water.

They sat like that, holding hands, sharing space and watching the lily pads buoy in the water.

"Last night, after you fell asleep, I got to thinking about your dad, which led to thinking about my dad and I knew I wanted to bring you here."

He felt Frankie's chest rise and take in a breath, then slowly let it out. "What were you thinking? About my dad, I mean?"

"That you are a lot like him and he knew that. Maybe he didn't leave you any of the vineyards because he knew you didn't need it. Your brothers have never been connected to that land like you have, they needed the ties. But you, you don't." He felt her tense, but she didn't move, so he continued. "What if it was his way of showing you his love? Doing what he thought was best, not for the winery, but for you."

Head still on his shoulder, Frankie tilted her face toward him, looking up with wide baby blues. "You don't think he did it because I chose to live with my mom?"

God, is that what she'd thought all these years? That her father hated her because of a single decision she'd been forced to make when she was six?

"No, I don't." He bent down and kissed her nose. "Your dad and grandpa went at it for years over how to run the winery. You being tied to that place would have made you miserable."

"Right, because we're such a big happy family now."

"*You're* happy though," Nate said gently and they both knew it was true. She might be hurt over Charles's behavior, but she loved making her own wine. "You are loyal and honest and you lead with your heart, Frankie. But you're also a dreamer. You'd rather take a huge risk on the off-chance that it produces something unique, than play it safe. And spending your life working Charles's land, following his rules and making his wine would have made you miserable, just like it did your dad. It would be a life of expectations, constraints, duty, and your dad knew that if you inherited those shares, you would have never broken free."

"Yeah, well, that vineyard was the only thing we had in common, the only tie I had to the Baudouin side of the family that had nothing to do with my mom or the divorce. So the only thing he broke was my belief in what I thought we had."

And my heart. It went unsaid but Nate knew that it had happened all the same.

"The funny thing," she continued, her voice so quiet he barely heard it over the lapping of the water. "I've worked that land every day since his death, next to a man who I idolized more than life only to discover that in the end, he didn't want me there either."

"Your dad loved you, Frankie. He wanted you to find happiness in just being you, without the weight of Charles. Maybe his plan just didn't go as he'd hoped."

"Maybe," Frankie whispered.

"And I think that Charles, although he is being difficult, is secretly proud that you went after what you wanted."

"I think," she said, leaning up and snagging his lower lips between her two plump ones and sucking him into her mouth. "That you secretly brought me here to go skinny dipping."

She untangled herself and stood, the dock shifting under her motions. Although skinny dipping sounded fan-fucking-tastic, and just the suggestion had him going from zero to fully-loaded, Nate wanted to finish their talk. But then Frankie stripped her shirt over her head and, hello, one problem solved.

No bathing suit or bra.

Then her fingers went to the button on her shorts.

Yeah, she was done talking. That much was obvious. He was starting to realize that whenever he tried to talk to her about something even semi-serious, she dangled sex in front of him. Not that he was complaining. Especially when she dropped trou and Nate finally got a look at the small tattoo on the upper curve of her heart shaped ass as she executed a perfect dive right off the end of the dock. And oh baby, now he was incapable of speaking.

He watched her tan skin glide beneath the surface, swimming farther and farther away from him and all the feelings that he just drudged up. He'd pushed a little, and she'd given a little. It was a start.

CHAPTER 14

Frankie waited until her lungs burned for air before she surfaced. She needed a moment of quiet to collect herself, to absorb what Nate had said and then store it safely away to revisit it—never. She was running, and they both knew it. More importantly, Nate knew when to push and when to let it go. And he had wisely let it go.

Diving back under, she allowed herself to just glide, let the water slide over her body. Everything seemed clearer under the water, the quiet flow made it easy to forget—about her grandfather, about her money problems, and most importantly about Nate and the genuine concern in his eyes, which made her wish for things that scared her.

When she was in the middle of the pond, she came up for air. Involuntary chills ran down her body. But it wasn't from the shock of the cold water lapping against her heated skin, it was from the strong, masculine hands that gripped her hips and ever so slowly slid up her body.

"Seems you forgot your suit," Nate said huskily in her ear, pulling her back against his front until every delicious inch was touching. She rested her head on his shoulder and floated while his hands shaped and explored, sliding over her wet body and finally finding a home on her breasts.

"Seems to be a trend today." Frankie turned, wrapping her arms around his amazing shoulders, her leg around his flat stomach and—hello. Nate was slick, and wet, and hard. Everywhere. "But if it bothers you, I can go to the bike and grab mine."

"And ruin a perfectly good skinny dip?" He watched her through water spiked lashes, while his hands slid all the way down her bare back before cupping her backside to pull her tight against him. The heat between their bodies doubled on contact, erasing the chills on her body and leaving behind a scorching flush. "Nah, I'm good."

Then his mouth was on hers. And, yeah, he was good all right. So good that she could actually feel her insides reaching melting point. So good that she was in trouble, serious trouble of falling in complete and total like with him. Especially when his mouth, cool from the water, gently worked hers, his tongue applying the faintest amount of pressure as he swam them backward toward the dock.

Tilting her head to the side, Frankie slid her hands up and into his wet hair, pulling him even closer. Then Nate stood, rising out of the now waist-deep water, which sluiced down their bodies. His hard chest glistened with moisture in the afternoon sun and a thin patch of wet hair trailed down the plains of his flat stomach, disappearing beneath the water.

His lips moved against her ear while his thumb brushed over her tattoo. "A daffodil?"

"It's a symbol of rebirth, new beginnings." It also symbolized unrequited love. She got it the day she'd turned eighteen, and since that was only a few months after her father had passed and she'd learned of his will, it had seemed fitting. But now, after what Nate had said, she wondered.

Feeling too serious in an already vulnerable position, she tipped her head back and guided his mouth lower, settling in just above the hollow of her throat. "What were you expecting, barbed wire-covered motorcycle handles?"

"No, I just wasn't expecting a cute, feminine, sunny flower," he said, pulling back, his eyes heavy and intense. "Nothing about this . . . about you is what I expected."

Nothing about this was what she'd expected either. The way he looked at her, held her, touched and molded her with his hands as though she were precious. Frankie never expected to fall—ever—but she was afraid that the warm ache that had taken up residence in her heart was a whole lot more than just complete and total like.

Frankie's chest started tightening, really fast and really effectively, damn near cutting off her air. Thinking about things such as "like"—or the other word that started with L and had four letters—made her lungs burn. Lust, chemistry, raging hormones she could deal with. She was good at physical, great even. This emotional crap—it was just too much.

So Frankie, taking it back to a level that didn't inspire hyperventilation, locked her thighs around him, sliding her center up the smooth underside of his hard length and then reversing to sink back down, enveloping him between her. Nate's eyes rolled back and his hips bucked a little, as though unable to get enough, increasing the friction and taking them away from cosmically connecting back to pure carnal need.

Her head began to spin, which was a good thing because she could almost ignore her heart going soft. Picking up the pace she rose and lowered, again and again, increasing the pressure until his arms tightened like a vice, smashing their bodies together. But it wasn't enough. Needing more, she rose up, her nipples scraping against his chest, until his tip was positioned at her entrance. The man was impressive and more than ready.

With a sigh, she eased down stopping after only an inch, loving the slight burn as she stretched to accommodate him. Relaxing her thighs she let gravity take over, and slowly began to slip down farther when suddenly his hands tightened on her ass, holding her in place.

"You feel so damn good." His words were a low rumble that vibrated all the way between her thighs.

"If you let go, I promise I feel even better." She rolled her hips and he growled.

"Can't. Condom. On dock. In shorts," he breathed, holding her still against him. The muscles in his neck tightened and his jaw clenched. Taking in a deep pull of oxygen he dropped his gaze to where their chests were mashed together and swallowed. "I want this so bad right now that I'm tempted to just say fuck it."

She wanted this too. Wanted so badly to feel him, inside of her, with nothing between them.

"Frankie," he warned and she kissed him quiet. She gave him a sweet, languid kiss that lasted for a long, erotic moment. They were touching everywhere, the sun hot on their exposed skin, while the water lapped around them as everything except their mouths remained perfectly still.

She pulled back, taking his lower lip with her. "Then fuck it."

"Frankie," he said again. But this time his tone was desperate, ragged, telling a different story.

She smiled. "I'm on the pill."

His eyes searched hers. "You sure?"

"Oh, yeah." And to show him she arched her hips back and down, taking him inside of her in one fluid motion. She inhaled at the pressure, breathing in his breath, completely lost in a wave of mind-numbing pleasure.

"Oh, fuck," he growled. "That feels so good, Francesca."

He lifted his hips as she sank back down and they quickly found a rhythm. The man was a master; after only one night he already knew how to touch her, tease her, drive her crazy. And he was fast learning how to shatter her defenses.

"You are so beautiful," he said against her lips.

"Harder," she rasped, pumping her hips faster, wanting his sweet words but not sure how to handle them.

"Slow and easy, honey," he whispered against her wet skin. "Just enjoy."

She was enjoying it—fast and hard and without the sugary endearments, thank you very much. But his hands settled on her hips, taking over and setting a leisurely but sensual pace while he whispered beautiful words in her ear. Words she'd waited her whole life to hear someone say, only she wasn't sure if she could believe them—that she was even considering it was a sign that she was in over her head.

"Harder," she demanded, coming all the way up before slamming back down and taking what she wanted. She dug her nails into his back and when he was too busy panting in her ear to whisper she finally felt her body relax, felt her walls tighten, and with one last thrust a pulse of pleasure washed over her, while a wave of emotion crashed into her stealing her breath.

Nate was right there with her. He buried his face in her neck and sunk his teeth into the sensitive skin at the slope of her shoulder as they came apart.

Drained and breathless, they stood there, tangled in each other's arms, swaying with the pond's gentle current. The faint pressure of his fingers danced along her spine, his lips soothing the sting of his earlier bite. There was so much weight in their unspoken connection she felt as though it would pull her under.

"I thought you said nothing ever bites here," she joked, but nothing about this situation felt funny.

"Sweet cheeks, it looks like you've caught the only thing that does."

"Caught?" The word stuck in her throat.

He pulled back, just enough to look at her. Just enough to see the awe in his eyes as he said, "You've had me hooked for over a decade, I've just been waiting for you to reel me in."

$\sim$

Something was wrong.

Frankie hadn't said more than four words to him after they'd had sex. And they were, "Not bad, stud boy."

Not all that encouraging for a guy who'd just had the best sexual experience of his entire life. Or for a guy who'd wanted today to mean as much to Frankie as it had to him.

Hell, he could still smell her on his skin, taste her on his lips and instead of lying naked together in bed talking about what was happening between them, he spent the better part of the night sitting alone on the couch watching ESPN while Frankie disappeared outside to brush Mittens. When she didn't come back in, he'd grabbed a bite, showered, and picked up a book. That had been two hours ago, giving him ample time to think himself into a serious state of frustration.

Being patient wasn't the problem. He was willing to give Frankie the time she needed if in the end she finally admitted what was going on between them was more than just sex. But he wasn't willing to let her fears keep them stagnant. And he sure as hell wasn't willing after today to go backwards, which considering the fact that Frankie stood in the darkened hallway, boots in hand, tiptoeing toward her room was exactly what she had in mind.

He stood at the fork in the hallway and clicked on the light. Frankie looked up at him and froze. To her right was his master bedroom, to the left her own personal space. Nate had a bad feeling that if he didn't fix this now, she would forever walk on the invisible line that had been drawn between them since he'd kissed her in high school.

"Helps if you turn on the light."

Frankie straightened as though startled to find him there. Her hair was back in its braid, but she still had on the shorts, tank, and no bra from earlier. She was windblown, covered in fur, absolutely beautiful, and confusing as hell. "I thought you were asleep, I didn't want to wake you."

"Was waiting for you to finish tucking Mittens in." Crossing his arms, he rested his shoulder against the wall. He could tell by her body language that talking wasn't on her top ten list. He could also tell by the way she was darting glances at his bedroom door that she wasn't planning on coming to his room. "But since you're sneaking down the hall I guess that was stupid. You are obviously avoiding me."

"How many times do we have to have this argument? I don't sneak and if I didn't want to talk to you, I'd just say so."

"Really? Because you came in the back door and rather than trample through the house in your dirty boots to piss me off like normal, they're in your hands." He stared her down. Spending the past two hours on a lumpy couch hadn't really helped his patience. It had, however, allowed him to spin himself into a mood, so he took a deep breath and lowered his voice. The last thing he wanted to do was rile an already cagy Frankie. "You're cautious. I get it. And with our history, I don't blame you. All I am asking is that you talk to me, because feeling like I'm being played or that this is still some kind of game pisses me off."

"Still?" she said her eyes filling with something even worse than anger.

Ah, crap. She thought . . . "No, that's not what I—"

Frankie held up a hand. "My boots are covered in mud and I know that you mopped the floor yesterday, so I was trying to be nice. My mistake. Won't happen again," she said sharply and dropped the boots. Now her arms were crossed, she was throwing up those walls she was so fond of, and she was ready for a fight. "And I'm not playing. But thanks for reminding me where we stand, since last time I played in one of your stupid games, I got fired, kicked out of my family, and lost my grandfather's respect."

Nate took a breath and ran a hand down his face. "Look, Frankie, I don't want to argue. And I'm not asking for some big declaration. I'm okay if you want to take things slow as long as we're both honest about what's happening between us."

"What's happening, Nate?" She took an aggressive step forward. "We had sex. We went to the lake. We fished. Then had sex again. It was fun. What about that is so confusing to you?"

Because that wasn't all that happened. They'd shared something, and she knew it—didn't she? Hard to say when she sounded so damn sure of herself. "I like you. You like me. So why are you making this so hard?"

"Because this is me, Nate." She sounded tired. "Everything is hard with me. I didn't mean to make you mad or ruin your night, I just . . . Look, do I like you? Yes. But I like lots of people. Do I want you? Obviously. That doesn't mean that there's anything more going on. Honest enough? Great then, I'm off to take a shower. Night, roomie."

Frankie brushed past him and went into the guest bath, shutting the door with a resounding thud.

Nate heard the water hit the tub before he pushed away from the wall, his chest doing stupid things, like not working. It didn't make any sense. She didn't make any sense. He liked her, she liked him. So why did the sum balance of their entire relationship always equal disaster? With Frankie he always felt like everything was spinning out of control.

He'd mentally weighed the pros and the cons of a relationship with Frankie, took into account that she needed to feel in control, felt more comfortable setting the pace. So he handed over the keys and she spun them right off the fucking cliff.

After slamming his own door, properly and like an adult, he plopped down in the chair. Pulling the footrest up, he leaned back and pressed a hand to his head. His heart was pounding, his hands twitchy, and he felt sick. He hadn't been this worked up since his parents died. And all over a woman who either A) didn't like him enough to even try, B) was too scared to admit she liked him, or C) had been telling the truth all along.

Maybe she was right. Maybe it was just sex and he was the one making this into something it wasn't. Hell, they were so completely opposite, maybe it was naive to think Frankie could even provide the qualities he needed in a partner—and vice versa.

Nate didn't allow the death of his parents to make him wary of relationships like his brothers had. He took their deep ability to love as proof that that kind of soul-deep connection and unconditional understanding did exist. And that was what he was looking for. But would he find it in a woman who would give the shirt off her back without question, but one question about feelings and she'd aim for the nuts?

Frankie was smart and sexy and honest and challenged him at every turn. But—Nate grabbed his legal pad and a pen off the end table—she was stubborn to a fault, could argue with an alpaca, and was awkward and unsure with kids.

Nate released a ragged breath and closed his eyes. He loved kids. The more time he spent around his nieces, the harder it was to leave without feeling the unsettling knowledge that there was a gaping hole in his life that needed to be filled—not tomorrow but soon.

Drawing a line down the middle of the page, Nate wrote *REASONS TO WANT FRANKIE* across the header, titled each column, and then numbered one to twenty down the margin. After he sorted and cleared out every emotion and thought, filled in every line, adding more numbers and even spilling onto the next page, he looked at the bottom entry in each column and swore.

Pro: I love Frankie.

Con: I love Frankie.

~

It was a quarter past four in the morning and Nate was still staring at the ceiling. He sat alone in his chair, head aching from frustration, body tense with worry. He was exhausted, the bone-deep kind that made thinking logically about anything impossible, which is why all the illogical crap was making it impossible to fall asleep.

Realizing he was in love with a woman who couldn't even say the word relationship without going into anaphylactic shock could do that to a guy. Admitting that he'd pushed too hard and may have blown it only added to the stress.

He'd taken a hot shower and reorganized his *REASONS TO WANT FRANKIE* list, but even that hadn't helped. He wanted to walk across the hall, tap on Frankie's door—and what?

Having sex with her would be a colossal mistake and yet she'd made it clear that it was the only thing on the table. Although he was pretty sure he'd screwed that up too when he'd stupidly implied that she was a game. God, how had their relationship become so complicated?

He quietly chuckled. Regardless of what Frankie was claiming, they did have a relationship. It might be more than she was willing to admit and less than Nate was willing to settle for. But three lists, two studies on how friends-to-lovers were seventy percent more likely to last, and a mental accounting of every encounter they'd had over the past three months and Nate was confident that they were both in deep. Which was why she'd gotten scared at the lake.

He got to her. Enough for her to pull back. She got to him unlike anyone he'd ever known. And beyond all reasonable explanation, they fit.

Now he just had to figure out how to take what they had, dysfunctional as it was, and make it into something amazing, something that fulfilled what they both needed. And right now

Frankie needed his understanding, his patience and her own space. She had a lot riding on this weekend, and the last thing she needed was more pressure.

With a groan, Nate pushed the footrest down and threw on a pair of jeans. Sleep was not his friend tonight so he'd have to settle for caffeine. He opened the bedroom door and stopped.

Dressed in a tank top, panties, and nothing else, Frankie sat against the wall, her legs pulled to her chest, her cheek resting on her bent knees. At the sound of his door opening, she lifted her head and it was like a sucker punch to the gut. Her hair was a rumpled mess, her eyes were red—from lack of sleep or crying, he wasn't sure—and the way she wrapped her arms around her body as though they were the only thing holding her together broke his heart.

"What are you doing up?" he asked quietly.

"Waiting for you," she said, her lavender-tipped toes wiggling nervously. "I didn't want to wake you but I also didn't want to miss you before I had the chance to say, to tell you that—Did I wake you?"

She was staring up at him, looking beautiful and confused and so damn lost he had to take a steadying breath.

"No. I was already awake and wanted some coffee." What he wanted was to take her in his arms and tell her that everything would be all right. But he knew that if he did, they'd wind up naked, and there went him giving her space. "Why don't we go in the kitchen?"

He offered his hand to help her up, and she let him, which turned out to be a mistake because now she was pressed against his body, looking attractive in a pair of cream panties that were barely there and quite—sheer. All he had to do was lower his head an inch and they'd be kissing, which would lead to touching, and groping, and eventually—

"Bed-sex."

Nate blinked. "Excuse me?"

"That's what I wanted to talk to you about."

"Bed-sex?"

"Yes. And to tell you that I wasn't trying to sneak past you tonight and I didn't think I was avoiding you, but I thought about what you said earlier and well . . . I think I might have been using Mittens as an excuse not to come inside. And I'm"—she took a deep breath and looked him in the eye—"sorry."

"You don't need to apologize, Frankie." Nate intertwined their fingers and brought her hand to his mouth, delivering a gentle kiss to each of her knuckles. "You have a lot going on right now and I get that—"

"I'm scared," she said, her eyes studying their linked hands. "I've never been very good at, you know, bed-sex."

No, he didn't know. Frankie was an incredible lover. She excelled at chair-sex, oral-sex, lake-sex, and he didn't know what bed-sex was, but he could guarantee she'd get a gold star in that too. "I'm not sure I understand what you're trying to tell me."

"That I like sex."

He couldn't help it, he smiled. "Definitely something to add to the pro column."

"And the whole holding-cuddling part afterward is kind of nice. But then comes the talking part." She forced herself to meet his gaze. "Not so nice. And finally the morning after." She laughed but it was self-conscious. "I hate that part, the not knowing, you know? Do I stay? Do I leave? Does he want me to stay or is he figuring out how to ask me to leave? And if he wants me to stay, then for how long? And what if I want to stay longer than he wants me to, then what?"

Nate wondered what would happen if he said never, that he never wanted her to leave. Frankie had spent most of her childhood being passed back and forth between families, and her adulthood trying to live up to unattainable expectations. It was easier for her to avoid relationships—even good ones—than to wish for something that might not want you back.

"Assuming I'm the *he* in your example," he said pulling her closer. "No. Yes. No. Yes. No. And for however long you want."

"You were the *he* in question," she admitted. She took in a big breath, and then studied her toes. "Are you sure?"

"Beyond sure."

"Even after I kick your ass in the Cork Crawl?"

He released one hand to cup her face and tilt it toward his. "Especially then."

She let that settle, then carefully said, "Because I'm going to win. You know that, right? I have to if I want to pay off Tanner *and* keep my grapes. Because if I lose, I have to sell and I can't sell to my grandpa or he'll go after Susan's account. And I can't sell to you because he'll see it as a betrayal." All the uncertainty may have been gone from her voice, but Nate could still hear the pain lacing each word. "So if I lose, I lose everything."

And wind up in the one place she's been her entire life—in the middle. Nate didn't want any part in that. Ever.

"Do you realize that you've spent the whole night worrying about Charles, your dad . . . me? What about you, Frankie? What do you want?"

"I don't know anymore."

"Do you want to stay? With me?" Although there was no expiration date on the invitation, since he figured that forever would push her too far too fast, they both knew what he was asking.

"So much that it scares me," she admitted on a whisper. One simple, honest statement that held so much hope, Nate felt the weight that had been crushing his chest evaporate.

"This scares me too, Frankie. I'm scared to push too hard and chase you off or not hard enough and make you walk away. I never know where you stand, what you're feeling, or what you need."

She padded closer, her body pressing against his. "Right now I'm standing in your arms. I'm feeling a little off balance and like I want to cry, and I never cry. And I really need to go to bed." She smiled shyly. "With you."

"Nothing would make me happier." He leaned down and kissed her gently, letting her know that bed-sex was not on the agenda. "But we're going to sleep."

Frankie wrapped her arms around his neck and smiled. "Whatever you say."

"I'm serious. We're both exhausted and we have a big week."

She kissed him again. And yeah, she was right. The second he got her under those covers he was going to strip her naked and the only thing that wasn't going to happen in that bed was sleep.

Not that he cared. Because there was also going to be a whole lot more going on between them than just sex.

～

Frankie stood on the steps of the wide back porch, sipped her coffee, and smiled.

The alpaca habitat was done. With its wood-slatted walls, green thatched roof, and white picket fence extending around the perimeter, it looked more like a miniature Victorian than a crate training device for a camelid. And the best part? Mittens loved it.

He pranced back and forth across the faux porch, humming while chewing on the fake flower baskets that hung from the window frames. Every third step he'd lift up his back right hoof and hop—alpaca speak for skipping.

Tanner and his hard hammers were on the other side of the field finishing up the last part of the tank installation. Nate was gone, but he'd left a detailed note on his pillow, explaining how he had to leave early to check on one of his vineyards in Sonoma that was being harvested, that he would rather have spent the morning having bed-sex and asked her to call him when she woke up. Now she knew why.

Smiling so bad it hurt, Frankie pulled out her phone.

"Morning." Just hearing his voice made her all giddy. She had it bad. "Did you sleep well?" he asked.

"Almost as good as Mittens, who sends his thanks by the way. You were right, he loves it."

There was a long pause and she could hear him smiling from the other side of the phone. "What time are you coming home?" she asked.

"What time does the kid go to bed?"

Frankie pressed the phone to her ear. "Brush and story time happen around seven, in the barn by seven-thirty."

"Are these kid friendly stories?"

"Very."

"Then I'll be there at seven-thirty sharp, with dinner." He yawned and Frankie realized that he had left the house before sunrise every morning that week. He'd spend all day in one of his fields, rush home to make her dinner—part of his "Pop Tarts for no more than two meals per day" campaign—only to stay up all night having hot bed-sex with her. He managed over twenty vineyards, kept his family from dramatically imploding, and somehow finished Mittens's house.

The man must be exhausted.

"Um, how about you take your time and be here by eight? I'll have dinner ready by then."

There was a long pause and Frankie shifted on her feet. She'd never offered to cook for anyone before. First, because she was terrible at it. And second, there had never been anyone she wanted to cook for. And the longer Nate held his silence the more nervous she became.

"I'm not really a great cook," she found herself explaining. "But I can BBQ some steaks and make a salad. Nothing fancy. As in lettuce and dressing. And maybe a few tomatoes. And for dessert I could—" and Frankie stopped herself.

Three nights. Three nights of bed-sex and she was already reduced to one of *those* women. Questioning every word. Analyzing the smallest pause in conversation. Desperate to please. This was why she didn't date.

She rested her cheek against her arm that was propped up on the fence and—*no way*— she was blushing. Her entire face felt like a giant solar flare. Not happening. In fact, the entire night was one girly snort away from being canceled.

"Dinner would be nice." Nate said, saving the night. "And maybe a movie. My DVDs are in the bedroom if you want to pick something out."

"I still have a bunch of leaf roses to make for Regan."

What had happened to her simple, no-frills life? A month ago she would have spent her Friday evening playing darts with

Glow and Luce, only to come home alone and eat a Pop Tart out of the wrapper while watching Formula 1 racing on television. Lights out by ten.

Now she had leafy greens in her fridge, craft supplies on her counter, and a date with her super-hot boyfriend. Lights out by ten, bed-sex until dawn. Yes, she'd just thought the words "boyfriend" and "bed-sex," all with Nate in mind and only suffered *minor* palpations—and a little perspiration on her hands.

"I could help you with the roses. I happen to be a pro at molding and shaping," Nate said with that I'm-here-for-you-babe tone that she'd come to associate with the let's-head-for-the-bedroom look. Which tonight translated into just how meticulous and efficient those hands of his would be. "Frankie."

Her head snapped up and she butted Mittens square in the jaw. "*Warkwarkwark!*" When had she laid her head back down on the fence post? "Yeah?"

"Whatever it is that has you breathing heavy," he continued. She could hear him smiling again. This time smugly. "I'm a pro at that too."

CHAPTER 15

Nate pretended to take a sip of his wine and laughed with his brothers and some buyer in a pair of loafers whose name he should have known but for the life of him couldn't remember. Not that it should matter. Nate made the wine and Trey sold it. But it did. Rubbing shoulders with the resident enologist always went the distance when finalizing sales, and was a big part of the reason that the Cork Crawl attracted so many respected buyers and collectors.

He prided himself on his ability to close. He was a master closer. But when one of the Cork Crawl volunteers walked out from behind the stage at the community park to collect and seal the DeLuca barrel, he gave up feigning interest.

"That makes it official," Trey said, shaking the man's hand and shooting Nate a hard look. "Cork Crawl is finally over."

"Good luck today," Loafers said and it was all Nate could do not to laugh. Frankie was right: loafers screamed uptight, snooze-fest. Good thing Nate had opted for boots today. Beat up, worked-in boots.

"I think this year is going to be a close race," Loafers went on and Trey said something Nate supposed was important but wound up sounding more brownnosing, Marc made a witty comment, Gabe chuckled his I-am-head-of-this-family chuckle, and Loafers laughed. Loud and nasally. "Either way, I'll be seeing you tomorrow."

Nate might have said goodbye, he couldn't be sure because a flat-cart of barrels rolled by on its way to the tally room. He started stacking and restacking the winery brochures. A clear sign that he was nervous. The sweaty palms, shouldn't-have-had-that-second-helping-of-chili kind of nervous.

After eighteen years of coming to the Cork Crawl, the past eleven making a Cork Crawl clean sweep, he wasn't used to nervous. He'd spent the past six hours fielding questions from amateur wine enthusiasts, wine critics, and his family. Although, ChiChi was less interested in wine and more into what was going on between him and Frankie, and his brothers' interest was securely invested into how he managed to stick his head so far up his ass.

A fair assessment since he'd been distracted at best, and flat out brain-dead at worst. Instead of focusing on his job, selling DeLuca wine into hearts and cellars around the world, Nate had fixated his entire attentions on Frankie who, one row over and two booths down, wore a red silky number up top, a black skirt that hugged every one of her incredible curves down below, and strappy black heels. Heels that had him wishing it were nighttime and they were alone.

A ping sounded from his back pocket. He fished out his cell phone and saw he had one text in his inbox.

YOU'RE STARING & MAKING LISTS. SHOULD I BE NERVOUS?

He glanced at the paper attached to the clipboard and smiled. Covered in lists. When had that happened? He caught Frankie's eye, she smiled, he smiled back, then replied.

IT IS MY *"WHAT'S UNDER FRANKIE'S SKIRT?"* LIST. LACE, SILK, PINK, THONG . . . SO MANY CHOICES . . .

His phone pinged again and man, just the sound had his body humming. Her two typed words had him breathing heavy.

ABSOLUTELY NOTHING

Nate looked up, trying to figure out if she was playing him. But she was in a deep conversation with a group of tasters. All men. And all checking out Frankie's packaging. Probably trying to figure out what she had on under her skirt.

"Couldn't you have at least stopped drooling over the competition for two seconds and pretended you were interested?" Trey said. "That was Alan Fielding."

Shit. Nate put his cell away. "Remington's VP."

"Yeah, and the one guy"—Trey held up a finger just in case Nate's head was lodged so far up there he couldn't hear—"I needed you to be on your A-game for."

Nate looked across St. Helena Community Park and watched Alan bypass Frankie's booth without a glance and walk right up to Charles, who was holding court under a flapping Baudouin Wines banner. Dressed in trousers, a sweater vest, and a floppy beret, he looked like the resident authority on wine. All Nate cared about was that the old man hadn't looked at Frankie once. And Nate realized that was why his stomach was in knots. He wanted today to go perfect for Frankie. He was nervous—for her.

For the entire morning and most of the afternoon, he'd watched her watch Charles and never once had her grandfather paid her any attention. Just like Nate hadn't paid his family—or his job—any attention.

"I'm really sorry guys. I've been distracted." Nate ran a hand through his hair.

Gabe picked up a brochure with lists scribbled down the back as evidence. "You think?"

"If you want, I can invite Alan to the vineyard, give him a private tour," Nate offered.

He hated giving private tours, and usually left that responsibility to Trey, who was a charlatan of the people-peddler kind. But he'd screwed this up, so he'd fix it.

"Don't worry about Alan," Marc said, patting him on the back. "I met him last year at a hospitality conference in Chicago. He can't stand Charles. Apparently, when Alan was just starting out, he tried to line up an exclusive deal with Baudouin Wines for some small hotel chain in Poland. Even though the offer was more than fair, Charles refused to sell, claiming his wine was too superior for their clientele."

That sounded like a Charles thing to do. Man couldn't even look at his own granddaughter. At least her brothers and aunt had taken turns helping her run the booth, so she hadn't been alone, but still.

"Plus, Susan said Remington is set on going with DeLuca. There is no way Charles can weasel his way into this," Marc added. "Lexi invited Susan, Alan, and his wife to the bistro for dinner last night. They talked food, we talked hospitality, and in the end Lexi closed strong with a pairing of a DeLuca late bottled vintage port and Pricilla's éclairs."

"Did they sign the contract?" Nate asked, surprised no one had told him. Then again, not all that surprising since he hadn't seen his brothers in over a week.

"What do you think? It was Pricilla's éclairs," Marc said as though that was answer enough. And it was. Pricilla's éclairs were world famous. A life-altering culinary experience, according to Martha Stewart.

"More important question," Trey asked, his gaze narrowing in on Frankie. "How do you think she's doing?"

Nate took a deep breath. He'd been meaning to talk to his brothers about Frankie's grapes, but between preparing for harvest and organizing everything for the Cork Crawl, he hadn't found the time. Okay, so he'd spent most of the time he could have been talking to his brothers about issues, which in the long run wouldn't matter, getting lost in things that would—like Frankie.

"I think she's going to win," Nate said and to his surprise Marc and Gabe smiled. Trey, not so much.

"Why is everyone smiling?" Trey growled.

Gabe laughed. "Have you tasted her wine?"

"If he did, he wouldn't be asking," Marc said and Trey glared. Being the youngest, Trey hated feeling left out. Even more so, he hated to lose.

Poor Trey, Nate thought. He was about to have a rough day. What Trey was missing was that Frankie winning wouldn't hurt their business. The DeLuca reputation was based on quality, quantity, and a long history of taste. Frankie was quality all the way. Her wine was bold and exquisite and would lure in the high-end brokers and collectors. Not that Nate didn't want to compete in that market—he would with his father's Opus—but he also knew that in the end it wouldn't matter who landed what account, as long as it was a fair fight they'd both win.

"She wins and we lose more than some stupid crown," Trey said.

"It wouldn't have mattered, Trey," Marc said, sending Nate a smile that he had a hard time interpreting. "Even if she lost, Nate wouldn't buy her grapes."

"Why not?" Trey asked. "She has to pay off Tanner somehow. If she loses, she'll have to sell to someone. Why not to us?"

Nate looked Trey directly in the eyes "I didn't hook Frankie up with Tanner in hopes that she'd fail and lose her grapes."

"Then why the hell did you do it?" Trey asked, sounding equal parts confused and pissed.

"And that is why you are single," Gabe said, slapping Trey on the back.

"No." Trey stepped back and shot each one of his brothers a horrified look. "I'm single because there seems to be a severe allergic reaction that happens when DeLuca males come in contact with domestication. The symptoms include but are not limited to, asinine diets, obsessive texting, and irrational and illogical decisions, all of which are hazardous to this family's stability. Hell, at this rate I'm surprised I'm not carrying around one of those needles that people stab in their hearts when they go into shock."

"An EpiPen?" Gabe offered.

"Yeah. A fucking EpiPen."

∼

Frankie stood in her booth and signed the questionnaire that yes, she'd had a great experience at the Cork Crawl, and yes, she would be coming back next year. Only she would be ditching the heels and black skirt. The location of her booth had brought more tasters than she'd anticipated and once the sun had come out from behind the clouds, the temperature had shot up to a suffocating ninety degrees.

A thin sheen of perspiration beaded on her forehead and, because there had been no mid-morning or late-afternoon lull as promised, Jordan's unwanted advice on shoes had cost her a blister on both big toes. Not that she was complaining, Frankie had spoken to more buyers in the past six hours than she had in the past fifteen years working for Charles—and she'd done great. She had a dozen business cards, all from prospective and very interested collectors and two brokers. Not Susan Jance level, but still impressive nonetheless. If it hadn't been for Abby reeling her back in, Red Steel would have sold out before lunch. Bottled and futures.

"There's a group of brokers and buyers standing over by the tree waiting to talk to you," Jordan said. How was it that her friend had stood in the same intense heat all day and wasn't even glistening?

Frankie walked out from under her tent. Sure enough, there was a group of about seven buyers, sweating like they'd just run a marathon in loafers, huddled under the tiny bit of shade offered by the mostly molted maple tree. They were talking among themselves, but when Frankie emerged they went silent, looking at her expectantly.

"They collected the barrels over an hour ago." Which was why most people had taken to the large tent set up on the south side of the park. It was shaded, air conditioned, and there was an abundance of hors d'oeuvre and wine—for those who hadn't already tasted themselves three sheets to the wind yet. "What are they doing?"

"What part of, 'Waiting to talk to you' did you miss?" Jordan said.

"They know you won," Abby said, her hair a cluster of wild curls from the heat. "They know that any offers not seriously entertained before the corks are finished being tallied will be tossed out."

"Do I go over and talk to them?"

"Nope. Let them sweat it out," Jonah said, coming up from behind. Even though he was dressed in jeans and a Red Steel Cellars t-shirt, his department-issued authority was still locked and loaded. "Most of those people are mid-level buyers. They don't have the money to compete at the level you're about reach."

"Which is why I told her not to accept any offers," Abby said with a smile. "And she's had plenty."

"Smart thinking." He tugged Frankie's hair. "After you win, those offers will be tripled. And I bet if you don't sell out tomorrow, whatever is left over will go straight to Chicago where it will fetch even more at auction."

Frankie rolled her eyes. "We don't even know if I made the cork court."

She'd had an amazing day, no question, but she didn't want to be talked into making a clean sweep only to be disappointed with a consolation prize.

"Just because I didn't follow in dad's footsteps doesn't mean I didn't follow him around for the first twenty years of my life." He leaned down and gave her a hug and Frankie clung tightly to his shoulders. A response that surprised them both. "He would have been proud of you today, Frankie. I know I am."

"He's right," someone said from behind. An extremely sexy someone, whose voice alone had the power to send a warm sensation sliding through her body. "You won."

She turned and her breath seemed to stick in her throat. Nate stood in his trademark uniform of khaki slacks and a

DeLuca polo and took her in with those warm, brown eyes of his that made her feel like giggling. Then she looked down and did. His feet, minus one set off stuffy loafers, were sporting a pair of muddy, rugged ball-buster boots, which Frankie had come to associate with the down-and-dirty grape grower. Which meant that along with the giggling came some squirming on her part because of the intense heat that pulsed below her belly button.

"We don't know that." But in her heart she hoped it was the truth.

"Oh, you won, sweet cheeks," he said. "No matter what Mrs. Rose has written on her tally, there was no other wine as talked about this year as Red Steel. I even had buyers asking *me* if I had tried it."

"What did you tell them?" she asked, feeling very girlie and not really caring.

"That it was a shoe-in for the win."

"I'll bet," Jonah said, eyeing Nate with suspicion.

Frankie hadn't told anyone about Nate being her boyfriend—even thinking the word made her chest go shifty. But it was pretty obvious by how they were all but mentally stripping each other that there was more than just a roomie situation at Sorrento Ranch.

Movement at the front of the stage caught Frankie's eye, as Mrs. Rose and the mayor took their place. Behind them, elbowing each other for the front spot, like a group of grannies at a high-stakes coupon bingo game, stood ChiChi, Luce, and Pricilla, each reaching for a tray with an award. ChiChi grabbed the King's crown and Luca ended up with the Queen's crown.

Frankie tried to tell herself that it didn't matter which lady carried what award, that she'd held her own with the big boys and she should be proud. But she didn't want to merely hold her own, she wanted to kick some ass. And that meant winning.

"Can I have some money?" Ava asked as she walked over. Today her hair was streaked teal, matching her bellybutton ring, and she wore a halter top and a strip of white denim on bottom.

Abby blinked. Twice. Then leaned in and whispered, "Where's the rest of her pants?"

"On vacation with the rest of your legs," Ava said. "What are you, like four-feet tall?"

"Five-one," Abby huffed.

"Whatever." Ava rolled her eyes then turned to her mom. "Can I have some money? I'm hungry."

Jordan handed her a twenty. But when Ava went to take the bill, Jordan didn't let go. "If I find out that you gave this to Mr. Sexy Syrah two rows over, who promised to sneak you a couple of bottles if you met him behind town hall—"

"You'll do what, mom?" Again with the eye roll. "You already took away my internet and phone."

"You want to try me, young lady?" Jordan said, all business. Even Jonah took a step back. "I will have Mr. Sexy arrested for soliciting a minor, you thrown in jail for being underage and in possession of alcohol, and you will spend the rest of senior year taking Tiny Tots Tap with me at the Tap and Barre School of Dance. Now, you still need money?"

"Gawd." Ava drew out the word for so long Frankie was convinced she'd pass out from oxygen deprivation. Bad ass mom with wicked game: one. Bad attitude teen with a wardrobe disorder: zero.

The mayor tapped the mic and it echoed through the loud speakers. "Good afternoon, everyone."

Silence settled throughout the park. A light breeze picked up and rustled some of the last leaves from their branches. Mrs. Rose snagged the Cork King crown from ChiChi and walked to the center of the stage. ChiChi settled on the Cork Prince award, but not before shooting the current Wine Commissioner a sharp look.

"Over five thousand corks have been cast, counted, and tallied. And the results are right here in these envelopes." The mayor held up four gold-embossed envelopes and the crowd cheered. "It is with great honor that I get to present this year's St. Helena First Harvest Cork Crawl's royal court and crown the best wine of the harvest with the coveted title, Cork King."

"About the party tonight," Nate whispered, his breath tickling her ear. He hadn't touched her yet; in fact he was keeping his distance today. Something that she had asked for when she saw that her grandfather was just a few tents away, but was now regretting.

She turned her head slightly and had a hard time speaking. He was still a companionable distance away, but she could feel his presence press through her entire body. "I haven't decided yet."

His eyes dropped to her lips. "Holding out for a better offer?"

"No, just making sure the offer still stands after the results are in."

She had been putting off her decision because she didn't want Nate to feel obligated to bring her if the results swung in her favor. Or if they swung his way, she didn't want him to bring her out of pity. She wanted him to bring her because he liked being with her. So she'd wait until the results were in, gauge his interest level, and then make her decision.

"And the new Cork Princesses of this year's harvest comes from . . . the Stags Leap District. Chiappa Vineyards for their Petite Syrah reserve."

"Ohmigod Ohmigod Ohmigod," Abby chanted harshly over the cheering. "We won. I mean you won, well I was on your team, but you freaking won." She looked at Nate. "Sorry about being number two. You do know that it is the first loser."

"What are you talking about?"

"Look," Abby practically screeched. "Look at Nora Kincaid. Look where she is standing."

Nora Kincaid had been huddled with her ear pressed to the tally tent for the past thirty minutes. After sharing a few hushed words with Mrs. Rose, she had taken up residence next to Charles's booth. And she wasn't just standing there, she had her phone set to camera, and her fingers were hovering over the snap-and-load-to-Facebook button.

"That doesn't mean anything." But Frankie knew that it did. "It could mean that *he* won."

Something that would not be the end of the world. Sure, it would burn to lose to Kenneth, but Frankie knew what kind of boost being crowned king could give her grandfather. She'd spent most of the day watching him, partly hoping to catch his gaze and silently wish him good luck. But mostly she was worried over how tired he looked, how fragile he appeared. When had her hellion of a grandfather gotten so old?

"Nope," Jordan said, clapping her hands. "If he won, then she'd be filming you."

"Can you guys be quiet?" Ava hissed. "You just missed winner of the Cork Prince."

"Who was it?"

"Doesn't matter, it wasn't you."

Frankie looked back at her grandfather. It wasn't him either. Which meant that between her, Nate, and Charles someone was going to have a really crappy night.

Frankie felt a warm hand engulf hers. She looked up and saw Nate smiling down on her. He didn't say anything, but then he didn't have to. He was doing the one thing that she needed but was too embarrassed to ask for. He was supporting her no matter what.

"And the Cork Queen of this year's harvest comes from the St. Helena Appellation area." The mayor took a dramatic pause and Frankie's heart literally stopped. Her hand tightened around Nate's and he gave a quick squeeze back. She looked up to find him not watching the mayor, but staring down at her. "Please give a warm hand to DeLuca Vineyards for their Cabernet Sauvignon."

Frankie wasn't sure what she expected, but it hadn't been for his smile to widen. For his eyes to go soft and him to look genuinely happy for her. And proud of her.

"I'm sorry," she whispered.

"I'm not."

"We still don't know if I won. Charles could take it."

He shook his head. "You won, honey. This is your moment."

Frankie looked at Charles whose eyes were firmly fixed on the mayor. "And finally, I am honored to say that this year's Cork King also hails from the St. Helena Applications."

She watched as Charles finally looked her way. His eyes weren't warm, but they weren't angry either. They looked desperate, scared, as though everything he had was riding on the mayor's next words. And suddenly Frankie got an awful feeling in the pit of her stomach.

"Please welcome our new King Cork, Red Steel Cellars for their Cabernet Sauvignon reserve blend."

Frankie's breath rushed out of her. She heard people calling her name and felt congratulatory pats on the back but all she would do was look up at Nate. There was no surprise, no hesitation, no ulterior motives.

He knew. Knew she would win.

"How did you know?"

He turned to face her, but still didn't take her in his arms. "Because it's you in a bottle, Frankie. What can beat that?"

At his words Frankie had to fight the urge to launch herself into his arms at the overwhelming sense of happiness that filled her chest. This was what Nate had been talking about. This was what it felt like to connect, trust, open up and share. This was the completely, one hundred percent, forever kind of right.

But when he still didn't move, still didn't put his arms around her she asked, "Why aren't you kissing me?"

He laughed. "Because your grandfather is watching. Nora has her phone aimed this way. I'm pretty sure your brother is packing. And if you need another reason, the last time I did that, you kneed me in the nuts. So, sweet cheeks, if you want that kiss, you have to make the first move."

And move she did. Fast and furiously, putting her hands on his shoulders and rolling up on her tiptoes, not stopping until their mouths collided. Right there in the middle of St. Helena Community Park, in front their families and most of the town.

His mouth met hers, soft and giving and so right that she didn't care if Charles was there, or that Nora had moved to catch it all on tape, or that after this everyone would know that Francesca Baudoiun and Nathaniel DeLuca were a couple. All that mattered was that he had believed in her. And that he was hers.

Hers.

How had that happened? Frankie found someone that she wanted and he wanted her back.

Her fingers slid into his hair and she felt his slide down her back—gentleman that he was, stopping at her waistline. And when his tongue glided over hers all of the earlier insecurities vanished and were replaced by hope.

It had been a long time since Frankie had allowed herself to get caught up in the dream of something more. With wine she was bold, a risk taker. With her heart she was usually so cautious, convincing herself it was better to go it alone than risk knowing what you're missing out on. But nothing about her feelings for Nate would allow her to proceed cautiously.

Frankie pulled back and ended the kiss. Partly because people were cheering now, and the mayor was calling for a representative from Red Steel Cellars to please come to the stage. But mostly she pulled back, because if he kept kissing her like that, she'd forget what she wanted to say.

"Okay?"

Nate tilted his head to the side. "Okay, what?"

"I want to go with you to your family's party tonight. As long as you know that I don't cook."

"Oh, honey, I think you made that clear last night."

Right, when they had pizza for dinner and Pop Tarts for dessert because she charred the steaks until they were nuggets and her cupcakes collapsed in the middle.

"How about I bring the wine?" she said. "I hear it is a real winner."

CHAPTER 16

One hour later, Frankie stood in Judge Pricket's private chambers feeling like anything but a winner.

"I don't understand," she said. She knew that she hadn't done anything wrong, but had a gut feeling that in the end none of that would matter. "What kind of grievance?"

Judge Pricket, looking ever so official in his jacket and tie, sat behind his massive desk. To his right, staring enviously at his gavel was Mrs. Rose.

"Someone is claiming that Red Steel was grown, fermented and aged on Baudouin property," Judge Pricket said.

Frankie would bet the vineyard that *someone* was Shady Katie or cousin Kenneth. "Yes, sir. That is true, I leased the use of the barrels from my aunt and some of the grapes were grown on Baudouin land, but they are mine. I grew the grapes, harvested them, and aged the wine myself. All by myself."

"That's what I told him," Mrs. Rose harrumphed, arms folded over her ample chest. "And if he hadn't insisted on taking his claim to court, we'd all be out celebrating instead of in here accusing someone of nothing good."

"Ed, could I have a word with my granddaughter?" Charles said from the doorway. And just like that, Frankie's heart broke.

"I think we should call Lucinda. She needs to know what's going on," Mrs. Rose said, standing and putting all of her two hundred pounds between Frankie and her grandfather.

"I wish you wouldn't," Charles said, but his eyes were on Frankie.

"That's all right, Mrs. Rose. Judge—" Frankie stood as well. So did Pricket. Now they were all standing, waiting for Frankie to finish her thought, but she couldn't because she knew if she did that she was going to lose everything.

But then she thought of Nate, and how she'd risked her heart with him and he hadn't let her down. And a small part of her, the little girl who missed her dad, who tried so hard to prove that she was worthy of her grandfather's love, hoped that maybe this was the time, this would be when she put herself out there and not be let down.

"I think I'd like to talk to my grandpa for a minute alone," she heard herself say.

"You sure?" Judge Pricket said, resting a hand on her shoulder. Because the judge, just like the rational part of Frankie's mind, knew that there wasn't a happy ending to be had. At least not for her.

"Yeah, I'm sure."

The room cleared out, leaving Frankie with the one person she'd been trying to get alone for months. Only now she wished her brothers were there, or her aunt. Or Nate.

Charles walked to the empty chair beside Frankie, leaning heavily on his cane, his body deflated with every step he took. He lowered himself and stared at his feet.

"I need you to say that Red Steel is a Baudoiun wine," he said.

And any hope that Frankie had died. Her heart expanded too fast for her chest to contain and her throat tightened, cutting off all air. "I'll lose everything. You know that, right?" she said. "Without that wine, I'll have to sell my grapes and still I won't be able to pay off Tanner completely. And Katie will deny me the loan."

"I know," was all he said. He still hadn't looked at her, or hadn't even really spoken to her about what happened over the past few months. He'd just come in and asked her to give up her entire world without giving her anything in return.

"Can I ask why?"

"Because if you don't, the family will lose everything." His voice cracked and he cleared it before continuing. "The vineyards, the house, the wine, everything."

"I thought you only lost half the grapes in Santa Ynez?"

"I may have well lost the entire thing. With only half the expected harvest, I will need to sell each barrel for double the cost and without placing in the cork court . . ." He shook his head.

"You can't sell central coast wine for Napa Valley prices," Frankie finished for him. "So it takes you a few more years to break even. You've been here before."

"Never here." Finally, he looked up and Frankie wished he hadn't. Outside of anger and pride, she had never seen her grandfather show much emotion, and she had never seen him cry. But his eyes were red and glassy. "I had to take out a hard money loan."

"Please tell me you didn't use the St. Helena property as collateral."

He gave a shaky nod and Frankie braced herself for the impact his answer would have over her future. "After the mess with the Showdown—"

"You mean when you tried to be sneaky and ruined the family name?" Frankie clarified, because if they were going to go there, then there wasn't going to be any skating around issues. She wouldn't get his love, but she would damn well get his honesty.

"Yes, I got greedy, messed up, and the buyer I had lined up for those grapes pulled out. But I found a new buyer," he said and Frankie already knew where this was going. "Without that title, I can't get the prices I need to make the first balloon payment."

Stomach churning, Frankie collapsed back against the chair. "Oh, God, Grandpa. Does Luce know?"

That land meant everything to her aunt. If Charles didn't make the payment, her aunt would lose her cottage that she loved so much, her garden, and everything that Luce's father had left her. The entire Baudouin legacy would end.

"And that's where Red Steel comes in?" she ventured. "He'll take your supermarket select at a mid-range price if my wine is part of the deal?"

"I'm so sorry, Ches-ka."

Frankie wasn't sure if it was the utter sorrow in her grandfather's apology or the use of her childhood nickname, but her eyes began to burn. "How much is he asking for?"

"All of your bottles and the last two harvests when they age."

Frankie forced herself to breathe. It didn't help. She was going to be sick, so she dropped her head between her knees. "That's all the wine I have."

"It will get us through until the next payment, which is after the next harvest."

"You," she corrected sitting up. "It will get *you* to the next harvest. It will set me back four or five years."

"No, Ches-ka. I want you to come home. Come home and work with me. By my side. Make this winery what it used to be. We make a great team." Charles leaned forward and took her hands in his bony ones.

His touch brought nothing but a deep, resonating sadness and she was surprised that she could feel anything beyond the pain in her chest. She tried to remind herself that he was just trying to save his business, save the family, and that this wasn't personal. But nothing had ever felt so personal to her before and nothing had ever felt like such a betrayal.

If she said no, then her grandfather lost everything. If she said yes, she lost everything. But if Charles lost, then so did her aunt, and Luce was the only person in Frankie's life who had never let her down. Frankie wasn't about to allow Charles's pride to destroy someone else's dreams. She knew all too well what that felt like.

"Is your buyer Pierce Remington?"

Charles shook his head.

"Okay, I'll give you the win, but be clear, if I find out you are going after Remington, I recant."

Charles stood. "Your dad would have been so pr—"

"Disappointed, Grandpa. He would have been sad and disappointed that I was giving up what I wanted. But let me be

clear. You will not get the two acres of grapes. I will sell those
to anyone but you in order to pay off Tanner. Ah," she held up a
hand when he looked ready to argue, "that part is not negotia-
ble."

Of course, stubborn man that Charles was, he started negotiating. "As long as it isn't those damn DeLucas."

"Grandpa, not too long ago, I would have given up everything, done anything if it meant that I could come home and
work with you again." Although the term "with" applied loosely
since it would have been Frankie working "for" Charles. "But
now . . . I'm going to have to decline."

"I don't understand."

She feared he never would.

Frankie wouldn't have either if hadn't been for Nate. He
showed her that love doesn't have to have attachments, conditions, or the fear of rejection.

"Because you showed me that Baudouin Vineyards isn't my
home. Not anymore. I love you and you taught me everything I
know about wine, but if I go home, things will go back to the
way they were and I deserve more than that." Frankie stood and
pressed a gentle kiss on her grandfather's cheek. "And Luce deserves more than what you've done. So I'll give you my wine,
under the condition that you promise to not let Kenneth and
Uncle Tom take over. Promise that you'll be honest with Luce
and my brothers, and that you'll hire someone who cares about
the land as much as we do."

After a long moment, Charles whispered, "I promise."

With a gentle kiss to her cheek, her grandfather slowly
made his way toward the door, only instead of opening it he
paused. "And Ches-ka, earlier when I said that your father
would have been proud, I meant that he would have been proud

of the winemaker you've become. Proud of the person you've grown into. The only disappointment he would have felt over the past years would have been directed at me."

And then he walked out, leaving behind a weighted silence.

Above the sound of her breaking heart, Frankie heard herself explain everything to a surprised and understanding Mrs. Rose. Frankie didn't remember leaving town hall or walking into Nate's room. She vaguely remembered sitting in the shag chair, pulling the afghan around her and calling Regan to explain that she wasn't going to make it to dinner.

~

ChiChi's normally formal living room was littered with leaf-rose streamers and green and red balloons gathered to looked like clusters of grapes. A giant cornucopia sat in the middle of the coffee table, overflowing with festive-colored presents while Holly the Harvest Worker, dressed in overalls and a pair of Gabe's ratty work-boots, pushed around a stroller with a shrieking Baby Sofie inside. Nate couldn't tell if St. Helena's Official Harvest Baby was supposed to be a giant grape leaf or a red and yellow starfish.

"Thanks for taking the time to talk to Alan," Trey said, leaning back and swirling the deep red liquid around his wineglass. He watched it coat the sides, only to do it again. Which looked ridiculous since he was wearing a harvest tiara made out of leaf-roses—ones that glittered. "You had him so rapped on Opus that at one point I thought the guy was going to openmouth kiss you."

"I told you, I'm a good closer." Nate leaned across the couch and, careful not to spill his wine on ChiChi's cushions, socked

Trey in the arm. "And you weren't so bad either. We did great."
And they had. For the first time in months, Nate and Trey had
tag-teamed like old times and it had paid off. Huge.

And there he was smiling again. Big and stupid. Sitting in
a room that looked like a harvest confetti cannon exploded and
wearing a party tiara of his own. But he couldn't help it. Everything about today was smile worthy. They had more hard offers
than they had wine, Remington was officially on board for
Opus, Frankie had her moment to shine, and man had she
shined. Then she had kissed the hell out of him.

In. Front. Of. Everyone.

"Did I see you talking to the rep from Stanford Specialty
Markets?" Marc asked Gabe.

"They are looking for a winery to partner with. I guess they
want to create their own brand of wine to sell in their stores.
Quality for a bargain kind of thing. Sounded interesting."

"No way," Trey said, looking exhausted. "I need at least
three years to recover from the last distribution deal we made."

"That's what I told him," Gabe said, losing all focus when
his wife walked into the room. He took his wife's free hand and
tugged her onto his lap. It didn't take the guy but a second before his hands were around her waist. "What took you so long?"

Regan paid her husband no attention, instead looking directly at Nate. "Did Frankie call you?"

"No, why? Is it time for pin the cluster on the vine?" Nate
checked his cell for the sixth time in so many minutes. Nope.
No text or messages. He had considered giving her a call, but
hadn't wanted to rush her. Tonight was a big night. If she needed
two hours to enjoy her moment alone, then he'd give it to her.

But when he'd left the Cork Crawl to head to ChiChi's, he
had assumed Frankie wouldn't be far behind. He wanted to

drive her, but then Mr. Rose had needed to finalize a few things with Frankie, so Nate had gone ahead. That was two plates of Lexi's wasabi-gouda fritters, a glass of Red Steel, and a game of twenty questions with Holly ago.

Apparently, in Holly-land kissing a girl in public meant that he should propose. Nate wondered what kissing Frankie in private should lead to. He thought about all the options and found himself shifting to get comfortable.

Maybe he should call her. If anything just to hear her voice and tell her again how proud he was. Something he wouldn't get to do at the party because he knew that it would embarrass her in front of his family. Yeah, he'd call her.

"No, I was just checking my voicemail," Regan explained, her usually confident eyes swimming with concern.

Trey on the other hand looked perplexed and irritated. He held the bottle of Red Steel in his hand and studied the label. A thorough investigation later, his mouth flattened and his head bobbed side to side. Trey for *Not bad.* After sniffing the cork he poured himself a glass of Frankie's wine, a gift from Lucinda who was busy in the kitchen with his nonna, and swirled it around. He took a sip and there it was—the how-did-she-do-it look of perplexed ecstasy.

Trey had been trying to find fault with Red Steel since the crowning, with no luck.

"There was one from Frankie," she said and the tone in her voice had Nate setting down his glass.

"What'd she say?" Nate asked, a sinking feeling settling in his gut as Regan looked over at Lucinda who stood in the doorway. She was holding onto Mr. Puffins so tight his eyes were slightly bulged. Lucinda's eyes, on the other hand, were filled with worry.

"That she regretfully declines tonight's dinner invite." Regan managed to look even more concerned than Lucinda. Then she shot a sad look at her husband. "And to see if Gabe would be interested in buying her grapes."

"What?" Nate sat forward. Definitely time to give her a ring.

"Are you serious?" Trey also sat straighter but for a totally different reason.

"We aren't buying them, Trey," Nate growled, then looked back at Lucinda. "Why would she do that?"

Lucinda stepped forward and for such a solid woman she looked strangely fragile. "Because Charles petitioned the decision, claiming that since Red Steel was partially grown and fully aged on Baudouin land that the wine and the win belonged to him."

"There is no way that the Wine Commission would uphold that. People lease land, buy grapes, and rent storage all the time. Plus, there is no way Frankie would cave. She needs this." Nate was already on his feet, gathering his keys and dialing Frankie. It went straight to voicemail. He tried again. Same result.

"Sit down, Nathaniel," ChiChi said and he did. It was a command not a request and even though Nate wanted nothing more than to go find Frankie, he took his seat. It wasn't years of conditioning had him pausing; there was something about the way ChiChi had said it that made breathing, let alone walking difficult.

Lucinda sat next to him, her bony hands tucked securely around her cat. "Charles is about to lose everything. Everything that my father built all because of this stupid feud and his pride." She shook her head and Nate could feel the sorrow rolling off her body. "Charles doesn't know that I know. Stupid man forgets that although I haven't been as active in the vineyard, I do remember how to read a loan document."

"The Santa Ynez property," Nate guessed.

Lucinda nodded and Nate heard a murmur of a sniff. Ah shit, if Lucinda was getting teary eyed he needed to find Frankie. Now.

"Last summer Charles took out a five-year hard money loan using the St. Helena property as collateral. His first balloon payment is due at the end of the year. I think he was hoping that his sales tomorrow would be enough."

"He lost half the vines in the fire and didn't even make the Cork Court," ChiChi added. "I can't remember the last time he didn't make the Cork Court. He must be devastated."

"He'll get over it," Lucinda said quietly.

Nate noticed the way the older woman rubbed her cat behind the ears. Gentle and loving, stroking him as though the act provided her with as much comfort as it did the cat. It reminded him of Frankie and Mittens.

"I've got to find Frankie," Nate said, standing again. He'd heard enough. "I can't let her do this."

"Frankie needs to do what she thinks is right."

Nate froze. "Are you willing to stand by and watch her give up everything she has worked for, everything she's achieved for some selfish son of a bitch who has done nothing but break her heart?"

"No," Lucinda said quietly, but there was nothing passive about the look she was leveling him with. "I know my niece and she will bounce back from this. It might take her longer to get to where she needs to be, but she will survive. If Charles loses that property though, and she believes she could have saved it, she will never forgive herself. That is something I'm not willing to stand by and watch."

"Well, then." Nate grabbed his jacket, since it was better than punching a wall. "I guess we need to figure out a way to save the land and Frankie's dreams, because I'm not going to do nothing while that bastard crushes her world. Again."

~

Nate took the front steps three at a time. Frankie still wasn't answering her phone, Mittens had chewed through the bay windowsill and was working his way through the front door, and Frankie's bike was parked out front—engine cold. Meaning she'd been there for a while. Alone.

Son of a bitch, he should have gone looking for her earlier. Two hours is a long-ass time to finalize things.

"Frankie?" he called as he opened the door.

He quickly scanned the front room and kitchen. There wasn't a single light turned on in the entire house. "Honey?"

That's when he heard it. A small sob coming from his darkened bedroom. Nate flipped on the light and his heart nearly exploded. Frankie sat on the shag chair, her legs to her chest, and enough wadded up tissues to know that she'd been crying. His Frankie had spent the past few hours alone, crying.

"Frankie," he said softly, taking a step forward stopping when she jerked to her feet.

Rubbing at her eyes with the back of her hand did nothing to erase the red-rimmed eyes and wet cheeks. Those eyes made him want to go next door, grab Charles by the neck, and shake him until he admitted what an amazing granddaughter he had. Then shake him some more to put the fear of God into him in case he ever considered using Frankie again.

"Honey, I heard about . . ." The words died fast and hard. Frankie took a single step forward and held up her hand. Every thought left his head, and he couldn't speak past all of the words on the paper staring him down. Words he had written.

He recognized the eight by eleven piece of paper that was crumpled in her hand, recognized the stubborn tilt of her head, but the one thing he didn't recognize was the look of utter devastation and defeat on Frankie's face.

"You're crying."

She choked out a mirthless laugh. "Is that something you want to add to your *Frankie* list? Because there's room right here in the margins," she held up the list he'd stupidly made in a moment of frustration and pointed to the middle of the page, between 'is messy at best, a disaster at worst' and 'drinks from the carton.' "Or even better, at the bottom of this page." She flipped the paper over. "Right below 'selfish with her emotions.'"

She wiped angrily at her cheeks again, but the tears fell faster than she could wipe. "Was this your goal all along? A way to get back at me for buying the land? Was this part of your *game*? Make the . . ." Her chin started quivering in an attempt to stop the flow of tears, and God, it nearly did him in. "Make the 'socially awkward' tomboy fall for you then crush her? Well, congratulations, once again. You win, golden boy."

"Frankie," he said, but knew there weren't enough words on the planet to make up for the ones he'd so callously scribbled on that page. "When I wrote that list I was angry, trying to sort out my feelings."

"Oh, you made your feelings more than clear." Her chest started trembling and he could hear her struggle to get a breath in past her sobs. "I'm not worth your time or apparently," she took in a shallow shaky breath, "your love."

"That's not true."

But he could tell by the look in her eyes that regardless of what he said, she believed he didn't love her. Couldn't love her. "You promised never to lie to me."

He stepped forward and took her by the arms. She stiffened but didn't pull away. "Honey, I'm not lying."

"Yes, you are. It says it right here in black and white next to every failing I possess as a woman, person, and partner." She shoved the paper against his chest, hard enough that he stumbled back. "I might be 'uninformed in the current political climate' due to my 'obsession with NASCAR' and I might not have graduated from a fancy school like you, but I can read."

Nate took the paper and looked down at the last line and felt his chest tighten to the point of pain. He blinked, but when he opened his eyes it was still the same heartbreaking statement staring back at him. The *I Love Frankie* in the pros column was scratched out, leaving it only on the cons' side. Shit, he hadn't remembered crossing it out.

She shook her head, sad and slow, so much fucking pain and heartache in her eyes that he felt his own begin to burn. She was slowly falling apart and it was his fault.

"I could have handled Charles, losing my grapes, everything you wrote on this list. But the last part, I just don't know how to deal with, because everything else is true so this one must be as well."

Frankie was the strongest woman he knew. She'd suffered on the outskirts of her family for a lifetime, bounced back after

Charles publically humiliated her, even stood up to Nate and his family without even shedding a tear. And the one person who destroyed her world was him. And he had no idea how to make this right.

"You know what's funny? You always say I'm not open with my emotions, that you never know where I stand?" She sniffed. "You want to know?"

No he didn't. Not right now. Not when her eyes told him everything and the humiliation he saw there made his chest hollow out. Because for the first time since high school, Nate saw a flash of that girl who believed she was broken, undeserving of love.

"Right now," she whispered. "I'm *standing* in your room with a list detailing every single insecurity about myself that I hate and don't know how to change without changing me." A fresh wave of humiliation spilled over her lashes. "I'm *feeling* like an idiot for believing that this could work between us and thankful that I didn't tell you today that I was actually in love with you because that would only make this moment all the more awkward."

"I don't care what I wrote. That list is all bullshit, Frankie. Everything there is bullshit. What matters is in here." He hit his chest. "This matters. *We matter.* And we can make this work."

He reached out to cup her cheek but she turned her face. "No, we can't. You have twenty, I mean thirty-seven, clearly outlined reasons why we can't. Love can't beat logic. I guess not my love, anyway."

Nate's gut clenched to the point of pain. He would have given anything to take back what he'd done. Because seeing her cry was breaking his heart. Watching her grab her helmet and keys and head for the door had his heart exploding out of his chest.

"Frankie, wait—" he grabbed her hand and she stopped, her shoulders slumped in defeat.

"Right, I nearly forgot, the *need* part of your emotional equation." She turned around and wham, the look on her face shattered his fucking world. "I really *need* you to understand that *this* is over."

He knew what *this* meant. The past, their friendship, hope of a future, all of it was gone. Frankie didn't do things halfway and he'd just rationalized his way out of the most important thing in his life.

CHAPTER 17

"Am I awkward around kids?" Frankie asked, smashing soggy cereal against the side of her bowl with a spoon.

"Well, I'm not the best person to ask," Luce said, ripping the kitchen curtains open. God, the morning sun was so bright; it practically flipped Frankie the big, fat sunny finger. "I showed up to Joshua's Boy Scout badge ceremony with a male escort."

"I bet grandpa flipped," Frankie said, observing Luce walk to the counter in her fuchsia house robe and crocheted slippers, to watch waffles toast.

"It's why I did it." After buttering, plating, and dousing the toaster waffles with half the bottle of syrup, she set three plates on the kitchen table and pulled out the chair between Frankie and Mr. Puffins. "Now, what's with all the questions? You got a bun in the oven?"

"No, I was just wondering if everyone had that, you know, maternal thing." Frankie mumbled, digging into her plate.

The toaster waffles were warm, crunchy on the outside and soft in the center, and coated in liquid sugar. Too bad Frankie was too numb to notice.

"You went over to your house this morning after crying yourself hoarse last night to get your goat, didn't you?"

Frankie looked out the kitchen window and saw Mittens eating Luce's wagon wheel while tethered to the fence. "He's an alpaca, and yes I did because I didn't want him to worry. I left without telling him where I was going."

She had gone over at the crack of dawn so that she wouldn't have to run into Nate, but his car was gone. He'd moved out. Not surprising since she'd texted him that he had three days to vacate the property or she would tell Pricket to call in the bulldozers.

Four months. It had only been four months since the Summer Wine Showdown where Nate kissed her, but her life had changed so much. She started her dream winery, found a happiness and confidence that she'd never known before. Fallen completely and helplessly in love with a DeLuca of all people. Only to have it all taken away in just one day. It was like she was six all over again and her parents were divorcing and her life would forever be changed.

"Well then, that sounds maternal to me." Luce cut up one of the waffles and pushed the plate in front of Mr. Puffins, who was in a terry cloth robe and bunny slippers. "I don't know what happened between you and Nathaniel, but I know that he's sorry."

Frankie studied her waffle. It was easier than letting Luce see any more tears. "I don't know about that, but I do know that I'm not really looking for anyone right now. Or ever. I mean, you are as responsible for this place's success as Grandpa and you did it all on your own. No man."

Luce put down her fork. "I did do it all alone. The key word being alone." She placed a hand over Frankie's. "I don't regret my life, I've had a fun and full one, but I did it all alone. No husband, no kids, no grandkids. And it's been hard."

That startled Frankie. She'd always thought that her aunt had chosen her life. "Then why didn't you marry?"

"Because I was so busy making sure Charles wouldn't cut me out of the family business that I spent all my time working. And when I finally decided that maybe I wanted more, all the men my age were married with families, and then, well it just didn't seem to make sense. But that's not what I want for you."

"Yeah, well the only prospect I care about doesn't really care back."

"I call bullshit," Luce snapped, sending Mr. Puffins and his syrup-coated whiskers scurrying under the coach. "That boy has it so bad for you, he's walking around town like a fool. Everyone knows it."

Yeah, well by the end of the day everyone would also know that he and Frankie were over. And they'd all assume that she did something wrong.

"Apparently loving me is some kind of hardship," Frankie admitted and felt her throat tighten. She was not going to cry again. It was embarrassing enough that Luce heard her last night in bed—and then again this morning in the shower—but to actually have her witness it would be humiliating.

"Loving you is the best thing that could happen to a person, I know. You have the biggest heart of anyone I've ever met, enough passion to run a small nation, yet in relationships, slugs move faster than you. Which means loving you is as much a blessing as it is an experience—and it's an experience that's not for everyone."

"I don't care about everyone," Frankie whispered. She only cared about one person, and to him her love was something that made his life harder.

"I know you do," Luce said gently. "And you know what's wrong with people today?"

"No." Frankie didn't feel like sitting through one of Luce's lectures on the world. Not right now. Not when her world hurt too much to live in.

"They're lazy," she went on as though Frankie hadn't spoken, and she could tell by the way Luce was winding up that it was going to be a long one. "You kids think that loving is the easy part, but it's not. It's the liking part that's difficult. Love, once it happens, is always there no matter how angry you get. But like, that takes compromise and honesty and understanding and a lot of hard work. Look at that grandpa of yours. I love him with all that I am, but I don't think I've liked that SOB since JFK was in office."

Frankie thought long and hard to find a time when she did like her grandpa, and she couldn't think of one. She idolized him, respected him, even loved him enough to give up everything to save his winery, but liking the man was difficult.

What if she was the same way?

"You really want to know why I didn't marry? It took me too long to figure out that although 'like' fluctuates over time, love is always there and as long as there is something in there that you like, the love will hold you together." Luce let out a sigh. "My guess is that right now you'd have a hard time telling me one thing you like about Nate. And I'm betting he'd have even a harder time finding something he liked about himself."

"I could actually tell you over a dozen things I like about him," Frankie whispered, knowing it was true. She was mad and confused and didn't know if this hollow pain in her chest would ever go away, but the reason why she hurt so bad was because Nate was an incredible guy—lists aside. And for a moment she knew what it was like for him to be hers.

"I bet you could also tell me a dozen things about him that drives you crazy." Luce raised a brow when Frankie didn't answer. "People make mistakes, Frankie. Nate made a big one in breaking your heart, but don't let your mistake be pride and fear."

"What if he doesn't like me?" Frankie asked, her voice sounding small even to her own ears.

"Ah, Ches-ka, that boy doesn't just like you, he adores you, bad attitude and all. But most importantly he loves you. That's forever." Luce leaned up and gave Frankie a surprising and sweet kiss on the cheek. "Now, go feed your goat. We have to be at the hotel in twenty minutes."

"God, do I have to go?" Frankie asked. Walking into the Cork Crawl Wine Open and talking to buyers and brokers about a wine that Charles already sold to some bottom-of-the-barreler was going to be bad enough. Having to see Nate and knowing he wasn't hers was going to wreck her heart.

"You're my niece, aren't you?"

And Frankie had her answer.

~

Frankie stood at the back of the ballroom at the Napa Grand Hotel as buyers and brokers finished their coffee and

pastries, staging their strategy of attack on the provided conference maps while vintners took their places behind assigned
linen-covered tables.

She watched as one by one, the winemakers displayed their
sales brochures and logo embossed labels, signaling a go and
sending the brokers scrambling to get in the line of their first
choice.

The Cork Crawl Wine Open was almost ready to begin and
even though Frankie was the belle of the ball, she didn't have a
ticket or a date.

Her eyes scanned the massive glass-domed room, looking
past the swelling crowd, past the mahogany bar in the center of
the ballroom that functioned as Lexi's pastry shack, and past
the line that ran the length of the room, until they settled on
her table. Her stomach went hot with emotion and everything
seemed unreal as she took in the sight.

Jonah and Adam. Her brothers. Sat beneath the Red Steel
Cellars sign, wearing company shirts and smiling and greeting
interested parties. In a matter of moments, the queue for Red
Steel was twenty deep with some of the most respected buyers
and brokers in wine. It was as if the who's who of wine collecting had come specifically for her.

This couldn't be happening. She had reached the pinnacle
most winemakers only dream about, and yet she was even farther from her dream than she had been a month ago. She had
lost everything. And yet she couldn't even feel the loss over the
gaping hole Nate left behind.

It had taken a brisk walk around Luce's lavender garden with
Mittens, a long motorcycle ride, and polishing her ball-buster
boots to get the courage to walk into that ballroom, because she

knew everyone would be expecting her to sit behind her booth and sell her wine as though it were still hers. As though her world hadn't completely fallen apart.

"Thought you fell in," Luce said.

"What?"

"You went to the bathroom, said you'd be right behind me, and that was a half-hour ago."

"No," she said and her voice sounded raw and empty. "Just needed a minute to get my game face on."

"That a girl." Luce smacked her rump like this was the Super Bowl and she was the defensive coach. "The negotiating starts in about fifteen minutes, so get over there and make me proud. And remember, Ches-ka, they fell in love with your wine. They might not like that you are sold out, but in three years that love for what you created will still be there."

Frankie made her way through the crowd, but even before she could take her seat, Jonah pulled her into his arms and gave her one the best big brother hugs in history. Frankie didn't hesitate, throwing her arms around his middle and holding on.

When he pulled back, he didn't say anything about Charles. He didn't have to. His face said it all.

"I can't talk about it right now," she whispered and took a small step back. Any more emotion from her normally stoic brother would be the end of the brave-Frankie she'd struggled to pull together.

"Sorry I missed everything this weekend," Adam said and, after a quick glance over her shoulder and wiping his hands on his jeans, pulled her in for his hug. When had they become a family of huggers?

"I'm just glad you're back and not hurt."

"Me too, but I'm sorry we didn't tell you about the fire."

"I think we all have a lot of talking to do if we want to fix everything, so I figured that since Frankie loves wine coolers so much," Jonah teased, "we could pick up a few cases when this is over and go back to my place. Maybe braid each other's hair. And . . . talk."

Frankie felt a hysterical laugh bubble up from her chest and break free. She couldn't help it. So instead of trying to hide it, she let it out and pulled Jonah in for another hug. It took him a minute to catch up, but when he did he hugged her back.

"Now, if we're done with all this touchy-feely shit, can we sell some wine?" Jonah said gruffly. "I think they are about to ring the bell, and I figure it's going to take us at least three hours to get through that line of uptight trousers."

"Oh. I uh . . . " Frankie looked up at him. God, the man was a tower. "I thought you guys knew. Charles and I—"

"Oh, we know all right," Adam said fiercely. "And Charles is handled."

"What?" Frankie asked, she looked at where the Baudoiun table sat, empty. "Where is Grandpa?"

"A better deal came along and he wisely took it," Jonah explained through a clenched jaw.

"What?" No, this couldn't be happening. "What about the house, Luce's cottage, the vineyard?"

"All taken care of. It seems that last night some guy from Stanford Specialty Markets heard that grandpa was sitting on thirty thousand cases of six dollar wine."

"Oh my God," Frankie had to take a seat. Knowing what Charles had to do and actually knowing that it was going to happen made everything so much worse. This would save the family vineyard, but ruin the family name. No longer would the Baudoiun name be connected with quality and flavor, it would be associated with double coupon days. "Our name is done."

"Actually, it's not," Jonah sat down. They kept their voices low, and since the tables hadn't officially opened, the line was back far enough that they couldn't be overheard. "The way the deal was negotiated was that Stanford Markets would contract all of the Santa Ynez grapes for the next fifteen years to be bottled and sold exclusively at their stores."

Adam held out a mock wine label attached to a memorandum of understanding, outlining all of the basic agreed upon points for the finalized contract. The bottle front label read, STANFORD SPECIALTY COSTAL. Not a Baudouin anywhere to be seen. She flipped the page to the back bottle label.

VINTED AND BOTTLED BY SANTA YNEZ VINE-YARDS, SANTA YNEZ VALLEY EXCLUSIVELY FOR STANFORD SPECIALTY MARKETS.

"Santa Ynez Vineyards?" She flipped the page to the memorandum. "When did that become its own entity? And how did Charles negotiate that kind of deal?"

Her grandfather was a shrewd business man. But shrewd only worked when one didn't reek of desperation. And this was way too out of the box for her grandfather to come up with.

Adam and Jonah exchanged loaded glances. After the glares and eyebrow raising and non-verbal argument, it was Jonah who finally spoke. "The new corporation will be finalized end of this week, Stanford Markets is in the bag, and all Grandpa had to do is sign."

"I don't understand."

"I think you do," Jonah said, resting his hand on Frankie's shoulder.

Frankie's eyes scanned the room and immediately found Nate. Their eyes locked and so much sorrow and pain and something that Frankie wasn't ready to admit passed between them it was hard to breathe. He gave her a small, hopeful smile but she was afraid to smile back. Unable to hope or even hold his gaze without dissolving into tears, she busied herself with straightening the already immaculate table. But as she stacked the brochures that Regan had made, her hands froze.

At the corner of her booth sat a plain vase overflowing with dozens of daffodils. She reached out and ran her finger along one of the petals when her phone chimed. She pulled it out of her pocket.

DAFFODIL: A SINGLE DAFFODIL FORETELLS UNREQUITED LOVE WHILE A BOUQUET OF DAFFODILS INDICATES RETURN OF AFFECTION.

Frank read and reread the text until the words began to blur. She wanted to go back to yesterday when everything felt right, when she felt as though she finally fit, when she didn't know that she was one dirty sock on the coffee table away from losing Nate. Because that was what it came down to, wasn't it? The fear that she was one annoying habit away from losing the only man she'd ever loved.

How could she move forward knowing that there were parts of herself so ingrained into the fiber of her being that could be the deciding factor between heartbreak and forever?

"Frankie." Nate's deep voice poured over her like a well-aged Bordeaux.

She looked from the phone in her hand to the pair of dirty boots standing in front of her table—and then higher.

Nate looked so handsome in his black slacks and dark blue button-up, but the look on his face nearly did her in. Dark circles outlined his eyes, and his expression was nervous and un-sure. She hadn't seen him look this way since the day of his parents' funeral

"Nate." She stood, then sat back down, only to pick up the Stanford memorandum and stand again. "You did this."

"She's as bad as you are at this," Adam said shoving Jonah.

"Do you have a minute?" he began, clearing his voice twice before continuing. "I know everything is about to start and I don't want to ruin your day . . . again. But I'd like to explain—"

"What's that?"

He was holding a single yellow rose and matching legal pad.

"It's for you," he said, offering her the rose.

Frankie had never had a man bring her flowers before and she wasn't sure what to do. If she accepted it was she saying that she forgave him? If she didn't, would he walk away and it was over? And if he walked away would she regret not having the courage to take a flower for the rest of her life?

Jesus, her entire future had come down to petals and thorns.

Nate must have understood her panic because he pulled it back and twirled it in his hand, gently probing a thorn with his index finger. "Lexi said roses are cliché, but I disagree. Did you know that the yellow rose is quite a complicated flower?"

She shook her head.

"I never understood how a single flower could possess so many contradicting meanings. Friendship, betrayal, heart-break." His eyes met hers. "Apology. It's all in one beautiful package."

"We looked for a flower that meant stupidest motherfucker to walk the earth, but there isn't one, so he got you the rose," Adam shot off.

Frankie shot off something back at Adam. The finger.

The most romantic thing anyone had ever said to her and it would forever be associated with the words "stupidest mother-fucker."

"I know that sorry doesn't make up for how I hurt you, but know that I never meant to hurt you."

"But you did," she whispered.

"I know. God, I know, but I don't know how to make it better." He set the rose down and flipped through the legal pad. From what Frankie could see every page was triple-columned and completely filled. "Last night after you walked out, it hit me that I may have lost you for good. And it hurt. But what got me was the idea of you never hearing all of the things I love about you. All the things that if you walked away I'll never get to tell you. So I started making a list and," he swallowed. "I want you to know how I feel."

Frankie just stared at the pad and her knees went wobbly. She had a mental barrel of what drove people crazy about her, but she'd never once considered what it would feel like to know what someone liked—no, wait, the list was titled *Why I Love Frankie* —loved about her.

He loved her. Frankie felt her throat start to burn. Luce was right: love was forever. It didn't matter that he hated when she drank from the carton or used his electric razor to de-knot Mitten's coat, because even though his need to wash the dishes before putting them in the dishwasher drove her crazy, she still loved him. Always would.

And he loved her.

Nate took her hesitation to mean something else because he quickly added, "I have another two at home. All filled, but I was told it would make me look desperate." He glared at Trey who stood three booths away and waved. In fact, Nate's entire family was standing three booths away, listening and watching. "I should have brought the other two. I knew it."

"I don't need the other lists," Frankie whispered and took the pad.

Glancing at the first page, she felt a small smile tug at her lips. Then she took Nate's hand and pulled him past his smiling family and hers to a small utility room off of the ballroom floor. She didn't even let him get the door closed before she asked, "Boobs, really? They are number two and number nineteen."

Nate laughed. It was raw and thick with emotion. "You seem to do better with the heavy stuff if I start with sex as a warm up. And yes, number two refers to how they feel, and number nineteen has to do with taste and page three, number two-hundred and seventy-six, is how they look wet in the water."

"Isn't that redundant?"

He shook his head and ran a gentle hand down both of her arms. "I remembered the way they looked after we made love in the lake, and it's different than in the bath with bubbles. That's in journal number two. But it doesn't matter what's in there, Frankie. What matters is—"

"In here." She placed her hand over his heart.

"I love you," he whispered and Frankie stepped forward until their bodies were gently brushing.

He smelled like home and felt like forever, and the way his hands slid around her, pulling her close and trapping a dictionary of words on a legal pad between them, she realized that the only three that mattered crept inside her heart. "I love you, too."

Nate kissed her lips. "I know."

"And what you did for my grandpa, for my family."

He cupped her face between his warm hands. "I did that for you, Frankie. Everything I did, I did it for you."

She leaned up and when their mouths came together, everything that she'd been too scared to say, too scared to think rushed through her chest. Things that four months ago would have terrified her, now made her feel happy, hopeful, free.

"I'm *standing* in a utility room." She wrapped her arms around his neck and a small smile tugged at Nate's lips. "I want to cry because for the first time, in a really long time, I *feel* as though I fit." She delivered a gentle kiss and whispered against his mouth, "With you I fit."

"Which is why I need you," Nate said roughly. "To understand that aside from all logic, I am ridiculously in love with you, Francesca."

With a final brush of the lips Frankie pulled back and when she looked up into those warm-brown eyes she knew she was staring at her forever.

READ ON FOR A SNEAK PEEK OF MARINA ADAIR'S NEXT ST. HELENA VINEYARD ROMANCE!

Be Mine Forever

Available February 2014 on Amazon.com

Trey DeLuca hated hospitals. Almost as much as he hated himself right now.

Seven calls. He'd received seven calls over the past two days from his family, which he'd selfishly chosen to ignore. Three texts came in while he'd been in transit from Paris to San Francisco. All from his oldest brother, Gabe. And all with the same message: *Call me.*

So he finally had. And was sent straight to voicemail.

Trey hurried through the emergency waiting room of St. Helena Memorial and was hit by the smell of ammonia and a nervous hum that gave him the willies. It was a pretty quiet night. Most of the industrial-grey seats in the waiting room were empty. Then again, St. Helena, California with its not-quite six-thousand residents wasn't exactly a hive of activity.

Finding the room where the hospital attendant had directed him, he rested his hand on the doorknob and closed his eyes. God, he just needed her to be okay.

With a deep breath he opened the door, took one step inside, and froze.

Holy Christ Almighty, if the smell of Bengay didn't make him want to run for it, the sight of saggy breasts slung up in sequins did.

He'd been played. His brothers had dangled his grandmother's health in front of him and he'd come running. But instead of lying on her deathbed with his family standing in silent vigil, Nonna ChiChi Ryo stood at the back of a small cafeteria, where the tables and chairs had been shoved up against the wall to create a makeshift dance floor, draped over some silver fox's arm as though he'd caught her mid-faint.

Dressed in a flowy red dress, matching orthopedic shoes, and enough hairspray that would ignite with a single spark, ChiChi sashayed around the floor, twirling through a good portion of the town's retired sector, and going for the dramatic dip under a giant poster that read: ST. HELENA'S SALSA SOCIETY. WE PUT THE HEAT BACK IN WINTER.

"Trey?" ChiChi said mid-toe-flick, looking about as startled to see Trey as Trey was when she adjusted her goods and—ah, Christ, he had to look away. "You came?"

"You say that as though you didn't leave a half-dozen cryptic messages on my cell implying I needed to come home before it was too late."

"And here you are, such a good boy," ChiChi praised, smoothing a hand over her grey up-do and coming over to give him two kisses to the cheeks. "Just in time for—"

"You'd better say to resuscitate." He ran a hand down his face. "I thought you were . . ."

Dead. He'd thought she was dead. He'd spent the past eighteen hours on an airplane after rushing out in the middle of a business meeting, praying he'd make it in time to tell his grandmother that he loved her, berating himself for being a selfish prick for staying as far away as possible from his family. He wasn't even sure what time zone he was in anymore. "Christ, Nonna, you said it was a matter of life and death."

"Watch your language," she chided. "And this is life or death. The Winter Garden Gala is just three weeks away. And you, my favorite grandson, get to be my dance partner. Isn't that wonderful?"

Yeah, wonderful.

Trey ran a hand down his face, working overtime not to lose it. St. Helena might not be *Dancing with the Stars,* but people here took their swing time seriously. And the Winter Garden Gala, a Valentine's celebration put on by the St. Helena Garden Society, was pretty much the hottest ticket in town. The last time he'd gone, Trey had been fifteen and his mom a nominee for Winter Garden of the Year. With his dad stuck in a snowstorm in Chicago, his brothers cursed with two left feet, and Trey having seven years of enforced dance lessons, he was the only possible candidate to partner with his mom in the Winter Garden Waltz.

Only Mollie Miner, with her blonde hair and way-too-full Cs for a freshman, had asked him to meet her in the garden. Even at

fifteen Trey knew she wasn't looking to Waltz. And since dancing with his mom in front of the entire town sounded like social
suicide, he'd snuck out to meet More Than a Handful Mollie.

They rounded second that night, Mollie turned out to be a
bra stuffer, Trey missed the Winter Garden Waltz, and three
months later his mom died.

"Gabe is your favorite." *And better with this kind of stuff*, he
thought, pulling ChiChi in for a big hug. Underneath the anger
at being played, deep relief poured through his body. She was
okay. His nonna was alive and okay.

"Yes, well, Gabe is busy being a husband and proud papa."
She pulled back and patted his cheek. "And you drew the short
straw."

"I wasn't here to draw," Trey argued.

Every year the brothers drew straws to see who "got" to escort ChiChi and partner with her in the Winter Garden Waltz.
And every year Trey somehow managed to weasel out of it. Apparently this Valentine's Day, his brothers and Cupid had their
pointy little arrows aimed at Trey. Too bad for them, tomorrow
morning he was going to be on the next flight back to Anywhere But Here.

Being home was hard enough. Being home around Valentine's Day was not going to happen.

"No, you weren't," ChiChi tutted. "You were off to God
knows where, with God knows who." Trey had been at a wine
conference. In Paris. Alone. Selling the family's wine. "So, I
drew for you."

"And just how many straws were there to draw from?"

"One. Congratulations, dear." She clapped as though he
were the luckiest man in the world. And maybe he was. His
grandma was alive. Which was the only thing keeping him

from wringing her neck. But there was no way he was going to that dance. One of his brothers would just have to man up.

The door to the cafeteria opened, causing everyone in the room to turn, and every man in the room to smile. Trey glanced over his shoulder as a tiny woman, burrowed under a bright yellow rain slicker and a sorry looking blue and white knit cap that screamed handmade, entered. She was carrying a broken umbrella, which explained the drowned kitten look, and a duffle bag big enough to hide in.

"Sorry, I'm late," a sweet, but slightly harassed voice came from beneath the slicker as she struggled to pull it over her head, but the wet vinyl got stuck. "Some jackass in a minivan parked diagonally taking up three spaces so I had to circle the lot a few times."

"Maybe they were in a rush, had a family emergency," Trey said, sending ChiChi a stern glare.

"Yeah, well," the woman, who he assumed was the dance instructor, said, dropping the broken umbrella to the floor to work harder on her raincoat. "There were no more spots, I looked. So after five laps I decided to squeeze in beside him. I mean, I figured my car was a compact. It should fit, right?"

Trey hoped to hell it had. Otherwise he was going to have to explain to his brother Marc how he'd "borrowed" and dented his new minivan. Which kind of served him right for trading his truck in for one.

"Wrong." Giving up on the buttons, she reached down for the hem and tugged up. "I heard the scraping of metal and instead of stopping I panicked and gunned it."

"Oh dear, are you okay, Sara?" ChiChi said, concern lacing her voice as she took a step forward. Several other worried hums erupted from the senior gallery.

"Outside of eating my front bumper, the minivan looks fine." Which explained her shaking hands. And the way she was frantically fumbling to get out of her coat. "I left a note, but the wind blew it away. So I stood out there for a few minutes waiting for the owner to come out."

Her movements were jerky with what Trey thought was frustration and a good dose of adrenaline. In fact, if she wasn't careful in her disrobing someone was going to get hurt. One of the senior males with bad hips and dentures was already closing in to help.

With a frustrated huff, Sara dropped the duffle bag, bent at the waist and started shimmying out of the slicker and—*holy shit*—a shapely, sequined-clad, nowhere-near-qualified-for-a-senior-discount ass emerged from underneath the raincoat. He'd always considered himself a leg man, loved them long and wrapped around his middle. But after seeing that exquisite heart-shaped handful, he was a changed man. Not that her legs weren't toned and silky. But that backside. Perfection.

"You need help?" Harvey Peterson, the town's podiatrist asked, his hands already reaching for her waist.

"No, I'm fine. Really, Harvey." If anything, Mr. Peterson's offer got her moving even faster.

Harvey, however, looked disappointed. Trey felt for the guy.

He stepped around the forming crowd so as not to lose the view as Sara wrenched and yanked the wet material until she made some progress and—*thank you, Jesus*—it got stuck on an even more incredible set of breasts—on the smaller side, maybe a full B, but incredible all the same. And they were just as slick as the rest of her.

Always the gentleman, Trey stepped forward to do his part, lending his hands to the cause. "Here, let me help."

"I'm fine, really," she said, her hands batting at his, which rested on her hips to steady her. And yeah, she was tiny but packing a ton of delicious curves.

"Sorry, can't hear you through the material," he lied, grabbing her wrists and guiding them to the bottom hem of her thin, tank-style shirt. "But if you don't stop flopping around you're going to take someone out. Or give Harvey over there the chance to goose you and call it an accident." She froze. "So, work with me here. Hold your top down so I can pull the slicker up and . . ."

"Okay. Better?" Sara whispered.

Abso-fucking-lutly. First, the woman did just as he asked—that in itself was a miracle. Second, she pulled a tad bit too hard, causing the scoop of her neckline to ride blessedly low, giving him an inspiring view of teal-lace and tan cleavage. The best part was when he gave the final tug, and the slicker and knit-cap came up and off, leaving behind the most beautiful woman he'd ever seen.

Which didn't make sense. Trey had been around a lot of beautiful women. Spent the past ten years traveling the world and getting up close and personal with a lot of them. Women who were stilettoed, stacked, smoking-hot, and satisfied with one night. This woman was maybe five-two with bouncy brown hair, girl-next-door freckles, and a pair of no-nonsense shoes that were definitely more Mary Anne than Ginger. And he was a Ginger kind of guy. Always had been.

Nothing about her said simple, short term, or easily impressed. So why then was he having a hard time breathing?

Dry spell. That was it. The main reason he was staring at Pollyanna had nothing to do with the way those big brown eyes seemed to look right through all of his bullshit or the way her sweet kiss-me-mouth curved up into a smile that made his pulse pound. Nope, the simple truth was, it had been way too long since he'd gotten laid.

"Isn't this interesting?" ChiChi murmured, patting Trey on the back, no doubt already picking out great-grandbaby names. "This gentleman here is my grandson. My *favorite* grandson."

"Thank you, *favorite grandson.*" Sara smiled, two little dimples winking his way. He'd never been into dimples, but on her they worked.

"My pleasure," Trey said, wondering what kind of dance she taught and if she would be open to a private lesson—of the tangled-sheets variety.

He flashed her that smile he knew women loved, because why the hell not? Flirting with a pretty woman seemed like a much better way to spend his evening than arguing with his brothers or picking out funeral arrangements.

She tried not to smile, but one slipped out and—*hello sunshine*—it even lit up her eyes. Message received and reciprocated. Sara with her sunny smile and pert nose was aware of him in a purely male-to-female, let's get down and dirty kind of way.

"Shouldn't you two exchange information?" ChiChi nudged.

Right. The minivan. "It seems silly since I've already helped you undress, but it seems that we've reached the information portion of the evening where I ask for your name, number, and if there is anyone at home you can call?"

A hint of pink tinted her ears, which he found oddly endearing, and she looked up at him with those big bottomless eyes, practically slaying him right there on the spot.

"Information? Okay, um, no, there is no one at home." She wiggled a naked ring finger and before Trey could clarify the reason behind his questions, she pulled out a business card and handed it to him. "My number is on there and . . . what?"

"Bolder Holder?" He read the frequent buyer card she'd handed him. He was right—a 32-B. "Your local lingerie pusher-upper."

"Oh, God." She snatched it back and produced another card. Still not the insurance card he expected, but before he could explain, she looked around at the room of students who were all smiling back and damn if her entire face wasn't glowing with embarrassment. "I'm Sara Reese and as you can tell I'm not really good at this."

Even her name was sweet. And flirting disaster would be putting it mildly. Not that he minded. There was something about her shy interest that got to him.

"Trey DeLuca," he said. She placed her hand in his extended one. Her skin, soft and a bit chilled, packed one hell of a punch. "I'm the asshole who ate your bumper."

ACKNOWLEDGMENTS

Thanks to my editors Eleni Caminis and Lindsay Guzzardo, and the rest of the Author team at Montlake, for all of the amazing work and support throughout this series.

As always, a special thanks to Jill Marsal for being the best agent in the world and loving Mittens the alpaca as much as I do.

A huge thanks to my best friends and partners in writing. For all of the laughs, tears, and edits that you suffered through during the plotting, re-plotting, writing, deleting, restructuring, and re-writing (to the fourth power) of this book. To Diana Orgain, one of the biggest dreamers I know, thank you for sharing your dreams and allowing me to share mine. And to Miss Marni Bates for being my constant cheerleader.

A special thanks to my go-to-wine-guy, Gary Galleron of Galleron Signature Wines, for answering all of my questions about wine and grapes—even the ridiculous ones.

Finally, and most importantly, thanks to my daughter Thuy for being the most amazing kid in the world—and for loving

Buffy the Vampire Slayer . . . Buffy nights with you are some of my most treasured times.

Any mistakes I have made or liberties I have taken are all my own.

ABOUT THE AUTHOR

Marina Adair is a national best-selling author of romance novels. Along with the St. Helena Vineyard series, she is the author of *Tucker's Crossing*, part of the Sweet Plains series. She lives with her husband and daughter in Northern California.